100 DAYS

Nicole McInnes

FARRAR STRAUS GIROUX
NEW YORK

Farrar Straus Giroux Books for Young Readers
175 Fifth Avenue, New York 10010

Printed in the United States of America
Designed by Elizabeth H. Clark
First edition, 2016
1   3   5   7   9   10   8   6   4   2

fiercereads.com

Library of Congress Cataloging-in-Publication Data

Names: McInnes, Nicole, author.
Title: 100 days / Nicole McInnes.
Other titles: One hundred days
Description: First edition. | New York : Farrar Straus Giroux, 2016. |
    Summary: "A teen girl suffers from progeria, a rare disease that causes
    her to age rapidly. This is the story of three unlikely friends learning
    to live life to its fullest before ultimately letting it go"—Provided by publisher.
Identifiers: LCCN 2015036847| ISBN 9780374302849 (hardback) | ISBN
    9780374302856 (ebook)
Subjects: | CYAC: Progeria—Fiction. | Terminally ill—Fiction. |
    Friendship—Fiction. | BISAC: JUVENILE FICTION / Health & Daily Living /
    Diseases, Illnesses & Injuries. | JUVENILE FICTION / Social Issues /
    Friendship. | JUVENILE FICTION / Social Issues / Death & Dying.
Classification: LCC PZ7.M478654 Aam 2016 | DDC [Fic]—dc23
LC record available at http://lccn.loc.gov/2015036847

Our books may be purchased in bulk for promotional, educational, or
business use. Please contact your local bookseller or the Macmillan Corporate
and Premium Sales Department at (800) 221-7945 ext. 5442 or by e-mail at
MacmillanSpecialMarkets@macmillan.com.

For Jonah and Sarah

"In one of the stars I shall be living. In one of them I shall be laughing. And so it will be as if all the stars were laughing, when you look at the sky at night . . ."

—Antoine de Saint-Exupéry

100 DAYS

1

BOONE

DAY 100: MARCH 17

I STEP ONTO THE PACKED DIRT JUST OUTSIDE THE FRONT DOOR and rub my hands together. I blow on them for good measure, which never helps. There's something comforting in the gesture, though, like maybe I have some minuscule bit of control over this one simple thing, warming my fingers.

Of course, that's a complete joke.

Where the hell are the leather work gloves, the ones I've only recently started to think of as my own? The gloves used to belong to my father, like most everything else in my life.

I head to the paddock, say, "Yeah, same to you," as the gelding grumbles a low whinny. The sound is both friendly and demanding, like, *I love you, man. Now, throw my freaking breakfast over the fence.* For some reason, it makes me want to wrap my arms around the horse's neck in a hug. Diablo would never stand for it, though. Not until after he'd finished eating.

I grab a fat flake of alfalfa from the open bale on a pallet in the makeshift feed room. I take the purple bucket from its hook and scoop some sweet, expensive senior feed into it until the bucket's a third full. Try not to think about what me and Mom and Diablo are going to do now that my hours at the Feed & Seed have been cut to just weekends. Even though it's still cold, it's not the right season for loading up the truck with firewood and selling it on the side of the road. It's actually the opposite of the right season.

The horse is a ridiculous expense. If I wasn't able to turn him out into the big pasture from late spring until fall like I do, there's no way we'd be able to keep him.

For the past two-plus years, ever since horse chores fell to me (all chores, really), I've made a habit of checking Diablo's water trough for everything from slobbery clumps of half-chewed alfalfa to floating turds. Horses can be disgusting like that, and I like to clean stuff out of his tank before it gets too gross. When you live out in the middle of nowhere and have to haul your own water, you learn to conserve it pretty quickly.

This time, I don't find either of those things in the trough. Instead, I find two dead birds. Barn swallows, maybe, or wild finches—I can never keep them straight. Their wings are splayed out on the slushy surface of the water. The tip of one bird's right wing and the other bird's left wing are touching, like only seconds before death they reached for each other.

I just stand there, can't believe it. The backs of their wings are totally dry. For a crazy split second I think maybe they could still be alive. But, no. The birds are still, and the water is still. Which means they've been there for a while, possibly since right after I left for school this morning. I feel so awful all of a sudden—and so foolish for feeling awful about two stupid dead birds—that I clench my fists and hold them to my forehead. I tense all the muscles in my body as tight as they'll go until I feel like I might scream or explode. After a minute, I let everything relax again and drop my hands to my sides.

I walk to the shed for the mucking fork to fish the birds out of the trough. It occurs to me to wonder if they have a nest somewhere. Spring is just a couple days away, after all. It's not unusual at this time of year to see small birds trying to guard their nests from huge, pillaging ravens. Somewhere close by, a cluster of naked, wide-beaked chicks might be, right this very second, cheeping for their parents to return with some tasty earthworms. I could try to locate any potential babies, but then what? Their chances of survival with two dead parents would be nil, and it's not like I have time to nurse a nest full of newly hatched mouths to feed.

It does no good to linger on that thought. It does the opposite of good, in fact. Lingering on thoughts like that is just one more thing that makes me weak, so I push the image from my mind. Remind myself that nature can be a heartless bitch. Swipe at my eyes with the cuff of my jacket, then look around in case anyone saw. Which is moronic. Who'd be crazy enough to be standing around way out here in the middle of nowhere this late in the day in this kind of weather? *Don't answer that,* I think, trying to cheer myself up. It's probably the first sign that I've finally gone completely mental.

Back at the trough, I lower the mucking fork into the water and bring it carefully up under the birds. A part of me is half-afraid they'll startle and flap at the sensation, but nothing happens. One bird falls from the mucking fork as I lift it. Plops back into the water, wings akimbo. In the process of being scooped up again, both birds get twisted and tangled. When I finally get them onto the plastic tines, they're like feathered pretzels, dripping wet. They'll be frozen solid before some other animal finds and eats them in the next day or so. Circle of life and whatever. I say a few words in my head before flinging them as far over the pasture fence as possible, something like, *Thank you for these birds, amen.*

It will be getting dark soon. After hanging the fork back on its hook inside the feed room, I head toward the forest with a flashlight to look for a piece of wood to keep in the trough. Years ago, I overheard one of my dad's horseshoeing clients talking about how it was smart to keep a fat stick inside big water tanks so animals that got in could get out. Otherwise, they'd drown in there, creating a botulism threat. And when that happens, you have no choice but to empty the whole trough and bleach it, wasting potentially hundreds of gallons of water that you've spent precious time, money, and wear-and-tear on the truck hauling from town to your cistern.

Which is exactly, I realize, what I'm going to have to do now.

2

MOIRA

DAY 99: MARCH 18

ANOTHER DAY. SPRING ISN'T EVEN HERE YET, AND I'M ALREADY sick of it. Sick of the relentless beatdown from icy rain, screaming wind, and half-frozen puddles of mud that soak through the worn soles of my Doc Martens the second I set foot outside the building. Judging by how sullen the lunch line is today, I'm not the only one who feels this way.

Even normally peppy Agnes is zombied out. She's not chattering the way she usually does as we wait for whatever slop is being passed off as lunch. Instead, she's focused on nothing in particular, totally lost in space. I look down at the top of Agnes's wig. She's wearing the blond bob. High gloss. It looks like Barbie hair, or the hair of one of the insipid pop stars she's always trying to emulate. Give me 1920s silent film star hair any day. Louise Brooks (by way of Siouxsie Sioux) is the particular goddess my own hair's modeled after now.

If we can just get our trays and leave, things will turn around. I'm pretty sure the headache that's been inching its way up the back of my skull will go away once we make it to the home ec room and start working on the dresses that will be worth about half our grade in the class. The assignment is to design and sew an outfit for a special occasion. It has to fit, and it has to be something we'd actually wear. Agnes isn't sure yet how she wants her dress to look. Mine is inspired by two of Alfred Hitchcock's leading ladies: Eva Marie Saint in *North by Northwest* and Grace Kelly in *Rear Window*. I'm using gray silk with tons of slubs throughout the fabric, which gives it that wonderful, imperfect texture, almost like the silk is scarred.

The home ec room is, hands down, the best place to be during lunch. That's the only time the room is quiet and there aren't a bunch of other people hogging the sewing machines and spreading their fabric all over the workstations. I don't know what we'd do if the teacher didn't let us eat in there almost every day. Agnes and I both adore Mrs. Deene. She looks like she time-traveled straight from the 1950s. I imagine her crafting molded Jell-O salads and greeting her new husband with a martini every night when he gets home.

Sudden mayhem erupts in the lunch line behind us. An argument, probably, or a practical joke. Who knows? It's always a madhouse in here, which is why I prefer to bring my own food whenever I'm not too rushed, like I was this morning.

I sigh and adjust my posture, instinctively transforming myself into a human shield to protect Agnes from whatever's going on back there. It's too late. An unstoppable domino effect is happening in line, and there's no time to get out of its way. Someone shoves me hard from behind, almost knocking me off my feet. *Tipping point,* I think. My hands fly up and brace against whatever's in front of me.

It's some guy I don't recognize right away. He's a mountain of a humanoid. Not fat exactly, not like me, but solid and tall, like the side of a barn. My hands are planted between his shoulder blades, my arms ramrod-straight and forming a bridge over Agnes's head. Agnes looks up at the bridge and smiles, has no idea how close she just came to being a pancake. Crushed by her protector. God, the irony. I regain my balance and clear my throat. Think about how to apologize to the person I just shoved, but apologies have never come naturally to me.

The guy turns around and glares at us through long, frayed bangs. Looks first at me, then down at Agnes, and back at me. When he does, a little shooting star of recognition fizzles across my brain. I ignore it. An unreadable expression passes over his face, and he turns away again. Like we're not worth his time.

I shoot Agnes my "What a dick" look, but she's busy fishing

for the lanyard looped around her neck. So she recognizes him, too. She finds the strap and follows it down to the little digital camera hanging from the end. "Hey, you," she says to the dick's back.

When he turns around again, she points, clicks, and shoots in one fluid motion.

"Not now, Agnes," I say (too late) from above. I blink away the unexpected flash and listen to the sound of my molars grinding together. Remind myself to breathe. Remind myself that it's Friday and that there are only a few hours to go before I'm free of this hellhole.

The guy blinks, too, says, "What the . . ." He notes the way Agnes is smiling up at him and the way I am definitely not smiling. *What a piece of work,* he's no doubt thinking, *this whale of a girl I once knew bulging out of her Black Sabbath shirt. Skin like white paint now. Lips like coal.* He shakes his head and lets out a disgusted sigh before turning his back to us yet again.

My hands made indentations where I planted them against the rough fabric of his jacket. I stare at the handprints as the guy just stands there, not moving even when the line ahead of him thins out. "Sometime this *year* would be nice," I say, insulted by what I know he's thinking about me.

The guy turns back around like it's all just too much. He wipes his hand down his face, dragging his lower eyelids down with it. Sighs. "What the hell did you just say?"

That's it. I belly up to him the way belligerent drunks do in movies, just before a bar brawl. I force my voice to come out as low and menacing as possible. "I said: Sometime. This year. Would be nice."

"I'll move when I'm ready to move. *Shamu.*"

I shrink back at the sound of my old nickname. "It's Moira," I say in a voice so soft and wounded that it surprises even me. *You know that,* I almost add, but then I think better of it.

Before I realize what's happening, Agnes is standing on tiptoe between the two of us. "That's mean!" she says, coming to my defense, her lower jaw thrust forward.

The guy lets out a bitter laugh, points his face in her direction. "Whatever, Gollum."

Agnes looks dumbfounded. One hand rises up, index finger punctuating the air. "Shame on you! Just . . . just . . ."

Nervous laughter bubbles up from the line behind us. Nobody calls Agnes names. Not to her face, anyway.

"Agnes, don't. Let's get out of here." I take hold of my best friend's hand and lower it down, my eyes never leaving Dickhead's face as I pull Agnes away from the line. God knows what he might do. It kills me that I can't come up with a decent comeback. No doubt I'll think of one tonight as I'm falling asleep.

Traces of adrenaline are still pulsing up my spine and through my veins once we get to home ec and start working on our dresses. We never did get to eat lunch. I don't say anything about it, though. Don't bring up the fact that I'm still feeling shaky and combative, even once the weather lets up and a strip of sunshine cuts through the clouds.

After school, Agnes climbs into the booster car seat I installed for her inside El-C, my beater of an El Camino. "You're lucky I have an old car," I told her when I got my license a few months ago. "No airbags in this baby, so we can put your seat in front." El-C does have a truck bed, though. Also big black polka dots that I painted all over her primer-gray paint job.

"Anarchy in the UK" blasts from the ancient speakers as soon as I turn the key in the ignition. Agnes puts her fingers in her ears, even though I know she likes this song. She once told me her favorite part is when Johnny Rotten's voice cracks as he's singing about the Irish Republican Army.

Ever since we left the cafeteria, Agnes has stayed quiet. Now she's staring out the passenger side window. When we're a few blocks away from school, she reaches toward the stereo and turns down the music. "Did you recognize him?" she asks me.

"Who?" I'm already pretending that what happened didn't happen. Already stuffing it down the way I do.

"That guy from the lunch line. Boone Craddock."

"Of course," I respond. "What an ass." I'd say something worse about him, like the word that's been at the tip of my tongue since lunchtime—the one that starts with *mother* and ends with -ucker—but Agnes doesn't like it when I use words like that.

"He didn't use to be an ass."

"People change, Agnes." The words come out harsher than I mean for them to, and I instantly wish I could take them back. But just the name of that, that . . . I can hardly stand to even *think* his name, much less say it.

"Hmm. I guess so," Agnes says. "I've never even seen him at school, probably because he's been in those at-risk classes." Then she says, "I wonder if he remembers us."

I almost say, *How could he not?* But I don't. Instead, I reach for the volume knob and crank up the Pistols as loud as they'll go.

BOONE
DAY 98: MARCH 19

I REMEMBER THEM, ALL RIGHT. WAKING UP SATURDAY MORNING, yesterday's incident replays itself over and over again in my head, like a scene from some lame after-school movie special.

Standing in that lunch line, I'd been ready to slug who-ever just shoved their hands into my back. People are always giving me shit. And for what? *For what?* What have I ever done but try to survive? Just last week, some guy in the hall-way called me "retard" under his breath, hit himself in the chest with the back of his wrist when I walked past. A girl standing nearby gave the guy a little slap on the arm. "That's so mean," she said. And then she laughed at me, too.

It's the kind of thing that makes me miss the Alternative Classroom Experience track I've been on since starting high school last year. So what if being an ACE student marked me as an "at-risk youth"? The Bad Seed Track, some ACE kids liked to call it. Maybe we *were* bad seeds. At least there was a placc where we could hang out and be bad seeds together without getting into too much trouble. Now, thanks to budget cuts, that place is gone. ACE has only been shut down for a few weeks, but I can already tell things aren't going to end well. Being mainstreamed into "normal" high school classes is going to mean constant vigilance. Daily navigation through a minefield of the kind of shit that might just get somebody killed because there won't be an ACE teacher there to talk me down.

I get out of bed and head for the bathroom, wonder if I have any reasonably clean clothes. I have to hustle if I'm going to make it to work on time.

Judging by how dark the kitchen is when I go in there, Mom's not up yet. Big surprise. I flick on the light and head to the cereal cabinet, the cafeteria scene from yesterday still replaying in my mind.

Feeling those hands shove against my spine, I turned around in slow motion, like whoever did it was going to get what they deserved. Who cared if there was no more Alternative Classroom Experience for guys like me? Who cared if juvie was my next stop? I was done. *Done.* The shover was about to learn what a heartless bitch nature could be.

But.

It was Moira Watkins who shoved me. Of all people. At first, I didn't even recognize her under all the makeup. We haven't said zip to each other in . . . well, it's been about four years now. And it didn't make sense why she would have put her hands on me. Then I saw the fight or whatever it was that had broken out farther back in line and realized she'd been shoved, too.

I tried to hide my double take by glaring at Moira for a second and then down at Agnes Delaney, who was standing between us, as easy to miss as always. Then I turned back around like nothing out of the ordinary had happened.

But I kind of had to pull myself together. Had to just stand there for a minute and get the kinks worked out of my brain. Had to refocus and breathe. I was just waiting in the lunch line. That was all. It was fine. It was a normal day. Nobody had punched me. Nobody needed to be punched. One of the things ACE teachers kept trying to teach us before the program shut down was to listen to the voices of our higher selves when we felt overwhelmed. That was supposed to help neutralize whatever negative energy was about to get us in trouble. *Bring it down, dude,* the voice of my higher self urged as I stood in that line. *Everything's okay. Just bring it down.*

Then Moira said, "Sometime this *year* would be nice."

When I turned around again, it looked like she was trying to melt my face with her laser-beam eyes because I wasn't moving fast enough. Which made sense. I was, after all, standing between her and a counter full of food. Okay, so maybe that wasn't the most charitable thought, but with the adrenaline and the barely held back rage pumping through my bloodstream, it was the first thing that came to mind. At the same moment, images of a sixth-grade dodgeball game popped up before I could stop them. It was a pointless memory, one of those things you're embarrassed to think about. I've put it out of my mind in the four years since. Who wouldn't?

I took a deep breath. Thank God I hadn't knocked Moira out before realizing who she was or even that she was a girl. She definitely didn't make that second part easy with the black hair and lips, the white face, the crap around her eyes. Don't goths realize how ridiculous they look? Total freaks. *If you want to be dead, then be dead already! Stop inflicting your hideousness on the rest of us.*

My father's voice in my own head stops me cold.

We had words, me and Moira. Then she crossed the line by getting right up in my face. If I'd done that to *her*, I'd be kicked out of school so fast, it would make your head spin. True, some part of me instinctively felt cornered when she came that close. Still, if I'd had time to think, I know I wouldn't have called her what I did. Agnes, either.

The second I said it, the second I called her "Shamu," Moira's expression changed the way a just-punched guy's expression changes right before he hits the ground. Her face looked like something from the pain chart I saw in the school nurse's office after my first fight this year. Ten faces on the chart ranged from smiling (*Feeling good!*) to scowling and tearful (*The worst I've ever felt*). Moira's face was roughly a seven, but at least she backed the hell off when I insulted her.

God, my head is a muddle this morning. I look down and realize I've poured and eaten two bowls of cereal without knowing I was doing it. I don't even recall getting the milk out of the fridge.

*   *   *

That afternoon, when I get back home from hauling a load of water from the standpipe in town to our cistern out back, Mom's in the hallway. She's wearing her threadbare bathrobe and she looks like a nervous wreck, as usual. Trembly and drained of her life force. Standing in the doorway of her bedroom like she's just woken up (which she probably has). *Who are you?* I sometimes want to ask her. *And what have you done with the woman who used to get up before dawn?* That woman used to fry up a big skillet of bacon and eggs just about every morning. She'd squeeze oranges and make French press coffee before waking me and Dad up so the three of us could start the day together.

"How was your day?" she asks me in the small, defeated voice she uses all the time now.

"Fine," I tell her. "You okay?"

Mom nods before disappearing into the bedroom. As soon as she closes the door, I grab my dad's hunting jacket to wear while I feed Diablo and chop some wood for tomorrow's fire. It still feels subzero outside, but at least the worst of the sleet has let up a little.

Sometimes I think the hunting jacket still smells like my dad. He was wearing it the first and last time he ever took me elk hunting. At one point, I had a clean shot at a mature bull, but I couldn't kill it. Instead, I raised the barrel of the rifle just a hair and missed on purpose, fired off the round just over the animal's shoulder. The bull bolted, and my father cussed as if he hadn't realized all along how misguided it was to bring me out there. I could punch guys out all day long for teasing me about being dumb, but I loved elk too much to kill one. I've always been much happier hunting for their antlers, which tend to break free in winter from the impact of the bulls landing hard on their forelegs after jumping over forest service fences. If I look carefully enough, I always find discarded racks along those fence lines come spring.

To keep my hands warm now, I bury them in the pockets of the hunting jacket as I walk toward Diablo's paddock. My right hand encounters something solid, and I pull it out. It's an empty snuff can I found in the forest last week. I hate litter, so I picked it up, meaning to throw it away later. I didn't give it any more thought at the time, but now a memory from out of nowhere catapults me backward to the day I first found a full can just like it. I couldn't have been older than eight or nine. The can was resting on the edge of the truck bed, beckoning me. I twisted off the wide, flat cap quick, before my father returned from whatever he was doing. Then I pinched out a gob of the mysterious brown substance that reminded me of wet mulch and stuffed it inside my bottom lip, the way I'd seen him do.

I didn't know you're not supposed to swallow. Within moments, I could have easily passed for the lead singer of a metal band called the Heaving Vomits.

My father returned shortly thereafter. It didn't take him long to put two and two together. Those cool gray eyes of his moved from the open snuff can to my pea-green face. He didn't cuss or remove his belt like I thought he would, though. Instead, he came toward me, looming large and blocking out the sun. I remember how huge his frame seemed to me at the time, even though he probably wasn't as big as I am now. "Well," he said, "I suppose you've been punished enough."

Back then, he could still be merciful like that.

4

AGNES

DAY 97: MARCH 20

MOIRA IS MY SHADE TREE.

I first met her when I changed schools halfway through fifth grade. I needed better help with my work as I missed more and more school due to doctor appointments, visits to out-of-town specialists, and time spent at home feeling generally not well. By then, I already had the blood vessels of a seventy-year-old and the beginnings of cardiovascular issues to match. No other Resource room in the district compared with Ms. Marilyn's Resource room at my new school.

I was wearing my Hannah Montana wig that first day, the one that best covered up my sticky-out ears. The fifth-grade teacher, Mrs. Bhamra, had obviously told the students about me already; not one of them dared to so much as look my way when she introduced me. Except Moira. She was sitting in the front row desk to my right. I saw her out of the corner of my eye, staring for so long that I finally turned with a frown and mouthed, *Can I help you?* Between dealing with my parents' divorce and changing schools, it had already been an especially stressful year. I wasn't in the mood to be gawked at today.

"Miss Watkins will be showing you around," the teacher said.

At that, the staring girl smiled and held out her hand for a shake. "I'm Moira."

"Oh," I said. "I'm Agnes." Her hand was huge when it closed around mine. Everything about her was huge. She could have squashed me like a bug, but the handshake wasn't rough at all. Just firm and certain, like something between us was being decided once and for all.

5

MOIRA
DAY 96: MARCH 21

MONDAY MORNING I PICK AGNES UP AT HER HOUSE AS USUAL and force myself not to protest as she slides her favorite mix tape into El-C's old cassette player. I know every song on the tape by heart, and not because I want to. The song she loves most, "Dream" by Priscilla Ahn, sounds a little warbly now, probably because Agnes has rewound and replayed it over and over more times than I can count. I guess it's a pretty enough song, if you like schmaltzy, tear-jerker stuff, which I definitely do not. Sometimes I find myself humming it for no reason other than because it has been drilled into my brain over the past couple of years. I'm actually grateful for the song this morning. It seems to be distracting her, because she doesn't mention the name of my old nemesis even once.

Sixth grade flashed through my mind for only a split second as I stood in that cafeteria line with Boone Craddock looking like he was about to go all postal. But that split second was enough to make me shudder.

Looking back, I think some major hormonal event must have happened to everyone the summer after fifth grade, especially to the girls. All I knew was that when I returned in the fall, there was a new glint of meanness in the eyes of my classmates. It was as if the queen bees had gotten together over the summer and decided what part each kid would play in the Stephen King movie we'd all be forced to reenact. Some kids, the smart, quiet ones, got to be innocent bystanders. Others, the bees included, got to be perpetrators.

I, as it turned out, got to be the star, if not the heroine. My parents are hippies, which meant I usually wore clothes my mom made from tie-dyed cotton fabrics. For lunch, I brought reusable containers full of kefir and tabouleh, sandwiches made with tempeh instead of store-bought lunch meat, everything vegetarian. To top it off, I was already five foot eight and weighed as much as my weight-lifting brother, Grant, who was a senior in high school at the time. It didn't make sense that I could weigh so much eating the way I did, but my mom has always been the same way. One thing she started telling me that year was: *We just have slower metabolisms.* Another was: *You're beautiful, Moira. Embrace who you are. Someday, you'll be the kind of woman Peter Paul Rubens would have painted.*

As if that solved everything. Who'd want to model for a seventeenth-century Flemish Baroque painter, anyway?

It didn't help that much of the weight was in my breasts, which were the most recent gifts bestowed by the Puberty Fairy during my own summertime hormone surge. It took the boys a while to figure out what to call me. The nickname "Dolly Farton" was in heavy rotation, as was "Booby McGee." But I was big everywhere else, too. Hence the moniker that topped all others during that year for sheer usage: "Shamu." Killer whale. Between the name-calling and the fact that Agnes, my only real friend at school, spent most of her time in the Resource room, it wasn't long before every day of sixth grade felt like a slow lead-up to Carrie's prom night.

Thing is, this wasn't a new story. People who are different get bullied all the time. Interesting adults who contribute to society in amazing ways got bullied when they were kids, too. Even back then, even in the middle of it, I knew this. I'd watched *Sesame Street* when I was little. I'd seen the PSAs. Plus, my parents reminded me of this stuff all the time. But knowing I might one day help save the world wasn't much of a comfort when I was twelve and just trying to survive the school year. I was, after all, the one who'd been cast in the starring role by the queen bees at school. I was clearly the girl destined to end up drenched in pigs' blood under the disco ball.

AGNES

DAY 95: MARCH 22

I WAS TWELVE WHEN I GOT MY FIRST DIGITAL CAMERA. IT WAS cheap and had only a handful of megapixels, but it seemed like no small miracle to be able to take pictures at school and then go home and look at them on the computer. In no time, I figured out how to crop images, adjust the brightness and saturation, even add some basic effects.

From that point forward, I never went anywhere without the camera. I used it mainly for taking pictures of my friends and family, but there was another reason I loved it. I couldn't remember not being stared at constantly every time I entered a public space. I couldn't remember strangers' eyes not taking me in, judging me, and then revealing the verdict of what those strangers thought of me. I was funny looking, scary looking, a complete oddity. All of it was out of my control. But holding a camera up to my face gave some of that control back. It gave me a real sense of power for the first time in my life. It was a way of saying, *I'm looking at you, too. And I have thoughts about what I see.*

7

BOONE

DAY 94: MARCH 23

THERE WAS ONE TEACHER IN GRADE SCHOOL WHO I ESPECIALLY liked. Okay, maybe the truth was I loved her a little. Ms. Marilyn ran the Resource room. Her job was to help kids who needed a little more time to figure out the stuff we were learning. Unlike my sixth-grade classroom, Resource was always quiet. It was a great place to concentrate, or would have been, anyway, if being around Ms. Marilyn wasn't such a distraction. She had dark hair and a warm smile, and she was curvier and softer looking than any girl I'd ever seen. She made me think of angel food cake and roller coasters, though I didn't exactly know why. Maybe it was because my insides felt like I was on a roller coaster any time she leaned over my desk to help me with a math problem or to correct my spelling. She smelled like the woods near my house in midspring, when the pine trees started releasing their vanilla scent.

She was also the first teacher who encouraged me to "explore my options" when I felt the need to give some other kid a beatdown. My dad always said I'd been born with his short fuse. When I was little, my parents both laughed about it, but they stopped laughing when my anger started flaring up at school. I tried explaining to them that it only happened when I didn't understand some of the concepts we were supposed to be learning or when I got teased about taking more time than anyone else to finish my work. That's when Mom insisted I get extra help. At first, I stormed around the house like my dad did whenever he'd had a hard day at work. I'd never thought of myself as stupid before. I'd always thought some stuff just took me longer to figure out. Now I wasn't so sure. I was convinced that being pulled out of the regular classroom to spend time in Resource was going to be the end of the world. As it turned out, it was anything but.

Ms. Marilyn taught me to count to ten when I got angry, to use my words instead of my fists when other kids teased me. "You're a good kid," she said. "You just need to learn to deal with frustration in healthier ways." The thought of not seeing her anymore the following year when seventh grade would start nearly did me in.

The two hours I spent in Resource were the best two hours of every day. Sometimes, though, when I got back to my regular classroom, I felt more like a visitor than a regular student, an awkward antelope that didn't quite fit in with the rest of the herd. It didn't help that I started kindergarten a year later than everyone else and so was older than my classmates. By all rights, I should have been smarter and surer of myself than all of them.

Like me, Agnes spent a good chunk of time in Resource. I thought of her as the "little old lady girl." There was nothing wrong with her brain, that much was clear right off the bat. She was there mainly to get help catching up on work she'd missed when she was out of school for medical stuff. A couple of times, she was even in the hospital. I never asked her for details when she got back, but I figured it couldn't be good. Sometimes, when Ms. Marilyn was busy with other students, Agnes helped me with reading. There's no way I would have read out loud in front of anyone else at school, but being embarrassed in front of Agnes just felt wrong somehow. Like, *Hey, I know teachers have explained to us how you have this terminal disease that also makes you look like someone's grandma when you're twelve, but I can't read out loud to you because I'm afraid I'll get some of the words wrong.* That would have been too self-conscious even for me, and I was about the most self-conscious person I knew, other than Moira Watkins.

Moira was Agnes's best friend and unofficial bodyguard. The only time I wouldn't read aloud was when she came to Resource to hang out and study with Agnes. Moira was smart and fierce, and she could be sharp-tongued when she wanted to be. I thought she was extremely pretty, too, though I could tell she didn't think so herself. She was almost as big as I was; she towered over the other girls, even when she walked around with her shoulders slumped and her head down, which was most of the time.

Ms. Marilyn clearly loved Agnes and Moira. In fact, I was pretty sure she loved every student who came through the door of the Resource room, which caused me no small amount of torment. She was like Miss Honey in *Matilda*, which Agnes read aloud to a group of lower-grade Resource kids over the course of a few weeks. I was right there in the room, as usual, and I couldn't help but listen as she read. It was a great story. I wouldn't admit that out loud even if someone was holding a Kalashnikov rifle to my head, but it was true. Matilda was a badass. Moira was probably a badass, too, underneath her shyness and the way she'd retreat when other kids teased her about her size. They were harder on her than they were on me, even, which was saying something. Maybe it was because Moira hadn't beaten anyone to a pulp yet. I thought about mentioning this as a potential strategy to her, but then erased it from my mind immediately.

Boy, was *that* ever a mistake.

One day at lunch, I came out of the boys' bathroom and found Jared Vandercamp cornering Moira in the covered corridor between our classroom and the playground. "Fat ass, fat ass, fat ass," Jared was saying over and over again, his face only about an inch away from hers.

I didn't doubt he was spitting on her a little as he said it. Without thinking, I stepped between the two of them and shoved Jared backward. "Hey! Leave her alone."

"Boone," Moira told me. "Don't."

Jared looked surprised at first, but he quickly regained his balance and squared himself. "What are you going to do about it, Tardboy?" He made his mouth all droopy and stuck his tongue out the side of it as if to demonstrate what I was, what I would always be.

And that was it. A few seconds later, I was standing over Jared, every muscle in my body tensed and coiled as Moira screamed, "Stop it!" The whole thing happened so fast that I didn't even recall the flats of my hands on Jared's shoulders, propelling him backward yet again, this time onto the concrete walkway. He looked up at me, wide-eyed and helpless. A brief wave of utter peace flowed through my veins at the sight. If he attempted to get up, I'd strike like a rattlesnake. I wouldn't even have to think about it. At a certain point, these kinds of things became instinct.

Meanwhile, Moira was still screaming at me to stop, to leave Jared alone. Over on the blacktop, other kids had registered the chaos and were running over to surround us with the usual chants and jeers that started up any time a fight broke out. Teachers were hurrying toward us, too.

Ms. Marilyn wouldn't even look at me when I returned to Resource after doing time in the principal's office. I'd been told to gather my things and wait to be summoned back. My mother had been called to pick me up early, and I was being suspended for three days. Moira wouldn't look at me, either, not at first, anyway. After a few minutes, she got up to sharpen her pencil. She dropped a folded-up piece of paper on my desk as she walked by, and I allowed myself to breathe a small sigh of relief. I'd been afraid she'd never talk to me again. Not that I understood why. She could have at least shown me a little gratitude for decking jerkface Jared. I waited until Ms. Marilyn's back was turned to open the note.

I can take care of myself, it read. *Go to hell.*

Five minutes before I was called back to the office, Ms. Marilyn finally spoke to me. She knelt down next to my desk and let out a big sigh. "I was really disappointed by your behavior today." She whispered it so the other kids wouldn't hear. I could feel Agnes's eyes on the two of us. Moira was acting like I didn't exist at all. Ms. Marilyn spent the next few minutes whispering about the whole "words instead of fists" thing. I felt awful, of course, but I forced myself to look at her out of respect anyway. It was a good excuse to watch her mouth as she spoke, like I couldn't quite understand what she was saying and had to lip-read.

Still, the message got through. I started to clean things up after that. I started to try harder in school and take pride in my grades. Mom was thrilled. Dad, not so much. It's not like he encouraged me to go around clobbering people or anything, but it was no secret that he was proud of the fact that I *could* clobber a guy if I wanted to. I spent less time in the Resource room and more time mainstreamed, even though the teacher that year, Mr. Carter, didn't try to hide the fact that he wasn't too pleased to have me back in the classroom for most of the day. The first time I got an A on a math quiz (thanks to Ms. Marilyn's tutoring), Carter was shocked.

"This can't be right," he said, dropping the quiz onto my desk.

I focused on my fists and braced myself for the usual remarks from my classmates. It was always going to be the same story. No matter how hard I tried, things were never going to change.

Then I heard Carter saying, "What is it, Miss Delaney?"

Agnes typically spent math period in the regular classroom, too. When I glanced over toward her desk, she was lowering her hand from the air. "Um, I'm sorry," she said, "but why not?"

Carter sighed. "Why not what?" he asked her.

"Why can't it be right that Boone got an A? He worked as hard as anybody else."

Our teacher didn't answer. Instead, he ignored her, walked toward the front of the room, and told us to open our textbooks to page ninety-one.

MOIRA

DAY 93: MARCH 24

AFTER AGNES STOOD UP FOR BOONE DURING MATH, SHE STARTED asking him to hang out with us. He obviously felt awkward about it, which was just as well. I'd already told him I could defend myself, that I didn't need a bodyguard. Now I made it clear that I wanted nothing to do with him. Agnes and I were just fine on our own. The last thing we needed was a third wheel.

Then, one week in the spring of sixth grade, I was out sick for a few days. When I got back to school, I found out that Boone and Agnes had been spending recess together, and they were friends now. Agnes was stubborn about it, too. Despite my protests, she wouldn't stand for Boone being excluded. Still, it always seemed like he was a little uncomfortable being around us. Sometimes, I'd catch him looking over at the other boys in the class as they held tetherball tournaments on the blacktop or flag football games on the field. But the three of us kept hanging out. For a while, anyway.

Usually, we'd walk out to the chain-link fence bordering the soccer field. It was the farthest point from the school buildings that was still school property. Boone would give Agnes a piggyback ride out there. Sometimes, whatever teacher was on recess duty would leave us be. Other days, we'd hear the shrill whistle calling us back to the crowded blacktop. I always felt myself deflating when I heard it. To me, it was the sound of a prison alarm ordering me back to the exercise yard to be tortured by the other inmates.

One day, as we were hanging out by that fence that separated us from the outside world, Boone said something that made me laugh. I can't even remember what it was now, but I do have a vivid memory of Agnes reaching for her camera and snapping a picture at the exact moment I cracked up. Later, Agnes showed me the image on her computer. I was looking a little sideways at Boone. It might have been the first time I really looked at him, now that I think about it. I was surprised by whatever he'd said and by the fact that he'd made me laugh. My smile was natural and relaxed. It was the last time I looked at my own face and thought it was pretty.

"I think he likes you," Agnes whispered when the bell rang

and the three of us headed back toward the classroom. Boone was walking several yards ahead.

"Ha," I said.

But Agnes claimed to know about these things. "Any day now," she whispered, "I figure the two of you are going to start holding hands."

AGNES

DAY 92: MARCH 25

THE COUNTER IN OUR HIGH SCHOOL'S OFFICE IS TALLER THAN I am, so I hold my hand up high to get the secretary's attention.

"Can I help you, Agnes?"

"I need to talk to Principal Weaver."

The secretary's eyes appear over the edge of the counter. "May I ask what this is about?"

I draw myself up to my full height, which isn't exactly impressive, but still. "You certainly may."

Blank stare.

"Something happened last week," I tell her. "In the cafeteria. My friend Moira and I were bullied. Threatened." I know the words to use to keep the secretary from trying to turn me away. It's not easy to get a spur-of-the-moment audience with the principal. "Something needs to be done."

"Why did you wait so long to let us know?"

"I . . . I needed some time to think about it." This was true. More specifically, I'd needed some time to think about whether or not to throw an old friend under the bus, even if he clearly isn't my friend now and hasn't been for a long time.

*　　*　　*

"And what did he call you?" Principal Weaver is squeaking from side to side in his chair, turning toward and then away from sunlight filtering through the window blinds. His entire office smells like the half-eaten sandwich sitting on his desk. Pastrami and Swiss, I'm guessing.

" 'Gollum,' " I answer. "Which is fine. I don't even care. But he called Moira 'Shamu.' Like the orca. And nobody should be teased about their weight. Isn't that what you're always trying to teach us here?"

"Indeed. But nobody should be called 'Gollum,' either."

I'm a bit taken aback by this. I didn't come here to defend myself. I came here to defend Moira. I'm wearing one of my favorite wigs today, the auburn one with old-fashioned Shirley Temple curls. The principal's smirk makes me realize that he's having a hard time taking me seriously. No doubt between the wig and my helium voice, I'm coming off as too adorable. It's a fairly common problem. I reach up and pull the wig from my head, exposing the nearly bald expanse of skin there. I have a few wispy strands left, but that's it. Give me a little styling gel and I can create the world's most hideous comb-over. Long, pronounced veins run like rivers across the map of my skull.

Predictably, Principal Weaver blanches and stammers. This is nothing new. Just yesterday at the grocery store, a toddler gaped at me until the pacifier fell from his mouth. Kids are usually the easy ones to deal with, though. All I have to do is smile or wave, and they'll do the same, like I'm a cartoon character come to life. Adults are the worst. They want to be able to check me out while pretending not to. But it's an impossible thing to hide, even when someone's wearing sunglasses or watching you from the corner of their eye. I don't bother to wave or smile at most staring adults because, usually, they just act like they never saw me. Which is preposterous.

Other people's fascination and pity are powerful, heavy things. They're as heavy as those lead-filled X-ray cloaks the techs put over me when I'm getting a scan to check my arteries or bones. Sometimes, when I'm out in public, it's like people are piling lead cloak after lead cloak on top of me until I can barely walk or breathe or see. People mean well; I understand this. I've had more bake sales in my honor than I can count. I've been the honorary mascot of my school and my town. If I live long enough, I could probably take the state, maybe even go national. With my nearly hairless head and beaky nose, I might even replace the bald eagle eventually. Who knows? Before I met Moira, it was like I was living in a glass display case with all these people (strangers and acquaintances) on the other side of the glass, telling me how much they loved me, how "there for me" they were as I "battled this disease." Then Moira and I became friends, and Moira became the freak, taking all eyes off me and onto herself. For years now, Moira has been protecting me almost constantly, in ways big and small. The question is, who protects Moira?

The pastrami smell is getting to me. My stomach does a nauseated little flip. "You need to do something," I tell Principal Weaver.

"We'll get on it," he says. "Trust me."

"When?"

"You can rest assured I will be speaking to Boone Craddock as soon as possible."

"Okay then." I put the wig back on and hold out a hand for him to shake, which he does. Then the principal follows me out into the hallway and watches as I turn on my heel and march away from the office. Before pushing through the doors separating the administrative building from the rest of the school, I glance back at him with what I can only hope is a *don't make me come back here* look in my eye.

Sure enough, Weaver gives me a quick but formal military salute.

10

BOONE

DAY 91: MARCH 26

YOU WOULDN'T THINK IT WOULD BE HARD WORK SETTING UP temporary housing for a bunch of chicks and rabbits, but it is. I'm on hour two of pouring poultry starter into feeders, making sure the water containers aren't full enough to drown the babies, transferring this last batch of chicks from their shipping boxes to their correct holding bins, and double-checking the heat lamps. I head into the storage room, where my boss, TJ, keeps the big steel trough that needs to be set up with shavings, water, and alfalfa for the last of the "Easter bunnies." People will buy them for their kids on impulse today and then abandon the rabbits at shelters or turn them loose in the forest, where they'll make easy prey once the kids get sick of taking care of them.

God, I hate my own species sometimes.

About an hour before my shift ends, TJ tells me that Cheyenne, one of the cutesy rodeo queens who works the register (and who also happens to have TJ wrapped around her finger), wants to get her older brother a job. Turns out I am—big surprise—the most disposable employee. Not that TJ uses those exact words. He doesn't have to. My place in the Feed & Seed pecking order is glaringly obvious.

"Cheyenne's brother is twenty, and he's not in school anymore," TJ says. We're standing in the hay barn, where I've been stacking the truckload of alfalfa bales that came in from Colorado last night. "He can work hours you can't. We have to prioritize guys who can do that."

I hope my boss doesn't notice the sudden cold sweat breaking out all over my body. Hay dust turns to a thin layer of green paste in the creases of my skin. "What if I can get out of school early? Maybe I can take a work-study elective."

"Can you do that as a sophomore?"

I look down at the ground and give a weak shrug. "You never know."

"It'll all work out," TJ says, clapping me on the arm. "For now, just start coming in every other weekend, and we'll go from there."

Easy for you to say, I think. More than anything, I wish I could tell TJ where to shove his every other weekend. I wish I could walk out of here with my middle finger high in the air and never look back. I'm not a total fool, though. It's not like anyone else is going to hire me, and I doubt TJ would give me a good reference if I walked out. The sad truth is that TJ took me on as an act of charity. It's only my strong back and work ethic that have kept me in part-time hours this long. Still, I have to say something.

"With all due respect, sir, I don't think those hours are going to be enough."

TJ, who was walking back toward the store entrance, stops and turns around. "Well, it's what I can offer you." His voice is sharper than it was a minute ago. "Your father put the roof on this place, and I've tried to help you out, but this is a change that's going to happen. As I said, I can still give you every other weekend. Take it or leave it."

I can't even begin to imagine what I'm going to tell Mom. Probably, I'm going to tell her nothing. Probably, I'm just going to have to step up wood sales, and now that spring is upon us, elk skull and antler sales, too. I'll have to go out and scout for racks as often as I can after school and on the weekends. Park the truck in one of the abandoned lots in town and set up my painted plywood sign nearby where it faces oncoming traffic: *BARGAIN BONES: Antler & Skull Sales.* Maybe Mom doesn't have to know about my hours being slashed. It's not like she checks up on where I am, anyway.

My boss is waiting for an answer.

"I'll take it," I tell him.

* * *

As usual, I haul a load of water after work. The Chevy's suspension hasn't been sounding right lately, and the five hundred gallons of water loading it down don't help. We'll be completely screwed if the springs flatten out. That's a major repair. I try not to think about how carefree Saturdays used to be when I was a kid, but images from that time rise up in my mind anyway. Me lazing around in the hammock, watching Mom teach horseback riding lessons all day. Dad coming home from his job as a roofer, opening up the smoker at dinnertime and pulling out elk or buffalo steaks from animals he'd hunted and processed himself. The three of us sitting around the kitchen table laughing about whatever funny things we'd seen or done or thought about that day. I took it all for granted.

Back then, whenever my parents argued about something, my dad always had enough sense to simply leave the house and go hang out in the tack room or work on the backhoe's engine. Once he'd cooled down, he'd come back inside and apologize to her. Maybe I'd find them hugging in the kitchen, smiling at each other. Maybe I'd find them sitting on the couch holding hands, her head resting on his shoulder. Whatever it was, they'd always make up. Things would always go back to normal.

Then, one overcast day when I was in seventh grade, he

slipped on some wet leaves and fell off the roof he'd been finishing as a private side job to supplement his regular income with the construction company. Had it not been for the stack of tarped shingles below that broke his fall, he might have died. "Concussion," doctors said at first. "Maybe a bit of mild brain swelling." They saw nothing amiss on his scans and ordered him to take it easy for a couple of weeks. But when he developed a nonstop headache that got worse and worse, they finally said, "Brain injury. It doesn't always show up right away." The question then became whether or not my dad would feel better and how long it would take.

The owner of the construction company he worked for tried to keep him on after the accident, but the economy wasn't doing well. "People just aren't building as many houses as they used to," he told my dad when he finally let him go. My dad was convinced he was really fired because he kept making rookie mistakes, like misplacing the nail gun and forgetting to check on the delivery of shingles and lumber to the worksites. His balance was off, too, and his boss had already expressed concern that he might fall off another roof. "He's just afraid I'd file a workman's comp claim and raise his premiums, the cheap SOB," my father said.

Mom gave as many riding lessons as she could to help pay the bills until he could find other work. She also picked up some part-time work as a cashier at the dollar store and started taking antidepressants. "Just to take the edge off these rough times," she told me when I asked about the prescription bottle sitting on the kitchen counter. "Just temporarily."

The pills actually seemed to help lighten her up. She didn't seem to get so down about the money stuff when she was taking them. They probably would have helped even more if my dad hadn't kept turning into somebody we recognized less and less.

"It's hard for him to not be able to fully provide for us," Mom told me when the two of us were alone. "He feels like he's no longer the man he used to be." She reminded me that his brain was going to need time to heal. Maybe she was reminding herself, too. I don't know.

What I did know was that my dad was noticeably different now. He'd never been an easy person before falling off that roof, but at least he was someone you could reason with. Now it was pretty clear that one of the side effects of his new personality change was that his already lightning-quick temper was even more intense than it used to be. The simplest thing, like misplacing his keys or a minor leak in the water tank, could set him off.

By that point, my dad was doing what he could to bring in some money. He'd learned to shoe horses as a teenager, so he started doing some of that again, even though his coordination wasn't what it used to be and bending over to trim the hooves and nail on the shoes killed his back. He'd bring me along to help when I wasn't in school. Sometimes, on the weekends, he'd take me out on his rounds. Other weekends, when there were no horses to trim or shoe, he'd drag me along with him to the woods to help cut firewood that could later be sold by the cord. On every one of those trips, the misery and frustration of not being the man he used to be seemed to leak out of his pores.

It shouldn't have been a surprise when he started drinking on top of everything else. It was your standard downward spiral, the whoosh of a toilet being flushed as the life our family once knew swirled down the drain.

After that, whenever things got heated between my parents, he'd stay and fight. Rather than going outside to clear his head like he used to, he'd follow Mom around the house and keep yelling. Sometimes he'd even give her shoulder a little shake or poke her in the chest to drive a point home. These were things he'd never done before his brain injury. Once, he tapped his finger in the middle of her forehead, and not too gently, either. I stood in a dim corner of the room, out of his way but keeping an eye on him, clenching my fists over and over.

"Stop it," my mother said. It was clear she was trying to keep from crying.

"Well, you don't *listen*," he told her, tapping again. "What else am I supposed to do?" His voice was slurred. I'd already seen him at the bottle that morning, pouring some whiskey into his coffee cup when he thought I wasn't watching.

"Cut it out," I told him, my voice shaking.

He rushed at me in silence as Mom screamed at him to stop. Grabbed me by the shoulders and threw me down onto the rug. "What did you say to me, boy? Don't you *ever* talk that way to me again, you hear?"

After that, we never knew what to expect, never knew how he might act on any given day or night.

11

AGNES

DAY 90: MARCH 27

MY EASTER BASKET IS FULL OF JELLY BEANS, MARSHMALLOW chicks, and more chocolate than I'll probably be able to eat for the rest of the year. I also got a fancy Victorian sugar egg, one with a peephole you can look through to see the little sculpted frosting rabbit mom with her two rabbit children opening their Easter baskets full of carrots. It's a pretty impressive panorama, really.

That afternoon, I log in to the online progeria community to wish everyone who celebrates it a happy Easter. The website isn't a huge part of my life or anything. There are no more than a couple hundred of us progeria kids alive at any given time, and we're all scattered across the globe. Still, I have bonded with some of the other kids, and I like to stay in touch.

The hardest thing is logging in only to see that someone isn't doing well, or worse, that someone I talked to only a month or so ago has died. For some reason, it's their parents I always worry about most.

Sometimes, like today, when people the world over are celebrating rebirth, I catch Mom watching me when she thinks I don't notice. Her eyes take in my gnarled hands with their oversize joints and brittle, misshapen fingernails. My bird bones and loose skin. I wonder if Mom is thinking that this is how she might look at eighty, at ninety.

A mother shouldn't be able to see her own future in her child. Then again, since she grew up not knowing her real mother, my mom doesn't have anyone to watch for these kinds of clues. I guess that makes me a sort of oracle. That can't be all bad, right?

MOIRA

DAY 89: MARCH 28

AGNES GOES STRAIGHT TO HER ROOM AFTER SCHOOL ON MONDAY TO finish homework and edit photos on her computer. I don't feel like doing my homework yet. I'm a straight-A student who manages to make procrastination work for me, and I'll be damned if I'm going to break my streak by getting stuff done early for a change.

Since I don't feel like going home yet, either, it's a relief when Agnes's mom, Deb, summons me out to their little backyard patio. Once we've settled into a couple of plastic chairs, Deb snags a partially smoked cigarette from an ashtray sitting on the little table between us. "I need to quit," she mutters, shooting a guilty glance at the back door. "Agnes hates it." She lights and inhales in one quick motion. I still like hanging out with her, though. Deb's one of the few adults who don't seem at all fazed by my clothes or my makeup. Probably it's because she's pretty much seen it all. Agnes told me a long time ago that her mom grew up as a foster kid who was shuttled from house to house and never really had any family to speak of until she met Agnes's dad.

Not that I have anything against spending time with my own parents. Sometimes, though, it just seems like they're too stuck in their own . . . worldview . . . to really relate to me. While I, for example, feel most at peace lost in thoughts of hard-core thrash music and general urban destruction, my parents are ardent worshippers of nature. While I can't get enough of distorted guitar licks and screaming vocals, they're late-blooming flower children who still listen to Wavy Gravy and Frank Zappa. In the nineties, when all the other twenty-somethings were climbing the dot-com ladder and flipping houses, my parents were camping naked somewhere along the Pacific Crest Trail, or gifting at Burning Man, or mourning Jerry Garcia.

The second my older brother, Grant, was born, they put him in a hemp baby sling and just sort of incorporated him into their lifestyle. It was only after I came along that they reluctantly settled down and got jobs with a couple of local nonprofits that focus on environmental education and the arts. My mom bought copies of the *Moosewood Cookbook* and *Tales from a Vegan Table*. She became the ultimate hippie homemaker, baking dairy-free carob chip cookies and tie-dyeing all of my T-shirts.

This was all well and good until that horrendous sixth-grade year, when kids decided that the only acceptable clothes and home lives were those patterned directly after the latest top-twenty pop videos and Disney sitcoms. It didn't seem to matter that nobody actually had a life like that. You just had to look and act like you did to be considered acceptable. It's probably the reason I find Agnes's interest in shiny, sparkly, bubble-gum pop star stuff so distasteful. I deal with it, of course, just like Agnes deals with my reaper-like taste in clothes and music, but it's not always easy.

For a while, I tried really, really hard to be the kind of acceptable the sixth-grade ruling class insisted upon. I tried to wear the right clothes and watch the right shows (always at Agnes's house, since my own parents are totally anti-TV. They even have a "Kill Your Television" bumper sticker on their restored Vanagon). It didn't take me long to figure out how expensive those acceptable clothes could be, though. And Mom refused to buy any item that wasn't a) practical and b) absolutely necessary.

Enter Deb. One day toward the start of junior high, she taught me and Agnes how to sew a few different types of stitches on her old Singer sewing machine. At first, we made basic things, like pot holders and Christmas stockings, before moving on to simple A-line skirts. Not too long after that, I started branching out and experimenting with my own patterns.

Unfortunately, no matter what style possibilities I could envision in my head or bring to life on the sewing machine, it didn't seem to matter. At school I was still just the big girl who got bigger every day. No matter how many diets I tried, I remained the easy-to-strike target for as many insults as my classmates cared to hurl my way. By the end of grade school, I'd heard it all: *Freakshow . . . Lard Ass . . . Ten-Ton Tessie . . . Humpback . . . Can't believe nobody's harpooned you yet.*

"You okay?" Deb asks, squinting at me.

"Yeah."

"So, what's this I hear about some guy insulting you and Agnes at school over a week ago?"

One of the things I've always loved most about Deb is that she'll never push you to talk if you just kind of want to hang out and say nothing instead. So it means something that she's pushing a little for information now. I can't blame her for wanting to know. Agnes is always trying to protect her mom from stress and worry, and I'm sure it makes Deb nuts that her own daughter thinks she's such a wimp. Because she isn't. Not only is she a single parent, but she's attending college online so she can get her teaching credential. When Deb's not studying, she works as a substitute teacher to make ends meet and get experience. Still, at the end of the day, she can't out-stubborn her own four-foot-tall daughter. I know for a fact that when Agnes decides to clam up about a situation, like this new one with Boone Craddock, nothing's going to convince her to do otherwise.

"Tell me what really happened," Deb says, sneaking another puff of her cigarette. "Tell me all the stuff Agnes won't."

"God, where do I start?" I answer. "I seriously wanted to kill him. Still do."

Deb blows smoke out the side of her mouth and smiles. "Well, he'll be coming here to rake leaves next week, so maybe you'll get your chance." She waves the smoke away with one hand.

"He's *what?*"

"Apparently, the school is trying to take a 'creative approach' to the bullying problem." She makes air quotes with her fingers. "That's what the principal told me, anyway."

"God."

"Yeah. I have to say, though, part of me feels bad for the kid. I'm pretty sure he and his mom had a hard go of it after that thing with his father. I mean, don't get me wrong—the principal told me what he called the two of you, and I think he's . . ." Deb glances at the back door again to make sure Agnes isn't within earshot. Then she lowers her voice to a whisper. "I think he's a complete shit for that."

We sit there for a while in silence while I relive the cafeteria scene in my mind, how I didn't recognize Boone at first from the back. Maybe I shouldn't have been so nasty when he started holding up the line. But I had the shakes, like I always do before lunch. Mainly, though, I was just trying to protect Agnes from the fight or whatever it was that had broken out in the line behind us. Boone's slowness in getting the hell out of our way almost seemed like a hostile act.

"You remember that thing with his dad, right?"

I nod, still half lost in thought. "Yeah. I never really heard details, though. And Boone left school right after, so . . ."

"I never got all the details, either," she says. "He was a nice boy back when you all hung around together, wasn't he?"

Agnes comes out to the patio before I can respond. She frowns at the ashtray and at the cigarette in Deb's hand.

"We should work on the dresses Saturday," I say in my brightest voice to distract her.

"I can't," Agnes responds. "It's my dad's weekend."

Deb rolls her eyes.

"Good luck with that," I tell her. "Just don't come back here and try to convert me or anything."

"They're not religious wackos," Agnes says. "Jeez." She turns to go back inside.

"If you say so," I call after her, unable to stop myself. "But don't let their churchy propaganda get inside your head. I like you just the way you are, snowflake."

BOONE
DAY 88: MARCH 29

I'm back in the principal's office, aka my second home.

"You're not a bad kid," Weaver's saying. "I know that. But, unfortunately, the world isn't going to know that if you keep going around knocking people out every time somebody gets in your face. You just can't do that, son."

Don't call me son, I think. Out loud I say, "I didn't punch her."

"This time." Weaver creaks back in his chair. "Look, I know things have been hard for you since . . . well, for a long time now. And I know things are even harder now that the ACE program's been cut. Some other former ACE students are struggling right now, too. But I think you'll find you can fit in to regular school just fine if you—"

I don't necessarily mean to snort, but I snort anyway.

"Is something funny?" Weaver sits up straighter now. Ceases to look like an ally.

"Just the way you call this 'regular' school," I answer him. "Like ACE was somehow irregular."

The principal sighs.

I look down at my hands, which are dotted with calluses where the ax handle and the sledge handle and the mucking fork handle and the shovel handle have rubbed in different spots. My fingernails are chewed down and grimy, and my wrists disappear into the ratty but still-hanging-in-there cuffs of my dad's old Carhartt jacket. I'm embarrassed by these hands. Nobody else at school has hands like these, but what am I supposed to do? Stop using them? That's a laugh.

Thing is, Weaver's right. I know I should chill out, but how can I when people are constantly trying to get a rise out of me? They have no idea what I'm capable of doing to them, either. I would gladly kill the next jock who gave me shit if I thought I could get away with it. But you can't say that kind of thing in "regular" school.

You have to keep it inside.

That's not how it was in my alternative classes. The ACE building is only about a hundred yards away from where I'm sitting now, but it couldn't have been more different from the regular version of high school Weaver's so proud of. Not that it was an endless group therapy session or anything. It was still school. Hell, it was *this* school, but at least we bad seeds had some time and space most days to chill a little and talk about whatever stuff might be eating away at us. At least I got to hang out with students from all four grades and not just other sophomores like me. Now that we're all mainstreamed, I only see the other ACE kids in the hallways and in a few of my classes. It almost seems like the new schedules were designed to keep the former ACE tenth graders apart. Everyone's so busy trying to assimilate that we barely talk to one another. Sometimes there's a *S'up*, sometimes a quick chin-jut greeting, but that's it.

"Getting back to this most recent incident," Weaver says, "we've contacted Ms. Delaney."

"Agnes's mom," I say, remembering.

"Yes. And she's agreed with our assessment that a form of . . . service on your part would be an appropriate response here. I'm thinking yard cleanup, maybe some heavy lifting she needs help with around the place. You're a strapping guy. You'll need to complete two days' worth of service, total. At least two hours each day. Weekdays after school or weekends are both fine."

I have to work and haul water on the weekends, so that's out. "Do I have to?"

"It's that or long-term suspension at this point. Possibly expulsion."

I don't need to think about this for very long. If I refuse

to do the service, I'll be out of school. And no offense to Mom, but there isn't a chance in hell I'm going to spend more time at home than I absolutely have to. I love her and everything, but . . . no.

"I'll do it," I tell Principal Weaver. "Yard work, lifting, whatever. I'll do the service."

14

AGNES

DAY 87: MARCH 30

"HEY, MUSCLES!"

Dad calls me this sometimes, especially when it's been a while since we've seen each other. He first said it when I was in second grade and he let me win at arm wrestling.

I climb into the backseat of his car Wednesday after school. I have a doctor's appointment, and since I'll be spending the night at his house anyway, Dad thought it would be nice if he drove me there for a change. Afterward, we'll go get ice cream. When he asked what I thought of the idea, I heard Moira's voice in my head saying, *Whatever floats your boat.* Out loud I said, "Sounds great."

Today's appointment should be pretty run-of-the-mill. Typically, a nurse will check my height and my weight, neither of which has gone up since I was seven. Dr. Caslow will ask if I have any new pain or mobility issues and give me updates on drug trials I've been invited to participate in. Occasionally, some specialist on aging or heart disease or Hutchinson-Gilford Progeria Syndrome (the fancy name for what I have) will ask for permission to publish the results of my various tests in medical journals. As a rare case (I'm almost sixteen and haven't croaked yet), I'm in pretty high demand that way.

Dr. Caslow is my main doctor. He's a gerontologist who also practiced pediatrics in his younger days. Sometimes I meet with him at the hospital instead of during his rounds at the senior center, like when specialized tests are needed, but that hasn't been the case for a while. I consider him family. Over the years, I've been poked and prodded by some of the top progeria doctors and researchers in the world, but he was the one who first diagnosed me when I was a toddler. Like most progeria kids, I looked totally normal when I was an infant. It wasn't until I was almost two years old that my growth slowed way down. My body was also starting to show some of the classic signs that a couple of doctors in nineteenth-century England first noted when they "discovered" the disorder that would one day be mine: there was my skinny little body and my comparatively too-large head to start with. Then there was my hair, which was falling out, and my skin, which looked and felt like it was drying up.

Today, Dr. Caslow is going to check my joints, which have been really sore lately, and my heart, which has started doing this flutter-kick sort of thing in my chest when I get even the slightest bit excited or upset. I know these things are to be expected. Kids like me deal with all the typical stuff old people do. We just do it sixty or seventy years early, when kids our actual, chronological age are cheerleading, skateboarding, and running track. I try not to let it get to me. Sometimes I even succeed.

*　　*　　*

Kitty's the first person I see when we walk through the big double doors of the senior center. She's a glamour queen in her dotage who used to be a foxy Chicago socialite. When Kitty moved here to be closer to her kids and grandkids, she refused to give up her makeup and diamonds and fancy clothes. Today, she's decked out in a silk pantsuit, lounging on one of the sofas in the lobby.

"Darling!" she cries, getting slowly to her feet when she spots me.

I walk into her open arms for a Chanel No. 5–scented hug. "Hi, Kitty."

She winks at my dad. "And who is this handsome gentleman?"

"I'm Tom," he says, holding out his hand.

"Kitty doesn't do handshakes," she tells him. "Come here, you."

"Oh," he says, glancing at me for a terrified second as she grabs his forearm and pulls him into an embrace. "Okay."

I try my best to keep a straight face. My dad has never been too comfortable around old people. The older I've gotten, the more he's treated me like an antique porcelain doll. We do less and less of the roughhousing I used to love when I was little and my parents were still together. Heck, even arm wrestling is out now. He's afraid I might get a dislocated shoulder or a broken humerus.

Kitty has released my dad. "Here for your checkup?" she asks, readjusting the elastic waistband of her suit.

I nod.

We check in at the front desk, and a pretty nurse who's new at the center shows us to the usual exam room. She hands me a gown and tells me I can change in the bathroom down the hall. "It could be a bit of a wait," she tells us. "The doctor's a little behind schedule this afternoon."

"No worries," Dad says, smiling at her.

When I get back from the bathroom (clutching the gown closed with both hands), he's engrossed in one of the well-worn tabloid magazines from a rack next to his chair.

Before too long, Dr. Caslow comes in and gives me a high five. I wonder if he does this with his chronologically old patients, too. "How is she doing with medications?" he asks my dad as they shake hands. "Any issues with the statins?"

66

Dad looks at me and then back at Dr. Caslow. He knows I was put on statins in addition to the baby aspirin I was already taking to help keep my arteries from getting too hard and narrow, but the truth is he and I only see each other a few times a month, not enough for him to know much more than that. "I'm doing fine, mostly," I say. "Sometimes my muscles get a little achy."

The doctor pulls a little flashlight from the pocket of his coat and looks inside my mouth. "Well, that's to be expected, unfortunately," he says. "While we don't really know if that's a medication issue or a progeria issue, we'll have a better idea of whether or not the meds are helping when we do your next round of blood work and scans." He pulls an otoscope from the front pocket of his lab coat and looks inside my ears. "Still doing your stretches at home?"

"Yeah," I say, grimacing. Every night before I go to sleep, Mom comes into my room and says, "Time for the rack." Then she proceeds to stretch my joints and limbs in different directions just a little farther than is comfortable. It's supposed to limber me up and prevent injuries by keeping my muscles and tendons flexible, but I'm not sure it actually helps.

The nurse comes back in, and Dr. Caslow says he'll need to do a full physical exam. He asks my dad if he wants to stay in the room.

"He can leave," I say, answering for him. Dad looks surprised and a little hurt, but I just say, "What? I'm almost sixteen!" *So what if my body's closer to a hundred? I'm still a teenager, darn it.*

*　　*　　*

My stepmother, Jamey, has dinner ready when we get to the house. She's wearing her usual homeschool mom uniform—long denim skirt, a man's oversize button-down shirt, and no makeup. (*Holy roller,* Mom called her when Jamey and my dad first got married. *Tambourine smacker.*) Even now, more than five years later, Jamey and my mom have still only spoken a handful of times, usually on those rare occasions when Mom has picked me up from their house or Jamey has driven me home to Mom's. Jamey is born-again, and she believes in modesty and not in physical affection. To prove it, she doesn't hug me or Dad when we walk in, but she does say, "Greetings, fellow Delaneys." (Mom also thought it was hilarious that Jamey's name changed to Jamey Delaney when she got married: "She sounds like a Dr. Seuss character!")

I help Jamey finish setting the table for dinner and then go upstairs to summon my siblings. There are pictures of all of us on the wall next to the stairs, including one of me as a normal-looking baby. Of the three kids who live in this house full-time, Isaiah's the oldest. He's eleven, and he's Jamey's son from her first marriage. Even though Isaiah and I aren't related by blood, I still consider him to be my brother. Then there are my dad and Jamey's twins, Obadiah and Nevaeh, who are five now. They're playing Legos on the floor of Obi's bedroom, and when they see me standing in the doorway, they jump up to give me hugs. When they do, I realize that they're officially taller than me now. "Will you guys stop *growing* already?" I tease them. The twins are also starting to look more and more like my dad. He's their dad, too, of course, so it makes sense. Still, I'm hit by strange pangs of pride and jealousy at these new developments.

Isaiah, ever the vigilant big brother, comes out of his room and sees the twins wrapped around me. "Be careful," he scolds them. "Agnes is delicate, remember?"

"It's okay," I say, giving him a smile. "I'm sturdier than I look." I grab the camera from my backpack and get the three of them to stand together in the hallway. "Say 'stinky cheese,'" I tell them. Isaiah rolls his eyes, but the twins crack up and flash these huge grins, complete with gaps from their missing baby teeth, right as the shutter clicks.

*   *   *

Obi and Nevaeh snuggle up on either side of me before bedtime that night while I read their favorite story out loud. *"The Very Hungry Caterpillar,"* I begin, holding open the title page. "My friend Moira loves this one, too."

"Who's Moira?" Nevvie wants to know.

"She's what you might call my BFF," I tell her.

Nevvie looks at me for a long moment. Then she looks up toward the ceiling like she's puzzling something out in her head. "Bunny . . . Foo Foo?" she finally asks.

Obi throws his head back and lets out a high-pitched laugh, but it's clear he doesn't know what the letters stand for, either.

"No, silly. It means 'best friend forever.' Seriously, you've never heard that?" I laugh, too, like my little sister made a funny joke on purpose, but I'm going to have to talk to Dad about this. What little kid doesn't know about BFFs? It's like not knowing about LOL or OMG. It's basic communication. I won't be around for too many more years to teach the twins these things, and I don't want any siblings of mine being treated like freaks when they go out into the real world.

"I've heard about Moira," Obi says, still laughing. "Your BFF is big and fat."

I freeze. "What did you just say?"

"You heard me. She has a big fat butt. Butts are *hilarious*."

Even though I'm completely aghast, I try to keep a lid on it. "It's not nice to talk about people like that," I tell Obi in the calmest voice possible. *Nice use of the word* hilarious, *though,* I think. I consider complimenting him on his vocabulary, but then I think better of it. The mixed message would probably just confuse him.

"But that's what Dad says," Obi continues. "He says she's big and fat and that people get that way from eating too much."

Wait, what? Breath is backing up in my chest now. Dad and Moira have only met each other a few times over the years. After the first time, he called Mom and raised a stink about "that scary girl" being a bad influence on me.

"Why?" Mom challenged him. "Because of her fashion choices?"

"You call that *fashion*?" I could hear Dad's voice bristling through the phone as she held the receiver away from her ear and rolled her eyes.

"I call it independent thinking," she fired back, "which is obviously something you're not familiar with."

"It's not nice to talk about people like that," I repeat to Obi in a stern voice. "Even if Dad's the one doing the talking. Do you understand me?"

My brother nods. His eyes are wide now, and he looks like he might be about to cry.

"It's okay, buddy," I tell him. "You didn't know. But Moira's my friend, and I don't want anyone talking bad about her. Friends have each other's back."

"Like SpongeBob and Patrick?"

"Exactly," I tell him. "Exactly like . . . Wait. When does your mom let you watch *SpongeBob*?"

For a second, Obi's eyes get even bigger. I've never seen his face so solemn. Then he locks his eyes on to mine, slowly raises a finger to his lips, and goes, "Shhhh."

I'm not sure why this makes me so happy, but it does. Jamey's not going to know what hit her when this one's a teenager. "Don't worry," I whisper. "I've got your back."

MOIRA

DAY 86: MARCH 31

BY THE END OF SIXTH GRADE IT DAWNED ON ME THAT THINGS were only going to get worse in junior high if I didn't take action. I'd heard the stories of what happened to kids on the dystopian fringe of seventh grade. Insults would turn into shoving and tripping; hallway confrontations would end in toilet swirlies.

Without a doubt, the socially acceptable course of action would have been to starve myself down over the summer and just get with the skinny-girl program for a change, but I couldn't do it. For one thing, my love of food has always been stronger than my hatred of my body. For another, even at the time, I suspected that it wouldn't end up mattering how small I made myself. I'd already been marked as an outcast. And I never wanted to look like the rail-thin girls in teen magazines, anyway. True, I wanted to disappear most days. If an invisibility cloak was ever invented, I'd be the first in line to buy one. But I knew it wasn't an option for me to disappear via starvation.

Instead, I figured it was better to flip my middle finger to the world and work on accepting the random stoutness gene or slow metabolism or whatever the hell it was that had somehow worked its way into my DNA. It was better to fight back.

I probably would have chosen to homeschool starting in seventh grade if it hadn't been for Agnes. Not that I blame her for all the sucktastic school years that followed. Agnes just wanted to be as much of an actual "normal" preteen as possible. As her best friend and protector, I vowed to do whatever it took to help make that happen. Which meant there was no turning back from the impending potential crisis that would be junior high if something didn't give and give quick.

For starters, the homemade clothes and hippie food weren't going to cut it. They just amplified my existence as an easy target, so they'd be the first to go. Instead of going back to tie-dye when seventh grade started, I decided to cultivate my own look. I moved away from creating clothes from scratch and instead started embellishing clothes that already existed, changing them to suit my needs. I convinced my mom to buy bowling shirts and full-length skirts dirt cheap at the thrift store. And because my parents encouraged self-acceptance at home, because they sincerely believed that I was a perfect, capable, creative being of light, they didn't argue with me. The same held true for lunch. As long as I packed my own most days and included at least a couple of healthy things, no questions were asked.

For the most part, it worked. I survived seventh grade, and I still got to hang out with Agnes for much of each school day. Boone Craddock was there, but our schedules didn't cross much. That was just as well, since I didn't plan on ever talking to him again anyway, not after what he did to Agnes. He was there for the first part of eighth grade, too, and then he was just . . . gone. It wasn't until after the winter break that I heard his father had died. I have only vague memories of Boone's dad. Sometimes I'd see him pick Boone up after school in a beat-up Chevy truck. Once he came to get Boone from Agnes's birthday party, but he didn't come up to the door and say hi or anything.

"Should we call him?" Agnes wondered out loud as soon as we heard the news.

"You can call him," I said. "If you want to." I felt bad about the thing with his dad, but what was I supposed to do? Just ring him up out of the blue like nothing had ever happened, like he hadn't gotten Agnes hurt? I wasn't that big of a person. Well, I *was* that big of a person, but only in the literal sense.

BOONE

DAY 85: APRIL 1

THAT FIRST WINTER MOM AND I WERE ON OUR OWN WAS THE
hardest thing I've ever had to get through. My dad had always
been protective of his expensive sledgehammer and wedge;
since he'd only recently allowed me to start using those tools
to split firewood by myself, I still wasn't very good at it. I
tended to either not tap the wedge into the wood deep
enough, so that it fell away when I brought the sledge down,
or I'd sink it too deep into a knot. In that case, my only option
was to hammer at the stump over and over again until it finally split open and the steel cone could be pried loose. God
knew we couldn't afford a new one.

Dad and I had loaded a bunch of big Douglas fir rounds
onto the truck bed the day of the accident. Weeks later, when

I realized how low the wood supply was already getting, I started splitting them. It wouldn't be any easier to chop and stack the stuff once the really serious weather set in come January, that was for sure. It was hard, inefficient work getting the rounds cut down to pieces that would fit inside our old woodstove, but the work helped me focus the blackness within. It helped me compartmentalize the near-constant current of rage running beneath the surface of my skin—rage at my father for not being there, for leaving me alone to take care of Mom, who had all but stopped speaking, who would mutter only single-syllable words through her closed bedroom door in response to my questioning: "Mom, are you okay?"

"Yes."

"Does soup sound good for dinner?"

"Sure."

I felt like a complete shit heel being so angry about the whole thing. If anyone was really suffering, it was her. She was the one who'd become a widow and a single mother in one fell swoop. I was just half an orphan.

For a while after my father died, I figured her inability to deal was just a phase. Life had thrown both of us overboard without any warning, and we were just trying to stay afloat. As the weeks went by, though, it seemed like Mom's grief was dragging her farther and farther out to sea. I was getting knocked around by the waves of sadness and fear, too, but I could still see the shore, and I could also see how life might someday get back to normal if we just swam hard enough in the right direction.

I waited one month after my dad wasn't around anymore before even thinking about whether or not I should go back to eighth grade. I didn't want to put more pressure on Mom, but it wasn't like anyone was coming around to offer me rides, either: my parents didn't really have friends to speak of, and my dad's family had pretty much all died off before he did. If we were a normal family, Mom's parents might have helped, but they lived back East. They hadn't been thrilled with her decision to marry my dad, from what I'd heard over the years, and I only met them once, when I was a baby and too young to remember them. Still, weren't grandparents supposed to help out at a time like this? Women from a couple of local churches had been dropping off meals at our house since word got out about what happened to my dad, but I knew the charity of local strangers would only last so long until we'd be expected to start standing on our own feet again.

Another reason I waited before going back to school was that I didn't like the thought of leaving Mom alone during the day when she was such a mess. What if she . . . did something during the hours I was away? What if I came home and she . . . wasn't there anymore? When the middle school secretary called about a week into my absence, I told her I was being homeschooled now. Which was a laugh, but it worked to get her off my back, at least for the time being.

"Can you have your mom send a note verifying this so we can add it to your file?" she asked me. "At some point we'll need the necessary paperwork as well."

"No problem," I answered. "My mom will send the note tomorrow." The next day I wrote a note, forged Mom's signature, and rode my bike six miles to the post office to drop it in the mail.

Not too long after that, the shock of my dad's being gone for good seemed to wear off for her, and the new reality of our situation set in. The man who'd once been the center of her life was never coming back. Even during the year after he fell off that roof and turned into more and more of a ragey drunk, there was always hope that things would get better. My mother took her pills and insisted on two things: his body and his mind would heal, and he would get back to being the man he once was. Now all that hope was gone. Without warning, she and I were on our own. There was no tidy wrap-up of my parents' marriage, no Happily Ever After to balance out the Once Upon a Time we'd enjoyed back when we were a relatively normal family with the same ups and downs as everyone else.

This realization, combined with her new refusal to stay on the antidepressants ("There's no point," she told me when I asked her about the full pill bottle I found in the bathroom trash), seemed to flip a switch somewhere inside my mother's brain. Within a matter of weeks, she stopped taking all but the most basic care of herself, and she became terrified of being out in public. Anything from a drive to the gas station to fill the truck's tank to a trip to the grocery store usually ended up with my mother acting as shaken and traumatized as if she'd just had a brush with violent death. I ended up doing everything—educating myself the best I could, cleaning the house, cooking our meals, and taking care of Diablo. When she was too freaked out or zoned out to leave the house (which was most of the time), I'd hitchhike to town and get as much done as I could. Sometimes I'd ride my bike, but it was a long ride. Also, it was almost impossible to balance the plastic bags of groceries on the handlebars without wiping out on the dirt road. This went on for a couple of months, and then something else happened. My mother became an addict.

Not a drug addict or an alcoholic, mind you. No sirree. She didn't knock back a few shots with her morning cup of coffee like my dad had, and she didn't suddenly start scoring heroin or meth from a local dealer. Instead, my mother developed a jones for jigsaw puzzles. I don't know what it was about those things. I do remember Dad buying one for the three of us to piece together on New Year's Eve when I was little. For some reason, Mom's brain must have latched on to that particular memory for comfort after he was gone, the way my brain latched on to the idea that I was the man of the house now, that it was my time to step up and there was no room for feeling sorry for myself. She'd stay holed up in her room for hours, trying to fit the borders of different pieces together. And because I didn't know what else to do to make her feel better, I started picking up the cheapest ones I could find on my bike trips into town. It wasn't long before every surface in her bedroom was covered with cardboard fragments. Eventually, she had to expand the jigsaw operation to the living room and the kitchen table. To this day, she goes through even the thousand-piece ones like wildfire, so I still pick them up for her at the thrift store whenever I have a few extra bucks.

The thing is, even though I'm the one most responsible for keeping my mother's addiction alive, something inside me starts seething lately whenever she emerges from her bedroom in the late afternoon, having clearly just spent the entire day trying to piece back together a complex picture of dolphins or kittens or a tacky pastel cottage scene. Something grabs the steel bars around my lungs and heart and shakes them in frustration until I can hardly breathe. I never let it show on the outside, though. I know she's had a hard time. And hell would have to freeze over before I'd allow my anger to escape, before I'd ever allow myself to treat her the way my dad did toward the end.

MOIRA

DAY 84: APRIL 2

I'M NOT GOING TO FEEL SORRY FOR BOONE CRADDOCK.

I don't care what Deb says about him being a "nice boy" back in the day.

Some things, like the thing from four years ago that I haven't let myself fully think about and remember yet, can't be forgiven.

18

AGNES

DAY 83: APRIL 3

SUNDAY AT MY DAD AND JAMEY'S HOUSE ALWAYS = CHURCH.

Moira thinks Jamey's a fascist for making us go, but I don't usually mind. I've only gone once or twice a month since Dad and Jamey got together, so I've pretty much learned to deal with it. Mostly, I just tune out during the sermon and use the time in the rickety pew to help with the twins. If they're behaving, I close my eyes and just think about stuff for a while.

The church we go to doesn't believe in using musical instruments, so all the songs are sung a cappella. The acoustics in the old building aren't great, and there are only about a dozen people in attendance on any given Sunday. Still, I love the sound of all our voices intermingling on songs like "Power in the Blood," "What a Friend We Have in Jesus," and "Rock of Ages." I hold the hymnal so Obi and Nevaeh can see it, too, not that they can read the music or the words.

When we're done singing, a preacher I've never seen before approaches a lectern that's been set up in the front of the room. He has a big belly and a long white beard, and it's clear he takes his service in the Lord's Army very seriously. He starts off by talking about who's going to hell and who isn't. Basically, the people in the room are safe, assuming they've been washed in the blood of the Lamb. Not so the heathen who are using the Lord's Day to conduct business or sleep in or fornicate. It's all pretty straightforward, really.

I look down at my gnarled hands resting in my lap and roll my eyes. *A real brimstoner,* Mom would call this guy. Sometimes, I almost want to invite Mom and Moira to attend a service just to see what would happen. Almost.

In the middle of this thought I feel a tapping on my arm. It's Nevvie, blinking up at me. "Heaven sounds lonely," the kid whispers, catching me off guard.

I try my best to hold it together, but I don't do a very good job. Attempting to cover my laugh with a fake cough only makes things worse. Nevvie starts giggling. Dad clears his throat as a reminder for us to settle down.

The new preacher must think I'm laughing at him, because he pauses and looks right at me. I hold my breath and lower my eyes.

Next, the preacher moves on to homosexuality. "It is a sin for man to lie with man and woman to lie with woman!" He's yelling a little now, which doesn't seem entirely necessary, given the size of the room and the crowd. "Doesn't matter what the wicked world thinks about it. The Scripture says it's wrong, so it's wrong. End of story."

A few quiet *amens* rise up from the pews. I glance at Dad, who appears to be half-asleep. Jamey seems to think the little ones need to hear this, and I wonder if he thinks so, too. What good could it possibly do them?

The preacher notices my fidgeting. "God is not always fair." He keeps his eyes on me when he says it and sort of gestures in my direction with his head. A few of the congregants sitting in the front rows turn to look. Some of the women who don't see me very often make pouty faces: *You poor little angel.*

This time, it feels like the wind's been knocked out of me. *You did NOT just do that,* I think. Forcing myself to breathe and keeping my face a blank, I stare right back at the preacher. *You did NOT just make me the poster child for divine discrimination.* Thank God Moira's not here, or all hell would have broken loose by now.

For the altar call, everyone stands and sings "There's a Fountain Free." It's never been one of my favorite hymns, but today it sounds particularly flat and oppressive. This is the time when anyone who isn't baptized is supposed to be so overcome with the Spirit that she can't stop herself from going down front, confessing her sins, and proclaiming her need to be cleansed. As usual, I stay put where I am.

Everybody here knows I haven't been baptized yet. I'm pretty sure Jamey asks them on a regular basis to please pray for her little geriatric stepdaughter who surely doesn't have much time left. This is probably why I feel the weight of the congregation's eyes on me as we sing. Obi and Nevvie have been really good during the whole service, but they're starting to get tired and cranky now. I wonder if maybe they're picking up on the tension in the room. "Do you want to go down front?" Jamey whispers, leaning toward me with a smile.

I shake my head and try to smile back, but I'm sure it looks forced. If there's one thing I know it's that I don't want to get baptized. Not yet and maybe not ever. I'm certainly not going to be bullied into it. For starters, I'm pretty sure people in the Bible got baptized in rivers and lakes—"living water" I've heard it called—which sounds pretty nice. It seems to me that a real baptism—one where you decide to trade your old, grimy life for a bright, shiny new one—should be outside in nature, where God can see you more easily. People you love should be there, too. All they have here at the church is a big fiberglass bathtub that one of the families donated when they remodeled. The tub sits on a platform in the back room. Not exactly the most spiritual water-based experience I can imagine.

Jamey doesn't try to hide her irritation with me in the car on the way home. I'm strapped into my booster in the middle row of seats next to Isaiah. Behind us, in the way back, the twins sit strapped into their own booster seats. "Have you heard of the bridge embankment theory?" my stepmother asks, turning to look at me.

"Um, no?"

"Jamey," Dad says, glancing at her.

"What?" she asks him. "It's what finally convinced *you*, isn't it?" She smiles at me again, but it's a tight smile this time. "It means you could drive away from this church and hit a bridge embankment and die without being baptized. Think about how awful that would be."

"But I don't have my license," I answer. "Which means you or Dad would be driving, and Isaiah and Nevaeh and Obi would be in the car, too. So we'd probably all be dead. Not just me." I immediately regret saying it. When I glance back at the twins, they're staring at me with eyes the size of dinner plates. "Which totally isn't going to happen," I assure them. "You guys are going to live a long, long time."

Behind the wheel, Dad clears his throat again like he did in church. "I think you've been hanging out with that friend of yours too much," he says. "That big girl."

Once again, I hold my tongue between my teeth to keep from saying anything I'll later regret.

Jamey, meanwhile, seems to think about what I said. "It may be true that we'd all die," she murmurs finally, "but the rest of us have been baptized."

I can't believe what I'm hearing. It's not physically possible to keep quiet any longer. "And your point is . . . ?"

Oops.

Isaiah's head swivels around toward me. I'm pretty sure he's never heard anyone talk to his mother like this. Dad says, "That's enough, Agnes," but I'm not sorry. I cross my arms in front of my chest.

"I think you know what my point is," Jamey says, ending the conversation. She turns back toward the windshield and gazes out at the road ahead.

* * *

That night before bed, I find Isaiah in the bathroom brushing his teeth. "I have a favor to ask you," I tell him.

Eyebrows raised, hand paused in midbrush, he regards me in the mirror.

"I was wondering if I could borrow your slingshot."

Isaiah frowns. When a little line of toothpaste foam escapes from the corner of his mouth, he slurps it back in.

"Just until the next time I come here," I tell him. The slingshot has a wrist brace, which makes it easier for me to shoot. The last time I tried it out, I discovered I had pretty good aim.

Isaiah spits and rinses, then stands there with the tooth-brush in hand, deep in thought. Finally, he says, "You're gonna die soon, aren't you." The way he says it, it's not a question.

I blink in disbelief. "What? That is so totally beside the point. Where did you even get such an idea?"

"It's what you and Mother were talking about in the car, isn't it?"

"Not exactly."

"Have you accepted Jesus Christ as your Lord and Savior?"

All I can do is sigh. Verily, the situation with these kids is worse than I thought. "I guess I'm . . . still considering my options," I tell him.

He seems to think about this for a long moment. Then he says, "It'll suck if you don't accept Him. 'Cause then you'll go straight to hell, and I'll never see you again."

All I can do is laugh. I know it probably confuses him, but I can't help it. All this talk of who's going to heaven and who's going to hell is ridiculous. As if humans have any control over that sort of thing. As if we have any way of really knowing whether or not there even *is* a heaven or hell in the first place. "If nothing else, you're going to make a great preacher some-day," I say. "So can I borrow your slingshot?"

Isaiah looks a little disgruntled. "What'll you trade it for?"

I think about this for a minute. I wasn't expecting to haggle. "Hey, you could have my old sling from when I broke my arm. A slingshot in exchange for a sling, right? Even Steven?"

89

He shakes his head. "Nah. I'm sure it's way too small for me."

Man, this kid drives a hard bargain. "I know," I tell him. "How about my old retainer? I'll bring it for you next time I come." A few years back, I had this fantasy that my teeth wouldn't grow in all funky and crooked like other progeria kids' teeth do. The retainer was my dentist's way of humoring me until I learned to face the facts, and I'm banking on it being both gross enough and cool enough to warrant a loaner on the slingshot. It is. At the mere mention of used orthodontia, Isaiah's frown disappears. He holds his hand out to seal the deal.

"Thanks, buddy." I shake and then reach up to tousle his hair. I'm not quite tall enough, though, so Isaiah puts down his toothbrush and bends at the waist, lowering his head to just the right height.

BOONE

DAY 82: APRIL 4

I MAKE SURE TO SHOW UP AT AGNES DELANEY'S HOUSE RIGHT ON time Monday afternoon. God knows I don't need any more grief from Principal Weaver.

I get out of the truck and squint at the yard before reaching into the bed for a rake and a big plastic bag for the dead pine needles and leaves covering the lawn. I'm wearing a flannel shirt and old work boots with brass hooks for the laces and steel toes shining through the worn-out leather. They were my dad's, of course. Next year, they'll probably be too small for me. A knit cap is pulled low over my head, pressing my raggedy bangs over my eyes like a screen, the way I prefer.

I remember this place. I was here once, years ago, for Agnes's birthday party in fifth grade. Agnes hadn't been at our school very long, and not too many kids went, if I remember right. Before presents were opened and the piñata was smashed to pieces, Ms. Delaney led us all out to the grass. With Agnes right there, she asked what we knew about progeria. Everyone was quiet. Nobody knew anything about progeria. A few kids peeked at Agnes to see if the questioning bothered her, but she seemed fine with it. Her mom told us Agnes's body was aging much faster than our bodies were (as if we couldn't see that), but that Agnes was still a kid.

"And you should treat me that way," Agnes chimed in.

"Be a bit careful with her," Ms. Delaney added. "But also remember she's not an old person. She's a young person, just like you guys."

Afterward, we played Pin the Tail on the Donkey. When it was time for everyone to go home, Agnes handed out party bags full of candy and little toys. I got a plastic maze with a ball bearing trapped inside that you were supposed to tilt through the maze and into a divot at the end. The divot wasn't deep enough, though, so the ball would just roll right past it. That thing drove me crazy.

My dad picked me up from the party. Right away, I could tell he was having what my mother called an "off day." His off days didn't happen too often back then, before his roofing accident, but when they did, watch out. When I got into the truck, he nodded at the toy in my hand and made a sarcastic "Oooo" sound, showing me how unimpressed he was with the quality of the party favors being handed out around here. Agnes and her mom waved at him from the lawn, but he didn't get out to say hello or anything. Instead, he turned his head away, scowled through the windshield, and pretended he didn't see them.

"You could have wished her a happy birthday," I told him once we were headed home. Probably I was emboldened by cake and punch. Normally, I'd just shut my trap.

"Watch it, boy," he said.

I stared straight ahead.

"That little freak makes me uncomfortable." I figured he was trying to make a joke, but it didn't work. It wasn't funny. At that moment, it felt like our matching father-son tempers were completely in sync.

My jaw clenched. "She's not a freak." I thought about shoving open the passenger side door at the next stop sign, flipping him off, and walking home. Or maybe just jumping out of the truck and running back to Agnes's house to stay at the party longer. Her mom seemed nice. I bet she'd let me stay until my own mom could come get me. But that would only cause trouble, and I'd wake up later in the middle of the night to the sound of my parents arguing. Even if they made up afterward like they always did, I wasn't going to put my mother through that if I could help it. A hot, dull ache rose behind my eyes. I closed them hard to make it go away and let out a slow, steady breath.

Neither of us said anything more for the rest of the drive home.

*   *   *

Heading toward the Delaneys' lawn now, I spot Moira Watkins standing on the top step with her hands on her hips. She's wearing old Doc Martens that have been painted bloodred. She's also wearing black-and-white-striped tights that look like they were issued by the county jail. Seeing her, I feel like I've arrived early for my appointment with death.

Agnes is sitting on the step below Moira with her arms crossed over her birdlike chest. The two of them stay where they are, watching as I come closer. Nobody says hello.

It's a small yard. I know I'm going to have to listen to their conversation whether I want to or not. At least the weather's dried out a bit. Otherwise, the carpet of oak leaves and pine needles would be too soggy to rake efficiently. *The only way out is through,* I tell myself, starting on the first pile. Thank God the girls make a show of ignoring me completely.

"So, how was your weekend?" This from Moira.

"My dad wants me to go to a chastity ball with him."

"A what?"

"A chastity ball," Agnes repeats. "It's a thing they do where a bunch of churches get together and host a dance for fathers and daughters."

"Is that like a chastity belt?"

I do not allow myself to smile.

"Kind of," Agnes says. "Jamey thinks it would be a good bonding experience for us."

"Jamey also keeps a display cabinet full of Precious Moments figurines. Clearly, her elevator doesn't go all the way to the top floor."

"Maybe."

"Definitely," Moira says. "And no offense or anything, but does your dad really think he needs to worry about your purity?"

Agnes smacks Moira's arm. "Thanks a lot."

Wow, I think. *Harsh.* I use a corner of the rake to perfect the edges of one pile so it will be easier to bag.

"I'm just saying." Moira's laughing now. It's a surprisingly pleasant sound. "So what did you say?"

"I asked if maybe we could just go see a Disney movie instead."

"Talk about birth control," Moira says.

A short laugh escapes my mouth before I can stop it. To cover it up, I pretend to cough. I can feel Moira's eyes boring into the back of my skull.

"What a piece of work," she mutters.

At first I'm not sure if she's talking about me or this Jamey person, but Agnes clears it up. "He'll have to go to your house next, I'm pretty sure."

"No, he won't."

"Why not?"

"Because he won't, that's why."

"If you're talking about *paid* work, I need the money so bad, I'd actually consider going to your house," I say under my breath. "But there's no way in hell I'm doing it for free. I don't care what the school says."

Moira looks like she's turned to stone. Apparently, the comment wasn't as under my breath as I thought, and it's pretty clear she can't believe the servant boy is daring to speak. It's beyond satisfying to leave her speechless for once. It's intoxicating, really.

"Maybe I'll show up at your front door with my rake and my leaf bags just to piss you off," I continue in a louder voice this time. "Man, I'd love to see the look on your—"

The comment is cut short by a red-hot pain shooting through my left butt cheek. I'm so surprised that I instinctively drop the rake and grab my own ass, hard, with both hands.

The girls howl like a couple of coyotes circling in for the kill.

Doing my best to act casual, I release my grip on myself and look around, trying to figure out where the pain came from. Did somebody shoot me with a .22, a neighbor boy, maybe? Finally, my eyes rest on Agnes, who's doing a poor job of hiding what looks like a wrist rocket–type slingshot inside her jacket. When I was little, my father tried to show me how to shoot birds out of trees with a weapon that looked just like it (of course, I kept missing the birds by "accident"). Agnes gets up quickly from the step, not taking her eyes off me.

As I stand there shaking my head and glaring at them, the girls exchange grins before turning around and disappearing into the house. "Show up at my place and a slingshot will be the *least* of your worries," Moira yells right before she slams the door.

20

MOIRA

DAY 81: APRIL 5

I'M STANDING IN FRONT OF THE BATHROOM MIRROR, PRACTICING my death scowl. I'm convinced it's the thing that makes other people nervous enough to leave me alone. I don't care what they say behind my back. I assume the worst, and that's fine. It is what it is.

But this scowl? It's my armor. More than that, it's my middle finger to the world, specifically to the world of high school and all the lame-ass cretins therein.

AGNES

DAY 80: APRIL 6

"YOU NEED TO STAY HOME TODAY." MOIRA'S VOICE IS HOARSE AT the other end of the phone line.

"I'm not sick," I tell her.

"But I am. I don't want you going to school without me. People are assholes. Sorry—jerks."

"I'll be fine."

"I'm serious, Agnes."

"I'm serious, too. I have a geometry test."

"You didn't mention anything about a test yesterday."

"So now I have to tell you every detail of my academic life?"

The line goes silent.

"Sorry," I say. "I just—"

"No worries." Now Moira's voice is suddenly breezy.

"Em—"

"Nope. It's fine. You'll be fine."

"I will be fine," I tell her. "But—"

"Have a good day."

*　　*　　*

When our homeroom teacher, Mr. Jeffers, realizes Moira's absent, he asks me if I want him to call the front office so they can assign another escort to walk with me between classes.

"No," I tell him. "That's okay."

There's a late morning awards assembly for the fall sports teams. Everyone's jazzed up when it's over, shoving one another toward the exits and creating a bottleneck of students at one end of the gym. I stay put in my seat until the crowd thins, but things aren't much better when I get to the main hallway. I want to be able to tell Moira how brave I was when we talk on the phone later, but the truth is I'm scared. I feel like a toddler trying to navigate her way through a crowd of drunken lumberjacks. I hug my books close to my chest as I walk toward my government class, trying to protect myself the way you protect a newly healed broken bone that's just had the cast taken off.

A swarm of burly football players approaches. It may even be the entire team. Without the coach there to keep them in line with his shouts and his whistle, they laugh and jostle one another. Even from a distance, I can tell they're still amped from the rally. I assume—hope?—the rowdy group will part down the middle so I can safely pass through their midst. But they're so wrapped up in whatever it is they're joking about that they don't even seem to *see* me. Not one of them looks down, and why would they? Moira's the one people always see when she and I are walking together. Moira's like one of those bright orange safety flags on the back of a bicycle, the importance of which you underestimate until the one day it's not there waving above your head and you're mowed down by a truck.

I scoot to the side of the hallway and flatten myself against the wall. The players are taking up the entire corridor now. They're shoving one another more aggressively, cackling and hooting and yelling obscenities. A bunch of other students stop and press themselves against the walls, too, but still nobody sees me.

My eyes dart from one side of the corridor to the other as I step away from the wall, searching for a classroom doorway. *This must be what it's like to die in a buffalo stampede,* I think, panicking now, as their shadows approach and then envelop me. A guy I recognize as the star quarterback looms large. It occurs to me (too late) to throw a hand up to catch his attention like I do with the school secretary anytime I'm in the office. I open my mouth to scream, but nothing comes out.

There's a sharp squeezing sensation in my chest, like something with talons has gotten hold of my heart. I scrunch my eyes shut and wait for the inevitable.

It doesn't come. After a while, I open my eyes, but it still takes me a few seconds to get the courage to look up. When I do, I see that a familiar sort of bridge has formed over my head. It's a pair of arms, just like that day in the cafeteria when Moira shoved Boone Craddock's back to keep her balance.

This time, though, they aren't Moira's arms.

Boone's hands are embedded in the quarterback's chest the way Moira's hands were embedded between Boone's shoulder blades. As far as I'm concerned, they are the Hands of Life.

"What the hell—" the quarterback starts to say.

Boone cuts him off and motions down toward me with his head. "Just watch where you're going, okay? Try to have some awareness." His teeth are clenched when he says it.

"Oh, I'll have some awareness, all right," the quarterback says.

He's about to say something else when I scurry out from under the bridge of Boone's arms and over to the other side of the hallway as fast as I can, my heart cathunking all loud and uneven in my chest. Other kids stay frozen in place, expecting a fight. I don't hear all the words they exchange after that, but I do hear the quarterback call Boone a dipshit before the team continues down the hallway. A few of them look back, like Boone's a pile of something disgusting they accidentally stepped in.

When he looks over at me, his face is red and his jaw is still tight. "You okay?" he asks.

"Were you following me?"

"Doesn't matter."

He *was* following me. I'm sure of it. As the athletes round a corner at the end of the hall, Boone relaxes a little.

"Did Moira put you up to this?" I ask him.

"She didn't put me up to anything."

Then we just stand there for a few seconds, neither of us saying anything.

"Boone?"

"What."

"Thank you."

"Yeah, okay. Whatever."

For the rest of the day, he meets me outside each of my classes and walks me to the next one in silence. Not another word is spoken about what happened in the hallway, but I do manage to snap a picture of him before the end of the day. He's standing by my locker with his arms crossed over his chest, waiting for me to get my English stuff before last period. "You just need a pair of sunglasses and one of those earpieces to complete your Secret Service look," I tell him, reaching for my camera. At the exact second a grin breaks out across his face, I point and shoot.

22

BOONE
DAY 79: APRIL 7

I'M STANDING IN A PUDDLE OF GRAY SLUSH BEHIND THE GYM, and it takes everything I have to use my words instead of my fists. At least the quarterback showed up without his teammates like he promised yesterday after school when we arranged to meet out here. "I'm not about to get kicked off the team because of you," he said. "And we don't need any witnesses, even though I'd love to have an audience watching when I take you down." He punched his fist into his other palm for emphasis when he said it, and I worked hard to keep from laughing. Somebody needs to tell this guy to lay off the steroids. He probably only made the promise to show up alone because he knew he'd look like a pussy if he came with a posse. I smile a little at the poetry. I could do this all day, people.

In response to my smile, the guy whips off his letterman jacket and holds his fists in front of him, old-school street-fight style. What a meathead.

"C'mon," he snarls, no doubt imitating some action hero he saw on late-night TV. "What's the holdup, tard?"

Damn, I want to pummel this guy. But, no. I'll at least try to talk first, try to reason. I'll force myself to rise above my baser instincts and—

The quarterback throws the first punch. He's stupidly obvious about it, and I duck. As I stand back up to full height, he's on me, throwing punches that mostly don't connect very well.

I never could abide the methods of subduing horses my father used during that year after the roofing accident. After he got laid off and went back to horseshoeing, he had to occasionally deal with animals who seemed to see it as their mission in life to kick the ever-loving crap out of him. In that sort of situation, my dad would grab one of the horse's ears and twist it down. That, or he'd tighten a chain twitch around its sensitive upper lip. It made me sick to see a frightened creature rendered immobile by sudden localized pain. I much preferred a simple hobble, which forced the horse to use its feet for balance rather than for violence against its handler. At the time, I understood full well that my queasiness about using brute force made me repulsively soft and sentimental in my father's eyes. Due to the new situation with his coordination, though, he forced me to learn the harsher techniques anyway. Doing so meant I could help him shoe the rankest stallions and most pissed-off mares on his roster. The two of us damn near got killed perfecting our team restraint procedure more times than I care to think about. But perfect it we did.

Now, sighing deeply, I respond to the barrage of sloppy punches by throwing the quarterback onto his stomach in the slush, planting my knee in the small of his back, and hoisting one of his legs and his opposite arm up behind him. Bound in this sort of modified scotch hobble, my opponent screams in hyperextended agony.

And it is at that moment, in the strangest, calmest way and for the first time ever, that I find myself grateful for my father's lessons in cruelty.

MOIRA

DAY 78: APRIL 8

HIS SWOLLEN FACE IS THE FIRST THING I NOTICE WHEN I FINALLY feel decent enough to return to school on Friday. The first time I see him is in English. The fat crescent beneath his eye is hard to miss, even with his bangs hanging down. It's greenish with dark purple splotches mixed in.

When the bell rings, I gather my stuff, take a breath, and walk over to his desk. "Agnes told me what happened."

No response.

"She didn't say anything about a fight, though."

Boone smiles. "Let's just say a friend and I got together for a . . . chat after school yesterday."

Standing this close, I catch a glimpse of a crusted-over gash on the side of his face as well. "Damn."

Boone shrugs and looks away.

I don't say anything for a minute. That gets awkward quick, though, so finally I just go ahead and blurt out what I came over to say. "I need to thank you for what you did the other day. For Agnes."

"Don't worry about it."

"No, I'm serious."

"So am I."

I decide to ignore him. "My parents might have some stuff for you to do around our place. I remember what you said about needing work."

"Oh, you mean the thing I said right before Agnes shot me in the ass?"

I look down. "Yeah."

"Are you for real?" He's smirking, but it's not an entirely unfriendly smirk.

This time, I roll my eyes at him. "Do you actually think I'm not for real? Like I'm playing a trick on you or something?" It comes out pretty harsh, but I'm annoyed. I may be many things, but I'm definitely not one to ignore a good deed done on Agnes's behalf. "Yes, I'm serious," I say, taking another breath and turning the sarcasm down several notches. "Our yard looks like something from the ninth circle of hell."

"Cool."

"What's cool, that our yard is a sacrilege?"

"Yeah," Boone says. "Cool for me, I mean." He grins, and

I half wish I could see what his eyes look like when he does it. I can't, though. Between the too-long bangs and the shiner, he may as well be wearing a mask, like Jason Voorhees or Leatherface.

"There's stuff that needs to be repaired all over the house, too," I add, glancing away so I don't seem overly interested in his eyes. "Little stuff, mainly, but my dad still needs help with it all. God, I swear, our house feels like it's falling down sometimes. And my parents are completely oblivious. It's embarrassing."

Boone doesn't say anything, so I don't elaborate further. I don't tell him, for instance, about the decency talk I had with Mom and Dad just this morning when I asked if they would pay Boone to do some work in our yard. Basically, it amounted to: *Don't you guys* dare *be naked if he comes over here.*

Sadly, this particular fear of mine is not unfounded. Once, during freshman year, I came home from school to find my father standing in front of an easel that had been set up in the middle of the living room. In the corner by the window, bathed in natural light, my mother sat posed with only a barely there, oversize silk scarf covering the parts of her body I didn't want to even think about, much less see. Clearly, she was trying to relive her college days when she earned money by posing as an artist's model for fine arts classes. And, apparently, my father thought he was Botticelli or something.

"Mom! Dad!" I yelled before turning back around and lunging for the door. "God!"

"What?" Dad asked, shrugging his innocence, paintbrush in hand. "We thought you weren't going to be home until later."

"It's just a human body, Moira," Mom said.

This was followed, predictably, by my dad saying, "A lovely human body, I might add."

"God!" I shouted again. I stomped as loudly as I could out onto the front porch and slammed the door behind me.

"You can come over this weekend, if it works for you," I tell Boone now, cringing a little inside.

"How about tomorrow at ten?"

I nod and start to walk away, but then stop and turn back around to face him. "Is that idiot quarterback going to get in trouble for this?"

Boone looks at me and smiles. "Yeah, right. The school offered to send him out to my house to rake leaves."

I can't help but laugh. "Well," I say, "if you just happen to have a bunch of rocks lying around out there, I know someone who's in possession of a mean slingshot."

24

BOONE

DAY 77: APRIL 9

A GRIZZLED LABRADOR RETRIEVER AMBLES UP AND WHACKS ITS tail against my jeans the moment I set foot on the Watkinses' property that Saturday.

"That's Bingo," Moira tells me. "The love of my life." She blushes a little when she says it. At least her neck does. With all the makeup she's wearing, I can't tell if the color reaches her face or not.

"Hey, boy." I reach down to rub the dog's ears before following Moira inside the house. Her mom is in the kitchen. She looks like a smaller, nongoth version of Moira. "I remember you," she says, giving me a hug. "It's been a long time. How's your mom?"

"She's good," I lie.

"Enough with the twenty questions," Moira says. She leads

me to the garage, where a man's legs are sticking out from under an old Volkswagen Vanagon. "Dad, this is Boone." She nudges her dad's foot with her own, and he comes rolling out on his mechanic's board.

"Boone," he says, smiling up at me. "It's been a long time. Last I saw you was—"

"You have grease all over your face," Moira says, interrupting him.

"What's going on with the van?" I ask, trying to make things less awkward.

"I think it's the transmission. I never was much good with this kind of stuff."

"I could have a look at it, if you want."

"Would you?"

*   *   *

I spend a couple of hours working under the van and figuring out what parts Moira's dad needs to order. Afterward, I'm standing outside the back door blotting sweat from my forehead with a bandana. A month ago, I didn't think winter was ever going to release its grip. Now the weather's warming up fast.

Moira comes outside, too. She holds a glass of lemonade out toward me.

"Wow," I say, taking it from her hands and chugging it down in about half a second.

"What?"

"Oh, nothing. It's just that this seems very . . . girly of you. Bringing a glass of lemonade to the menfolk." I mean it as a joke, but as soon as the words are out of my mouth, I start wishing I wasn't such an imbecile. What am I thinking, flirting so casually with her?

"How dare you." Moira makes a fist and holds it up between us. Thank God she's smiling. "Call me scary. Call me a fat hippo. But use the word *girly* and you're dead meat."

I frown. "You're not fat."

Moira holds my gaze seriously enough to make it a challenge. "Yes, I am," she says, taking the empty glass from my hand.

"Not to me. Real women have curves."

"Ha. According to you, maybe."

"Well, who says otherwise?"

Moira's laughing now. "I don't know. Our entire society?"

"Maybe our entire society is totally screwed up. Have you ever considered that?"

Moira doesn't say anything. Her expression is unreadable.

"And nearly anyone would feel big next to Agnes, by the way. Think about how *I* feel next to her."

She doesn't have a comeback for that, either. We stand there for a while, until it's time for me to leave. Surprisingly, the silence between us isn't as uncomfortable as I would have expected.

MOIRA

DAY 76: APRIL 10

I STAND IN FRONT OF THE MIRROR IN MY BATHROOM AND PULL my shirt tight around my waist and hips, squinting my eyes to try to see what Boone was talking about. "Real women," he said.

I'd have a nice waist if it wasn't for an extra roll or two, but my hips are enormous. Sometimes I wear loose shirts to conceal the matching humongosity of my boobs, but those shirts hang straight down in front, hiding my waist.

Sighing, I let my arms drop back to my sides and turn away from the mirror. No matter what I do, I'm always going to end up looking like the Michelin Man.

26

AGNES

DAY 75: APRIL 11

I HOLD UP A BIG PAIR OF WOOL TROUSERS. THEY'RE MEN'S PANTS, but rose colored. I can't imagine who would have worn them. Still, the fabric is so nice. It seems like nobody uses this kind of fine gabardine anymore. "I'm thinking of trying to incorporate these into my dress," I say. "For the trim, maybe?"

"I wouldn't," Moira says, biting off the end of a thread. "It's a cool idea. But it'll shrink in the wash like a son of a . . . gun and throw the whole outfit out of whack."

"Yeah, you're probably right. I could boil it first, though."

"I guess. But is it really worth your time?"

I don't have an answer for this. How am I supposed to know what is and isn't worth my time? "Ooh, look!" I say.

"What?"

I pull a scarf from the pile of clothes Mrs. Deene dumped on the table at the start of lunch. ("Old stuff from my closet," she told us. "Do with it whatever you want.") It's a pale, bluish gray chiffon wisp of a thing, hardly more substantial than air.

"Hey, I like that," Moira says, reaching out her hand.

I jerk the scarf away and waggle a finger at her. "Ah, ah, ah. Finders keepers."

"Okay, just let me check out the rolled edges, then."

I hand it over.

"Ha!" Moira cackles. "It's mine now. Bwahahahahahaha!"

"Traitor!"

"Yes, but I'm a traitor with a pretty new scarf." Moira wraps it around her neck. It's not very long, so it really only wraps once. It's so soft, though. Softer than the kinds of things she normally wears.

"Wow," I tell her. "That looks really pretty on you."

Moira unwinds it and frowns. "Not my color."

"What are you talking about? It's perfect. Sets off your eyes."

"Nah." She hands it back.

"Mine!" I cry, victorious. "I used reverse psychology on you, and it worked!"

"Scoundrel," Moira says.

"Indeed."

"This isn't over, you know."

I make a show of snuggling the scarf close to my heart,

and Moira growls. Then she smiles to let me know she's not serious. She gets up, collects our lunch trash, and walks over to the waste basket on her way toward the door. "I'll be right back," she says. "I have to pee." She draws out the word *pee* in a singsongy falsetto voice to let me know it's an emergency. Her head is turned to the side when she says it, and she almost walks right smack into Boone, who's standing in the doorway of the home ec room with his hands in his pockets.

"Hey," Moira says. Her neck turns pink. We all know Boone heard her, but his face doesn't give anything away.

"So, my truck's broke down," he tells us.

"Bummer."

"Yeah. The real bummer is that I need to finish serving my yard work sentence today." He looks at me when he says it. "Weaver's going to fry my ass if I don't have my signed completion slip to him by tomorrow morning."

"Fried ass," Moira repeats. "What a lovely image."

"We can give you a ride," I tell him. "Can't we, Em?"

She nods. "My car's parked behind the gym. It's the gray El Camino with polka—"

"I know which one it is," he says.

*   *   *

Mom isn't home yet when we pull up to the curb in front of my house. I show Boone to the garage, where we keep the rake and big plastic trash bags.

"I'm not going to shoot you again, if that's what you're thinking," I say as he unspools a bag from its roll.

Boone and Moira exchange a quick glance. "It's not what I'm thinking," he assures me.

"I was trying to be funny, but it was wrong, and I'm sorry."

"Don't worry about it."

Boone works for a few hours while Moira and I clean off a couple of lawn chairs and try to get some studying done in the late afternoon April sunshine. It's a glorious day. Boone's quiet the whole time, like he was in the car on the way over here. Every time I look up, he's getting rid of dead foliage from last fall, or mulching around new plants that are popping up in random places around the yard. There's no rhyme or reason to Mom's gardening style, but the flowers always look pretty come summer anyway. When Boone puts the rake away, I survey the yard. I can't remember it ever looking so tidy. "How were you planning to get home?" I ask him.

"Beats me. Hitch, I guess."

Moira laughs. "Out to Beacon Valley? Yeah, right. Who's going to want to drive all the way out there?"

"I don't know," Boone says. There's a tinge of irritation in his voice. "I've hitchhiked plenty. What does it matter?"

"It's, like, ten miles."

"Seven, actually."

As if that makes a difference, I think. In the silence that follows, I nudge Moira.

"You should just let me drive you," she says, taking the hint.

"Yeah," I agree.

Boone seems to know better than to argue with the two of us, but he doesn't look exactly happy.

I know what to do to seal the deal and get him to just accept the stupid ride already. "I'd worry so much less knowing you were getting a ride with Moira rather than with some potential serial killer," I tell him.

He looks at me.

"I'm serious. Worrying is really bad for my condition. Really bad." I let out a sad little cough to show how the stress is already making me sicker.

It works. Boone rolls his eyes a little, but then he follows Moira out to El-C and gets in.

27

MOIRA

DAY 74: APRIL 12

I OPEN MY EYES, BUT I DON'T GET UP. INSTEAD, I STAY WHERE I am under the covers and allow images from yesterday to scroll through my mind. There's no way my brain is going to let me think about this stuff once I'm fully awake. It will just confuse me all over again, and I don't have time for that. I have a day to get through.

I probably should have just let Boone hitchhike home like he wanted to, but I wasn't able to shake the feeling that I still owed him somehow for saving Agnes. It rankled me, that pressure of an unpaid debt. Then Agnes played the terminally ill kid card, and that was that. The sun was going down as we drove out to his house in the sticks. El-C fishtailed a little whenever we went around turns in the dirt road. Swirls of red dust rose up behind us.

Boone was quiet for most of the drive. At one point, he unlatched the lid of the big cassette case I keep on the floor of the passenger side and looked through the tapes, most of which I found at the used music store in town: Fields of the Nephilim, Sisters of Mercy, Suicidal Tendencies, and so on.

"Wow," he said. "Dark stuff."

I considered it a compliment. "What do you listen to?"

Boone shrugged. "I don't know. I like old stuff, too. Just different old stuff. Social D, Hank Junior, Johnny Cash."

I thought about this for a minute. "Social Distortion is okay," I said finally. "And maybe Johnny Cash. I like how he wore black all the time."

"What do you have against Bocephus?"

When I glanced over at him he was grinning, but I still couldn't really see his eyes. "Who?"

"That's Hank Junior's nickname."

"Ah," I said. I tried not to smile back at him, and I succeeded. An awkward silence followed. To break it, I asked, "How do you even drive on this road when it snows?"

"My truck usually works fine. Four-wheel drive."

"You know, I've never been out to your place. Not even back when . . ." My voice trailed off into Awkwardland once again. God, why couldn't I just shut *up* already?

"This road was even worse back when we were in grade school," Boone answered, saving me from feeling like a complete idiot. "The county didn't maintain it back then."

Both of us were quiet after that, as if we'd broken some unspoken rule by bringing up that earlier time when we used to be friends. At the last big turn in the road he shifted in his seat. I turned to say something, to try to break the ice that had formed during the past mile or so, but he looked way more uptight than he had a minute earlier. "My driveway's the long one coming up on the left," he said, pointing. "You can just drop me at the end of it here."

"I don't mind driving all the—"

"No. I don't want you getting stuck." Boone was talking fast all of a sudden.

"Getting stuck? Are you serious? The road's dry as a—"

"Ruts in the driveway," he said, cutting me off. "Deep ones." He grabbed his backpack and jumped out before I'd even brought El-C to a full stop. "Thanks for the ride."

I didn't have time to reply before he slammed the door and walked away quickly, toward a little house at the end of another long dirt road.

"Sure," I said to the windshield, my voice dazed and quiet. "Anytime."

BOONE

DAY 73: APRIL 13

TURNS OUT THE CHEVY JUST HAD SOME LOOSE BATTERY connections. Once I had time to pop the hood and investigate, it wasn't at all hard to get her back on the road. This time. Now I park the truck in front of the food bank where I can get a shopping cart full of groceries for just twenty bucks. I'd get everything free if Mom had a food assistance card from the state. She never has enough energy to go to the office where they give out the cards, though, even when I offer to drive her there and stay by her side throughout the whole paperwork process.

Today, the cart is filled with day-old donuts and birthday cupcakes, low-grade ground beef, and prespiced frozen chicken pieces in vacuum-packed plastic. Not a bad haul. I load everything into the back of the truck and throw a tarp over it. Sometimes, if it's the end of the day and they have lots of perishables left, they'll let me take two shopping carts. It's always a crapshoot, though. Some days there's nothing good left, just bags of carrot ends and boxes of dry rice cereal for babies. That or donated cans of random exotic things like coconut milk and canned lychees.

I know better than to ask Mom how long we can keep this up, how long I can keep spending money, even if I'm excruciatingly careful about how I spend it. The life insurance payout has been our main source of income for two years, but it's not going to last forever. I don't have to be a full-fledged adult to know that much. It's not like I can just pick up more time at the Feed & Seed, either, especially since TJ cut my hours in half. If it was later in the year, I'd probably do okay selling wood out of the back of the pickup when I ran out of skulls and antlers, but even then I'd need a working chainsaw. The Stihl I used to cut the last load has been acting up lately. It could take a hundred dollars or more to fix it.

And then there was the drive out to my place with Moira, the embarrassment I felt as we got closer to the house. From the road, it doesn't look so bad. A little weathered maybe, a little the worse for wear from having prairie wind, sun, rain, and snow beating down on it regularly, but that's to be expected out here. It's only when you get up close that you see the missing roof shingles, the chunks of old wood siding gouged and ripped from the exterior, the bowed front steps and warped window trim held in place by just a few remaining rusty nails. The Christmas lights dangling from hooks driven into the roof fascia. It wouldn't be so bad if the lights were from the holiday season that wrapped up just a few months ago, but this particular string has been hanging there for three years at least. It hasn't worked for two of those years. Standing that close to the house, a person would only have to take a few more steps to be able to look in through a window. And what would a person see then? That was easy. She'd see the interior of the House Hope Left Behind. She'd see my mother looking ten years older than she is, haggard from fear and sorrow, stooped over a table working a jigsaw puzzle like her life depended on it, like she was trying to figure out what went wrong, but couldn't quite piece it together.

When the house came into view and Moira acted like she was going to drive me right up to the front door, it was all I could do to stop myself from jumping out of the El Camino while it was still going thirty. The phrases "over my dead body" and "when hell freezes over" rushed into my mind. Probably because both of those things would have to happen simultaneously before I ever, *ever* allowed Moira Watkins inside the godforsaken shack that doubles as my home sweet home.

MOIRA

DAY 72: APRIL 14

BUILDING FRANKENSTEIN'S MONSTER.

That was the caption beneath the picture of me that circulated at the beginning of freshman year. I'd been reapplying my makeup in the fluorescent light of the locker room after PE when I heard giggling nearby. I hadn't yet applied lipstick, so my mouth was still open in a wide, pale O as I lowered the tube in time to see the reflection of three girls in the mirror, all of them juniors. *Oh God, my hair,* I thought. It was still spiky and wet from the shower, pulled back from my face with an old elastic headband. Seconds later, there was a flash from one of their phone cameras. By the next morning, copies of the photo were taped up in the hallways and posted all over social media. People started pointing at me and shouting, "She's alive!" It was the usual horror, really.

"Just ignore them," Agnes advised, biting her lower lip.

"I'm trying. Believe me."

"It could have been worse. You could have been wearing a towel or nothing at—"

"I know."

The irony was that I'd recently decided to be pretty much done with the whole goth thing. I was just tired of it. The makeup I was applying that day in the locker room was noticeably toned down compared to how I'd been wearing it since eighth grade. I'd even donated some of my edgier clothes back to the thrift store where I bought them. But after the photo went viral, I had no choice but to reembrace a style that screamed *Death!* and *Darkness!* It was the only way I knew to not show weakness, to let the bastards know they weren't going to get me down.

Still, more than a year after the Frankenstein picture got plastered all over the school, it doesn't help when I feel like a monster yet again. When it becomes abundantly clear, for example, how quickly any guy who manages to spend more than five minutes in my presence wants to get away. Take Boone, for instance, and the way he bolted from El-C before I even got to the end of his driveway. Clearly he was freaked out by my music, my cynicism, my entire existence. The feeling of utter rejection that washed over me as soon as he shut the car door made me want to say, *Hey, wait. I think you might be misunderstanding something.*

It also made me want to hurt him right back.

It makes me shudder in self-revulsion.

BOONE

DAY 71: APRIL 15

IT DOESN'T SEEM LIKE SO LONG AGO THAT WE WERE IN SIXTH grade and I came this close to telling her she was the most beautiful girl I'd ever seen.

At the time, I knew Moira would think I was being a dope. *Shut up,* she'd say. *You're just trying to make me feel better.*

But she would have been wrong. Not that it mattered once she shut me out. Maybe I would have found the courage to tell her she was beautiful later if things had gone differently. Who knows?

These days, it's pretty obvious Moira thinks I'm a head case. All I need is for her to get an eyeful of my house and my one remaining nonfunctional parent to really make my life complete.

And so it goes and goes and goes. Some days, it's surprisingly easy to ignore how most guys my age are out shooting hoops or playing in garage bands or hanging with girls at parties every weekend. Other days, not so much. I despise self-pity, hate it most of all in myself. Still, sometimes I can't help but feel like every other sixteen-year-old guy in the universe is boarding the party plane to some magical land of women and money and fun while I sit by the side of the road, broken down before I even reached the airport.

AGNES

DAY 70: APRIL 16

MOIRA'S FAMILY LIVES IN AN OLD, TWO-STORY VICTORIAN HOUSE that's in constant disarray. There's art all over the walls, musical instruments everywhere, and, in the middle of it all, a baby grand piano. When we were girls, Moira and I would sometimes build forts under the piano and huddle there while her dad played jazz melodies or sonatas, filling our world with sound.

The house is one of my favorite places in the world, especially on a Saturday like today, when there's nothing that has to be done and nowhere that I have to be. It's the only place where I can really get away from my usual routine, other than school, which isn't much of a getaway at all.

"B-I-N-G-O!" I sing the tune of the old campfire song as

Moira's dog comes up to me with his tongue lolling and his tail waving back and forth like a metronome. I've taken billions of pictures of him over the years, and I take another one now. Then I cup his muzzle in my hands, and he sighs. Back when we were in grade school, I loved throwing a tennis ball for Bingo out in the backyard. He knocked me down once, and Moira just about had a cow. I didn't hold it against him, though. "He's just being a dog," I said.

The picture of Moira I love best has Bingo in it when he was a tiny puppy. Moira is only about three or four years old in that picture, which sits framed on a shelf filled with books on yoga and meditation and classic art. There's a look of pure, ticklish joy on Moira's face as Bingo sniffs her ear. Even now, that old dog is one of the only things that can make Moira seem like a little kid with no worries.

After we've been hanging out doing homework for a while, Moira drives me back home. On the way, I spot an old Volkswagen Beetle sitting in traffic. "Slug bug!" I shriek, punching Moira in the arm.

"Jesus, Agnes! You just about gave me a heart attack."

"I got you, though," I say, grinning maniacally.

Moira pretend-glares. "Indeed." She has no choice but to be a good sport where this particular game is concerned. The one and only time Moira saw a Bug and punched me (ever so lightly) on the arm, she gave me a big purple bruise. After that, no matter how many times I tried to convince her it didn't hurt, Moira refused to be the puncher. She was only willing to play if she could be the punchee every single time a Bug was spotted, even if she was the one to spot it.

"That's not going to be any fun," I said at the time. But I was wrong. It was tons of fun. I estimate that a good portion of every car ride I take with Moira is dedicated to being on the lookout for VWs so one of us can shout "Slug bug!" and I can punch my best friend.

"Why don't you come over for dinner tomorrow after school?" I ask her now. "You can show me how to make those yummy chocolate caramel coconut bars."

Moira sighs. "My brother's coming into town with his new girlfriend, so I have to eat at my house tomorrow. You could come over, though. I'm sure Grant would love to see you. Plus, you can meet his new floozy."

"Moira!"

"What? Have you seen some of the train wrecks he's dated? Like the girl with the spray tan who became a vegetarian when they started dating but then made this big, teary confession a month later that she'd been secretly bingeing on hamburgers the whole time? Then there was the cheerleader who was convinced they were going to get married right out of high school. She had a dress picked out and everything. And don't even get me started on that one protester girl who chained herself to the elm tree in our front yard after Grant broke up with her. I have no doubt this new chick will be a total piece of work."

MOIRA

DAY 69: APRIL 17

MAN, I WANT TO DISLIKE FERN. I REALLY, REALLY DO.

The only problem is, I can't. Fern is too perfect, but in a nice way. In a way that's impossible to hate. She met my brother at the university library where they both work, and they're like two peas in a pod. Fern seems perfect in the same way Grant has always been perfect, which is no doubt why they started going out in the first place. Self-esteem and popularity always came so easily to Grant. All through school he somehow managed to strike the perfect balance between throwback hippie kid and pop culture dude, never veering too heavily into either one. Everyone loved him for that—teachers, other kids, other kids' parents. It was sickening. Thank God he was a guy. If he'd been an older sister, I no doubt would have ended it all rather than try to live up to her. *Let's hear it for the Y chromosome,* I think.

It's almost ridiculous how happy Mom and Dad are to have Grant home. It's probably nice for them to have their non–black sheep kid around for a change, the one who embraced their lifestyle by doing graduate work in environmental studies at UC Berkeley. I would probably resent him for this, too, if I didn't feel the exact same way about my brother that our parents do. Every time he comes back, I realize how much I've missed him. Then he leaves again, and I have to stop letting myself think too much about it until the next time we see each other.

"So what's new with you, sis?" he asks as we finish up the organic fruit compote Mom made for dessert. "Any love interests I should know about?"

Without meaning to, I blush. "Shut up. Of course not."

Grant smiles at me. "Okay, then! What else is new in your world? Which dreamy new boy band are you listening to?" Even Fern looks appalled.

"You suck," I tell him. Still, he makes me laugh. He always has.

"Okay," he says. "I'll stop. How's Agnes?"

"The same. But, you know . . ."

"Older," he says.

"Yeah, by, like, decades since the last time you saw her."

"Agnes is Moira's friend we were talking about," Grant tells Fern. "The one with that aging disease?"

"Progeria," I clarify. I always feel protective of Agnes when other people talk about her. Grant would never say anything mean, though. I know this. When Agnes and I first met and Grant was in his junior year of high school, he and his friends were all so freaked out about how fragile Agnes was that they'd practically tiptoe around the house when she was around.

After dinner, my brother lies down on the living room floor with Bingo. "Such an old man," he says. "Look at that white muzzle." In response, the dog stares adoringly into Grant's eyes and lets out a long, heavy sigh. Then he farts. Audibly. Wheezing, Grant gets up and settles himself on the big couch next to Fern.

He asks how things are at his old high school, and I let out an irritated sigh. I tell him about finals break, the school district's newest attempt at staying relevant and sucking less. For a few years now, most of the public schools in our area have been getting poorer and hemorrhaging students, losing them to the charter schools.

"Finals break?"

"Yeah, we're getting a week off in May, even though we just had spring break last month. Students are supposed to use the time to study for the upcoming exams."

Grant laughs. "As if."

"Right? It's idiotic. Plus, finals won't even start until a week *after* we get back from finals break, so it makes no sense at all. Everything we study during the break is probably just going to leak right out of our heads by the time the exams finally roll around."

"Gotta love administrative scheduling logic."

"Hey," Fern says as my brother drapes her legs over his lap and starts rubbing her feet. "You should come hang out with us for the week."

I look at her. Fern really is pretty, but not in an aggressive, in-your-face kind of way like some of Grant's other girlfriends have been over the years. This is another fact that makes her easier to like.

"Sounds great," my brother says.

"Uh . . ." I answer, an intelligent response if there ever was one. At least I manage to not say what I'm really thinking, which is, *Yeah, that's not going to happen.*

Grant sits up. "Seriously, Moira. You can stay at my place and check out Cal."

My hands are up in front of me as if to stop his words, but Grant's on a roll, and he won't shut up.

"What are you, a sophomore now? Yeah, it's totally not too early for you to start checking out colleges."

"But I . . ." I look at my parents, like maybe they'll help shut this thing down.

"I think it's a wonderful idea as well," Mom says.

Dad just shrugs and smiles, a pacifist to the end. "Why not? You could fly out to the Bay Area, take the train, maybe. Flying's a lot quicker, though. Two hours, max."

"Mom," I say. "Dad. A plane ticket is going to be too expensive. And it's, like, a twenty-hour train ride or something."

*   *   *

Later, after everyone's gone to bed, Mom comes into my room.

"I don't want to go," I tell her.

"I can see that." She sits on the bed next to me and tucks a strand of hair behind my ear.

"So why are you guys acting like you're going to make me?"

"Nobody's going to make you do anything."

"Well, it seemed like pretty much everyone in that room was in agreement about what I should do, but nobody bothered to ask me if I wanted to go or not."

"Just out of curiosity, why *wouldn't* you want to go?"

"God, why *would* I?" There are so many reasons going away for an entire week would be a bad idea. "There's Agnes, for one," I begin.

Also, there's the whole "traveling by myself to an unfamiliar place" thing (which, not wanting to sound like a total chicken, I don't mention). And I don't even want to know what kind of food Grant has at his place. Bean sprouts? Tempeh? Probably the same crap my mother keeps in the fridge here, but at least in my own house, I don't feel compelled to actually *eat* it out of a sense of politeness. I can't really say that, either, I guess. "I have . . . stuff I want to do over the break," I finally say. It sounds lame, like I'm making it up on the spot, which I am.

"Look," Mom says. "I know you're worried about Agnes. You're always worried about her, and I get that . . . to a point. But your dad and I have been thinking that it might not be a bad idea if you started branching out a little bit. Getting out of your usual experiences."

"Like sitting naked for a room full of people so they can sketch me?" It's a bitchy thing to say, and I don't even know why I chose this one thing from Mom's past to bring up now. I regret the words the second they leave my mouth and hang there in the air between us.

Mom raises her eyebrows. "Wow."

"It's just . . . God." I drop my head and rub the spot above my eyebrows with my thumb and forefinger. "What's so awful about my usual experiences? It's not like I'm out there hooking up with guys or doing drugs. I mean, seriously, I never even stay out past my curfew. Are you trying to get me to do the whole crazy-teenager thing? Because I'm sure I could find some freak kids downtown who would gladly—"

"Moira, hey." Mom puts her hand on mine and brings it down so I'm forced to look at her. "You are a wonderful, amazing young woman. And I think you know I don't want you doing those things. But can we admit that there's a pretty huge middle ground between having a very limited, very regimented social life and . . . expanding one's horizons a little? That's all I'm saying."

"Agnes doesn't have anyone else." God, how pathetic is it that I'm using Agnes as an excuse? But it's true.

"Well," Mom says. "You know, maybe she would if . . ." Her voice drops off.

"If I stopped being friends with her? That sounds pretty shitty, if you ask me."

"We love Agnes. I think you know that, too."

"I thought I did. Now I'm not so sure." I'm just throwing out whatever pops into my head at this point. It's like I'm trying to build a hasty wall of words to stop this conversation from happening yet again. Mom loves Agnes, but this isn't the first time she has expressed concern about the time and energy I put into "being there" for my best friend above all else.

"She's there for me, too," I've told her more than once. That always seems to end the conversation pretty effectively, which is a good thing. I don't want to have to explain all the ways in which our friendship is not a one-way street, the ways in which Agnes is a shield for me just as much as I am for her. The problem is, I'm not sure I could explain it if I tried.

Plus—and it's not like this is a major deal or anything, but it's definitely on my mind—how can I explain the movie that plays in my head when I think of traveling alone to a strange place when I've never even flown before? There's the opening scene of my fat self trying to squeeze into a too-narrow airplane seat, for starters. And what if I got airsick? Yeah, that would be a lovely new kind of performance art. I'd call it *Fat Goth Chick Puking in Front of a Hundred People at 30,000 Feet*. I imagine the disgust on the other passengers' faces, the flight attendants overwhelmed by cleaning up the mess. The bathrooms on airplanes are supposed to be minuscule, too. What if, instead of puking, I just had to pee like a normal person but got stuck in there, and they had to get me out with the Jaws of Life? Do they even carry the Jaws of Life on airplanes?

Mom sighs and watches me chew at a hangnail. "Just think about Berkeley," she says. "Okay? Will you do that?"

I look away and nod like I'm in agreement, but the truth is, I'm done thinking about Berkeley. It's not going to happen.

AGNES

DAY 68: APRIL 18

SOMETIMES I LIE VERY STILL IN MY BED AND PRETEND I NEVER existed. I'm not afraid when I do this, because death isn't a real thing for people who don't exist. And sometimes, on nights when pretending I never existed doesn't work, the thought of dying is still okay. Let's face it: when you're a kid with a rare genetic disorder for which there is no cure, worrying about death is just wasted energy. Sure, there have been some major advances—advances bordering on miracles, even. But the outcome for kids like me is still a given. Our blood vessels are going to age at warp speed, and our arteries are going to get progressively more rigid and clogged up until the day a heart attack or stroke takes us down. Once I started to grasp the inevitability of that fate, I realized dying might be my gift, my talent. Maybe I was born to be a death prodigy.

Other times, though, I can't even think about not being here anymore. There's no good way to describe how scary and lonely it feels when you're reminded how fast your clock is ticking compared to everyone else's. It usually upsets other people to talk about it, too. Nobody really knows what to say. It's those other people I always end up thinking about most, the people I'll leave behind. My parents. Moira. My siblings. And now Boone, too, I guess.

I remember being at the park in early spring with Mom when I was a little kid, maybe six. On our way to the bathroom we found a newly hatched chick on the ground. It was a robin or a swallow probably. I remember how Mom looked up, as if being able to identify where the chick had fallen from would solve anything. We could see the nest high above us, in a branch. Mom cradled the naked baby bird in her hand, blew on it to see if . . . but no. It was definitely dead.

"Go ahead," she told me, gesturing with her chin toward the bathroom. "I'll be out here taking care of this."

When I came back out, she was squatting near a fresh mound of dirt, tamping it into place with her fingers. Burying that tiny creature made her go stony for the rest of the day.

*　　*　　*

"I want to donate my organs to science," I tell Moira when she picks me up Monday morning for the drive to school.

"Jesus, Agnes. Good morning to you, too."

"Well, I do. I want them to figure out this disease."

Moira sighs. "I know you do. I'm sorry. It's just . . ."

"You have to tell my mom. It'll kill her coming from me."

"Are we seriously having this conversation right now?"

"Promise," I insist, holding my pinkie finger in the air between us.

Moira sighs again, louder this time. "Fine," she says, hooking her pinkie around mine.

34

BOONE
DAY 67: APRIL 19

I'M STANDING AT HER BEDROOM DOOR, ONE EAR NEAR THE wood. A minute ago, I heard sobs. Now I touch one knuckle to the door and knock, but just barely. This is always the moment when I am my most careful, refined self. Like a well-behaved boy in church. "Mom, can I get you anything?"

No answer.

"I'm going to go feed Diablo," I say to the door, "and then I'll be back."

Technically, Diablo is her horse, but I'm the only one who takes care of him now. There's a memory stored away in the back of my mind from when I was only three or four. Sometimes, like now, fragments of it appear. I remember playing in the yard under the old oak tree, just tooling around in the dirt. Something made me look up, and when I did, I saw

Mom riding Diablo. Both of them were backlit against rays of lowering sunlight, the horse's hooves kicking up dust clouds as they beat out a perfect rhythm in the arena. I didn't know that the two of them were working on flying changes. All I knew was that there was a cadence and a rhythm to what they were doing that was like a celebration, though I couldn't have put it into those words back then. The first time I heard the phrase "poetry in motion," this was the exact image that came to me. It's one of my earliest, best memories.

My dad didn't have much to do with Mom's horse activities, but he didn't usually complain about them, either. Not at first, anyway. After the brain injury and the rage and the drinking changed him, though, he started saying things like, "Damn horse is nothing but a liability, eating us out of house and home." I knew it hurt Mom to hear this. For one, there was truth in it, at least during the colder months when Diablo couldn't pasture graze and my parents had to buy hay. But Diablo provided income as a lesson horse. In that sense, the poor beast carried all three of us.

Plus, the lessons were an area where I could help out, and it made me feel good to do that. Over the years, Mom showed me how to clean saddles and bridles with saddle soap from a big tin before rubbing the leather down with neatsfoot oil. I learned how to paint the wooden cavalletti poles that Mom used to encourage horses to round their backs and to get the youngest students ready for their first jumping lessons. When I was twelve, she even taught me how to drive the Chevy. That way, I could drag the arena by towing a chain-link gate behind the truck in big, slow, swooping circles to level out the footing.

Several of her students trailered their own horses to our place for lessons, but not all of them had their own mounts. Fortunately, we had a pony at the time in addition to Diablo. Her name was Cherokee, and she was a little Shetland cross Mom had rescued from a bad situation. Often, I'd get Cherokee ready for lessons with the younger kids. Sometimes, I'd even teach the beginner lessons myself.

Afterward, when my father was no longer there, we held on to Cherokee as long as we could. That period of time turned out to be not very long at all. Hay was expensive, and a pony wasn't an expense we could justify, especially once Mom stopped teaching. We couldn't afford Diablo, either, to tell the truth, but Mom couldn't stand the thought of selling him. I was sad to see Cherokee go. When the new owner, another trainer who'd also taken on a bunch of Mom's students, loaded the pony into her trailer and pulled away down the driveway, Diablo went ballistic. He galloped back and forth along the paddock fence line, shoving the wooden rails with his chest. I was afraid he might actually break through. The tears that sprang into my eyes at the sight of Diablo losing his only friend enraged me.

Even now, nearly two years later, the memory of Cherokee being hauled away makes my jaw tighten and my teeth grind. I throw a flake of hay into Diablo's feed tub, pat the horse on the shoulder, and head back inside the house.

35

MOIRA

DAY 66: APRIL 20

I HAVEN'T HEARD FROM BOONE IN DAYS. HE'S RUSHED AND
pissed-off looking all the time lately. He has perma-bags
under his eyes, and he barely says two words to me or Agnes
in the hallways. No doubt it's because he's embarrassed to be
seen with us. Or with me, anyway. And who could blame
him? I should have taken the hint when he jumped out of my
car as fast as he could the day I gave him a ride back to his
place. He probably figured he'd already done his duty by
being nice to me in exchange for my setting him up with
some paid work at my house. He'd used the "real women
have curves" line. He'd humored the fat chick. As far as he
was no doubt concerned, we were even.

And if that's the way he feels, then good riddance.

Still. I look down and behold my elephantine thighs, which he must have noticed jiggling as we drove out to his place. And what about my chin—or should I say *chins*? Every time he turned to say something to me during that drive he must have felt like he was addressing Jabba the Hutt.

I cringe at the fact that I'm worried yet again about how he sees me. Long ago, I vowed to stop caring about what other people think, and I refuse to break that promise to myself now. With that thought, the walls that came down when Boone was nice to me start going right back up again. Brick by brick by brick.

AGNES

DAY 65: APRIL 21

MOIRA IS WEARING HER CRAMPS T-SHIRT ON THURSDAY, THE ONE with the psychopathic zombie smiling on the front that always gives me nightmares. She put on her makeup extra thick this morning, too, which is how I always know something's not right. For now, I'm letting it go. I can tell she's in no mood to talk. I'd ask Boone what he thinks might be going on with her, but lately he's been acting as funky as she has. I don't know what's happening. For a while there, it seemed like everything was pretty much perfect.

Moira did volunteer to drive me to my appointment today when Mom found out she wouldn't be able to leave her sub job early enough, so that was nice. But now I wonder if accepting Moira's offer might have been a mistake. It's pretty clear most of the senior center residents are afraid of her. I can't really blame them, since Moira looks like she's ready to start snacking on people's faces at any second. Even the receptionist looks at her sideways until my friend Kitty, the elderly ex-socialite, comes up to the desk and gives both of us big hugs.

"I'd know you anywhere," Kitty says. "You're Moira, aren't you?"

Moira nods, looks away.

"Agnes told me you were beautiful. A *presence*, she said. And she was right."

Moira glances at Kitty briefly. "Thank you," she mutters with a fake smile on her face.

"How are you?" I ask Kitty.

She shakes her head. "Not so good. Harold passed away last week."

"Harold?"

Kitty looks around before leaning closer to us and whispering, "My boyfriend. I have to be careful saying it because some people here don't believe in . . . having relations outside of wedlock." Even Moira is caught off guard by this. She blinks in confusion as Kitty looks pointedly at another resident, a white-haired woman in a housedress who's sitting on a couch by one of the big windows, working on an afghan. The crochet hook pauses in midair as she purses her lips at the three of us and shakes her head slowly back and forth.

"See?" Kitty says. "I'm a widow, for crying out loud. Harold was a widower. Where's the harm?"

"I'm really sorry," I tell her. Next to me, Moira takes a long, deep breath and then slowly lets it out. I can tell she's doing it to keep from laughing. At least it's good to finally see some lightness in her expression.

Kitty shrugs, but her eyes are dewy. "What is there to do? He was a good man. Loved his wife when she was alive. Loved his kids. Maybe even loved me a little."

"I'm sure he did," I say. "What's not to love?"

"Right?" she says, brightening. "That's what I was always telling him. Anyway, he's dead now. And I know I'm supposed to be grief stricken, but the truth is I see death as a promotion. I've had too many experiences with it in this life to think otherwise. Besides, at my age, what's the point in worrying? Silver lining, glass half-full, and all that."

"That sounds like a good attitude," I tell her.

Kitty nods. "Put it this way: nowadays, I only wear bright colors to funerals. As far as I'm concerned, it's all A-okay." She makes a little circle with her thumb and forefinger and then leads us over to some plush chairs arranged around a card table. "This life is just a stop on the way to wherever it is we're all going," she continues. "It's a sideshow, if you will."

"And I'm the freak," I say.

Moira and Kitty both stare at me.

"Oh, honey," Kitty says. "I didn't mean it like that."

"It's okay," I tell her, embarrassed by my weird outburst. "I don't even know where that came from, to tell you the truth."

When it's time for me to follow a nurse back into the exam room, Moira asks if she should come, too. She looks concerned.

"Stay here," I tell her. "It's just a routine checkup. Plus, it will give you ladies a chance to get to know each other."

"Suits me," Kitty says. "My dance card's pretty empty today."

Moira doesn't look so sure until I whisper that I'm going to have to get naked. "Yeah, I'll just go ahead and hang here, then," she says.

After stepping on the hallway scale and standing with my back to the measuring stick so the nurse can get my stats, I change into the gown that's been set out for me in the exam room. In reality, I'm not at all sure today's checkup is going to be routine. I've been having more and more issues lately, and my joints seem to be stuck in a rut of constant achiness. Even hydrotherapy sessions in the big heated pool at the Y haven't been helping as much as they used to. I choose a magazine from the rack near the door and settle in on the exam table to wait for Dr. Caslow.

Before long, he knocks and comes in, giving me a high five as usual. "No parent today?"

"Mom had to work late," I tell him. "My friend Moira drove me here."

"Ah," the doctor says, checking my chart. "Looks like you've lost a little weight since our last appointment. Are you drinking your breakfast drinks?"

"Unfortunately," I say, making a face. The drinks he's referring to are a concoction of vitamins and protein and calories in the form of watery, faux-chocolate or faux-vanilla breakfast gruel. I gag just thinking about the foul, evil cans of stuff that I wouldn't wish on my worst enemy, if I had one. Tragically, the drinks seem to be the most efficient way for my body to get as many calories as possible. Mom has tried masking the taste with real vanilla, cinnamon, syrups, you name it, but nothing works. I still feel like a baby eating food I'd rather fling onto the walls.

The nurse comes back into the exam room, and Dr. Caslow gives me the usual once-over. When I tell him about some of the stuff that's been going on, he says he's going to move my next appointment up a few weeks so he can keep better track of my symptoms. "It could just be leftover aches from winter," he says, "but let's not mess around with them, okay? Also, I want your mom or dad here for our next visit."

Out in the waiting room, Kitty is teaching Moira to play blackjack. The two of them hardly notice as I approach the table and snap a quick picture. I do it more from habit than anything, since my heart's not really in it this time. Still, the shot should turn out okay.

"Oh, hey," Moira says, looking up. "Check me out. I'm totally planning to clean up in Vegas someday."

I smile, but it's a weak one. Moira notices and gets up from the table.

"What's wrong, honey?" Kitty asks me.

"Nothing. I think I'm just tired. Can we go, Em?"

Moira starts organizing the cards into a neat pile, but Kitty stops her. "I'll take care of this," she says.

During the drive home, I stare out the window without really noticing what I'm seeing.

"You okay?" Moira asks.

"Yeah. I'm fine." I just wish I could stop being so tired all the time. I wish I could stop constantly having to see my doctor. And I wish I could stop feeling sorry for myself whenever someone mentions a place like Las Vegas, just one more thing I'll probably never get to see.

BOONE

DAY 64: APRIL 22

THIS TIME, IT'S THE RUMBLE OF A DIESEL ENGINE OUTSIDE MY window that hauls me up from the depths of a dream before my alarm even has a chance to go off. "What the hell?" I groan into my pillow.

"Boone?" Mom's voice is anxious outside the bedroom door.

"I'm on it, Mom." I sit up in bed and rub a hand down my face before grabbing my jeans from the floor. I know it makes her nervous when unexpected visitors appear. Whoever this is, I'm glad they showed up before I left for the day. Sometimes I wonder what she does when I'm not here to intercept. Probably locks herself in her bedroom and hopes they go away.

That's what happened with her riding students once my dad was gone. They waited a few weeks for her to get over the shock, and then they started showing up at the door, one after another, in their velvet-covered riding helmets and tan breeches, at their regular lesson times. Again and again, I had to tell them it was still too soon, that she wasn't ready, and they should probably call before coming for their next lesson. But the story was always the same over the phone later on. After the landline got disconnected due to lack of payment, and before I bought a pay-as-you-go cell phone, a few of Mom's most dedicated students showed up at the door one final time. They wondered if she was ever planning to get back to teaching, and if so, when. By that point, I had to turn them away with no explanation other than a tired shrug.

Now the unused arena is overgrown with clumps of buffalo grass and rabbit brush. I try to keep rocks picked up in the paddock adjacent to the pasture where Diablo eats and spends the night in the shelter my dad built years ago, the one in constant need of being shored up against the weather. During the winter I'm always afraid the roof is going to collapse right on top of Diablo in the middle of a bad snowstorm.

A one-ton Ford Power Stroke pickup sits idling in our dusty driveway. It's the newest model, top of the line, with chrome trim, sprayed-in bed liner, and a custom winch mounted on the front. Damn, the things I could do with a truck like that. Haul a trailer out into the woods and cut twice as much wood in a single trip, for one. Put the five-hundred-gallon fiberglass tank in the back without worrying about busting an axle with every water-hauling trip to and from town, for another.

The guy standing next to the driver's side door has small, close-set eyes. "Your dad around?"

"No," I say, tearing my attention away from the truck. "He's . . . not here right now. Can I help you with something?"

"I'm Jackson Tate, and I've just bought the forty acres adjacent to yours. Need to talk fence line."

So this was the new neighbor. I'd seen the For Sale sign go up not long after old man Wallace died, and I'd watched from Diablo's paddock as the Realtor took it down only a couple weeks after that. No big surprise. It's prime real estate out here for people who can afford to do country living the way it's advertised in magazines. Wallace lived on that property in his one-bedroom homesteader cabin for longer than anyone around here can remember.

"Gonna build a house?" I ask Jackson Tate.

"Like I said, I need to have a chat with your dad about the fence. Seems the entire south line of his t-posts are driven in about ten feet past my property line."

"That can't be right." As far as I know, my grandfather and old man Wallace agreed on that fence line back in the 1970s when my dad was just a kid. Wallace and my grandfather were friends sometimes and foes at others. Those two geezers could fight like a couple of banty roosters, to hear my dad tell it, but one thing they never fought about was the fence line. If it had really been an issue, shotguns would have been drawn, no doubt about it. Not to mention the fact that even the thought of pulling up the entire line of those old-school, heavy-gauge posts is a joke.

"Oh, it's right, all right," the new neighbor says. "I have the measurements to back me up on how right it is." Turning toward the Power Stroke, he makes an annoyed, dismissive gesture with one hand, like I'm just some dumbass kid not worth his time. "Have your old man get in touch."

Of all things, it's a laugh that bubbles up inside me first. At this point, I'm going to be late for school, but I don't even care. I'm dying to see where this conversation might go. "What do you think he's going to do about it?" I'm not necessarily trying to sound disrespectful, but words have a way of leaving my mouth that way whether I want them to or not.

Tate turns back around, ever so slowly. "I think," he says, his lips stretched into a taut smile now, "that's he's going to move his piece-of-shit fence back onto his own piece-of-shit property if he doesn't feel like having a nice long chat with my attorney. *Capisce?*"

I cross my arms over my chest and train my eyes on him. Keeping my gaze as steady as I can, I watch as he gets back into the truck and drives away.

AGNES

DAY 63: APRIL 23

IF YOU LOOK UP *PROGERIA* IN OLD MEDICAL TEXTBOOKS, YOU'LL see black-and-white photographs of miniature, ancient-looking naked kids. I can't say exactly why this bothers me so much. Maybe it's because, somehow, those olden-days kids feel like family to me. Like we're all connected, thanks to a single microscopic protein that decided to go rogue and do its own thing when our bodies were first being formed.

I'm sure the images were useful back then for doctors to see what progeria sufferers (I hate that word as much as I hate the word *victims*, but it's the one people always seem to use) looked like from head to toe. Still. Some of the kids in those old pictures are obviously trying to hide their nakedness, which they were undoubtedly told not to do. I imagine the photographer commanding them to "Stop it! Keep your hands at your sides!" But how could a kid help it? Especially a hundred years ago, when even a healthy adult getting naked for anyone, much less for a picture to be published in a book, was a way bigger deal than it is these days. Then again, maybe those kids were already too worn down from being treated like pincushions and science experiments to care.

I know how they must have felt. When I go to the hospital, I feel like a science experiment, too. But the truth is, I don't have to deal with half of what those kids went through. Sure, people stare at me. Sure, they make ignorant comments, often loudly enough for me to hear. But I'm not hated because of how I look. I'm not in danger. Many of the kids in those old textbooks no doubt ended up in the freak show tents of traveling circuses, or they were hidden away in cellars and basements, a family's shame—if they lived long enough to do either, that is.

Sometimes, my heart hurts just thinking about them.

BOONE

DAY 62: APRIL 24

THE CHEVY'S OUT OF COMMISSION AGAIN, BUT THIS TIME IT'S NOT because of loose battery connections. All I can do is cross my fingers and hope that it will be another simple fix.

It's all going to work out. It's all going to work out. It's all going to work out.

This is the mantra I force myself to recite in my head when life's pressing down so hard that I'm not sure I can take it anymore. Without those words, I'd just find a corner and start rocking.

Lately, my days are a blur of wake up, get dressed, do the chores, feed Diablo, make sure Mom has something to eat, panic about the fact that *oh shit I forgot to study for history last night and there's a test today*, try to remember to eat breakfast and grab something for lunch, race out the door, hope the truck will start, hope I have enough gas, wonder what I'm going to do if I have to buy gas, stress about payday not being until next week, hope I'm not late to school, race to first period, listen to the hallway insults, try not to kill anybody, worry about the new asshole neighbor instead of focusing on the history test, fail the history test, avoid Agnes and Moira, who (without question) regret getting reinvolved with me and my apocalypse of a life, hope Mom's okay, wonder what I'll do if she isn't, try to remember if we have something in the fridge or the cupboard that I can heat up for dinner, find an isolated spot at lunch, eat whatever I happened to grab that morning, make it through afternoon classes without falling asleep, get the hell out of there as soon as the bell rings, drive home, make sure Mom's okay, feed Diablo, figure out dinner, try to remember to do homework, face-plant onto my bed, wake up the next morning, and do it all over again.

It's all going to work out. It's all going to work out. It's all going to work out.

40

MOIRA
DAY 61: APRIL 25

"HEY, THAT'S BOONE," AGNES SAYS, TUGGING AT MY SLEEVE. IT'S Monday afternoon, and we've just pulled out of the school parking lot. Sure enough, he's standing at an intersection up ahead with his thumb out.

"We should offer him a ride," Agnes tells me. "His truck must be broken again."

I stare straight ahead at the road. "He'll be fine." It's not like he appreciated the last ride I gave him.

"Jeez, Em."

"What?" I glance over at her. The look of disappointment that's in her eyes now never fails to kill me.

"We can't just drive right past him."

"Fine," I say, exasperated. I turn on the blinker and roll El-C to a stop a few yards from where Boone is standing.

Agnes cranks down her window. "Hey," she tells him. "Hop in."

"Nah," Boone says. His eyes dart to my face before he focuses on Agnes again and smiles. "That's okay. Someone'll stop."

"Okeydokey," I say to the windshield, my voice fake-cheerful. Of *course* he doesn't want a ride. Not from me, anyway.

Agnes ignores me. "I don't know," she says, grinning at Boone from her booster seat, *teasing* him like they're regular buddies and not just people who were temporarily thrown together by a random situation in the cafeteria. "You're pretty big and scary. *I* wouldn't pick you up."

"You don't even drive," he tells her, still smiling. Whatever this is, this weird little faux-flirty banter, he's keeping it between the two of them. I sigh once more and check the rear-view mirror to make sure there's nobody behind us who wants to turn onto this street. Sure enough, a bunch of cars are coming. They're only a block away, stopped at the light. I breathe out slowly through my nose.

"Well, what are you going to do?" Agnes is still grinning. "Camp by the side of the road with your thumb out, waiting for a ride that might never come?"

"I hitched a ride to school this morning," Boone tells her. "Figure I can do the same to get home."

"Just get in, Boone," I finally say to the air in front of me. Someone needs to put a stop to this nonsense. Apparently, I'm the one person present who realizes we're going to have a bunch of road-ragey drivers lined up behind us pretty soon if I don't move the car out of the damn road. I want to floor it instead, just leave him in a cloud of exhaust. But Agnes would never let me hear the end of it.

Boone hesitates at first, but then he finally picks up his grungy, military-style backpack, steps toward El-C, and reaches for the passenger side door. Unfortunately, because Agnes's booster seat is strapped in on that side, and because the car has no backseat, he's going to have to get in through my driver's side door.

"Over here," I bark at him through the open window. Moments later, I'm standing on the street, keeping an eye on the rapidly approaching traffic. Sighing, Boone meanders toward me and ducks into El-C. As soon as he squeezes himself past the steering wheel and scoots toward the center of the seat, I jump back in, slam the door, and step on the gas.

The traffic light up ahead turns yellow, then red, causing me to brake hard. Both their heads flop forward.

"Whoa," Agnes says.

Instinctively, I reach my right hand out to brace against her, the way moms do with their kids, but I end up pressing firmly on Boone's stomach instead. *Jesus.* "Sorry," I say.

He ignores the apology. "If you guys are in a rush and need to get somewhere, I could seriously just—"

"No!" Agnes laughs. "Moira's just being a spaz." She sort

of shout-giggles this last part. The sound grates on my nerves, which makes me feel guilty. Feeling guilty always makes me angry, so there's that, but what was Agnes thinking, throwing me under the bus the way she did?

The light turns green, and I touch the gas as lightly as possible this time, easing El-C forward. For the next few minutes, I drive at turtle speed without saying anything, like a seething grandma. Out of the corner of my eye I see Agnes staring at me.

"Sorry if my boots reek," Boone announces after a while, breaking the silence. We've just turned onto the dirt road that leads to his place.

"Ew," Agnes says, laughing again.

"I was out mucking the paddock this morning and forgot to change them. I'm pretty sure Ms. Chavez was this close to kicking me out of history today."

Agnes turns toward him in her booster seat. "You still have horses?"

"Just one now. My mom's gelding."

"Oh, Boone, can I ride him?"

Boone hesitates. "You mean today?"

With a wild grin on her face, Agnes nods.

This has gone far enough. Glancing at her, I shake my head: *No.* The strap across her right shoulder looks like it's digging uncomfortably into her skin. I make a mental note to loosen it.

"Uh, that's probably not the best—" Boone starts to say, but Agnes cuts him off.

"I'm not allergic or anything."

"Seriously," I tell her. "You've never even been interested in horses. Plus, we'd really need to ask your mom first if—"

"Pleeeeeeeeeease? I'm interested in them now!" Thankfully, I'm getting more used to driving on this road. Otherwise, I'd have to pull over just to look at her and go, *What the actual hell, Agnes?* Eventually, the long dirt driveway leading to Boone's house comes into view. "Should I let you off here?" I ask him in the sweetest voice I can muster. Part of me is perversely interested in seeing just how long he thinks he can keep pretending I'm not in the car.

"I want to see the horse!" Agnes insists yet again. God, she's been acting like a caffeinated toddler since we picked Boone up. Usually, it's not too hard to get her to change her mind about something by simply reasoning with her. Every once in a while, though, she'll dig her heels in. Clearly, this is one of those times, and I know better than to fight it.

"You can see the horse if you really want to," Boone says, quietly capitulating. "If it's okay with Moira." He sounds miserable, and he won't look at either of us, but at least he's finally acknowledging my presence.

Again, I sigh. "Are you sure?" I ask him.

"No," he says, staring hard at the dashboard. "I'm not sure. I'd rather you guys not see where I live from even this far away, to be honest. But Agnes wants to see the horse, so . . ."

I wasn't expecting that particular answer. It never occurred to me that he was embarrassed about having us out here. I stop the car at the end of the driveway and nod without looking at him.

"I'm sure your house is fine," Agnes assures him.

Boone smiles a little. "It's not, actually," he says. "It's really, really not. But let's go ahead and get this over with."

I turn in to the driveway and keep going until we reach the end of it. Without saying anything more, Boone points to a parking spot near the horse shelter. A few hundred yards away, a little house sits on a bare patch of ground looking sort of small and sad and like it has seen better days. The three of us get out of the car, and the first thing I notice is how quiet it is out here. There are no traffic sounds, no sirens. Just the cry of a far-off hawk and the rustle of leaves as a breeze moves through the branches of a big old oak tree near the horse paddock.

There's a ruckus as Boone leads us toward the shelter. I can see the horse standing next to a steel water trough. He's holding a stick between his teeth, and it looks like he's sword fighting with an invisible opponent. There's a demented look in his huge brown eyes, like he's demanding satisfaction.

"Look at him!" Agnes laughs.

Now it's Boone's turn to sigh. "That would be Diablo. I think he may have been dropped on his head as a foal."

Every once in a while, the horse whacks the stick against the trough and then lifts his head up high to reposition the weapon in his mouth.

"Wanna try him out?" Boone asks. It takes me a second to realize he's talking to me.

"Right, whatever," I say, rolling my eyes.

"Oo! I do!" Agnes is standing on her tiptoes, waving a hand in the air, practically jumping in place.

"Like I said," Boone tells her, "you can ride him as far as I'm concerned." He turns his attention back to me. "Why 'whatever'?"

"Um, hello? Silk dress?" I look down at the black vintage smock I got for a steal at one of the thrift stores in town. They didn't know what they had. Puffy gray crinoline was sewn in between the silk and the lining when I bought it, but I ripped it out right away. The last thing I need is a bulk-enhancing underskirt.

Boone's watching me, apparently not convinced by my lack of proper riding attire. Even aside from the dress, me riding that horse is an absurd thing to consider. Horses are gargantuan and unpredictable. I've heard they have brains the size of walnuts. I can easily see myself getting bucked off and becoming one with the ground below, my dress hiked up, displaying God knows how many unmentionable parts of my body. Agnes is watching me now, too. Do they actually think there's a chance in Hades I'm going to say yes? Rolling my eyes again, I reach down and grab some of the silk between my hands. "Silk. Dress," I repeat.

"Those tights you're wearing really don't look all that different from breeches," Boone says. "It's totally doable." My face feels hot at the thought of his noticing my tights. My chunky legs. True, I've always kind of liked my strong calves and my ankles, but . . . God, I never should have gotten out of the car. We should have just dropped him at the end of his driveway and taken off like I originally planned.

"Do it, Em!" Agnes is pleading now, bouncing a little on her tiptoes.

That's when I look away from both of them. "I'd break his back."

Boone laughs—laughs!—like he has no idea how much he's risking his life by doing it. "You would not," he says. Diablo has ambled over to where the three of us are standing. Boone reaches across the fence and scratches a spot at the top of the horse's shoulder. In response, Diablo stretches his neck out and lifts his lips away from his teeth.

Agnes squeals in delight. "He's smiling!"

"Plus," Boone says, looking at the horse instead of at me, "this way, you can convince yourself that it's safe for Agnes to get up there."

Which makes me want to kill him. It's like he knows that my desire to protect Agnes is rivaled only by my desire to give her what she wants. All the people closest to Agnes feel this way, but I'm pretty sure none of them feel the tension between those two warring forces as strongly as I do.

I look Boone right in the eye. "Okay," I tell him. I say it in a quiet voice but with my chin raised, like I'm taking him up on a dare, showing how unafraid I am.

Ten minutes later, Boone has Diablo all groomed and ready to go. With the saddle on, the damn horse is even taller than he already was. I have to stretch my arm up as high as it will go to grab hold of his mane like Boone tells me to do. My leg shakes a little when I put one foot in the stirrup and start hoisting myself up, but there's no time to worry about that now. I need to focus on keeping my balance and my upward momentum. Once my other leg is up and over, I try to land as lightly as possible on the poor horse's back. Diablo makes an *Oof* sound anyway, his ears swiveling around toward me.

"Now see?" Boone says. "That wasn't so awful, was it?"

"Check you out," Agnes adds from behind that blasted camera of hers as she points it at me and clicks away. I don't answer. I'm too busy ignoring both of them and blowing my bangs toward the sky like this is the most asinine thing I've ever had to do. Boone says he's going to lead the horse around a little with me up there. I don't like the idea of my fate being so entirely in somebody else's hands, and my legs instinctively clamp down on Diablo's sides at the thought. Apparently, that's the equivalent of stomping on an equine gas pedal, because the horse bolts forward. It's just a few steps, but it's enough to throw me off-balance. I end up leaning way back, bracing myself against the top of Diablo's rump. At that, his ears flatten and he gives a little hop with both hind legs. Something like lightning shoots down my spine as I jounce around up there. *So this is it,* I think. *This is how I die.*

"Whoa," Boone says, placing a hand on Diablo's neck. "Easy." The horse settles down and lets out a long breath through his nostrils.

"Okay, I did it." I straighten up, forcing myself to keep my legs loose. "I braved the pony ride. Are you happy?"

Boone smiles up at me now. "Thrilled," he says.

I work my way out of the saddle and ease myself back down to the ground as gracefully as I can. I do my best to keep the dress from catching on the stirrup and bunching up around my waist. It isn't a pretty process, but at least I don't end up sprawled in the dirt. I'm still shaky, though.

Now that it's her turn to ride, Agnes is barely keeping it together. *For Pete's sake,* I want to tell her, *chill out.*

"I'll help you get up there," Boone says. He asks me to hold Diablo's lead rope, and then he fits an old, child-size riding helmet onto her head. After adjusting the strap, he turns Agnes around to face the side of the horse. "Reach your hands up and grab the saddle."

"That's not how you do it," I practically shout as he puts his hands under her armpits and lifts her into the air. Panic rises in my chest at the sight of Agnes trying to scramble into the saddle with her delicate joints. "Stop stretching her leg like that."

"Em, it's fine," Agnes says, her voice suddenly heavy with exertion.

"No, it's not," I shoot back. "He's going to throw your hip out."

Boone is clearly trying to keep a lid on something. "You actually think I'd hurt her?"

"Maybe not intentionally."

"Oh, gee, thanks. But I might *accidentally* hurt her, since I'm such a big, violent clod, right?"

"I didn't say that."

"You didn't have to."

After that, we don't talk to each other. Agnes rides, and she's beaming the whole time, really getting into it. When I tell her it's time to go, she insists on giving Boone a hug from the saddle before he helps her back to the ground. "Thank you," she tells him. "That was so much fun. You have no idea."

41

BOONE
DAY 60: APRIL 26

I'VE NEVER KNOWN ANYONE WHO CAN FREEZE PEOPLE OUT THE way Moira can. She reminds me of the arctic blasts that blew through Beacon Valley that first winter Mom and I were on our own.

When the pipes froze, I stayed up all night—or tried to, anyway. I kept nodding off on the couch and even on the wooden kitchen stool. I tried working one of Mom's unfinished jigsaw puzzles, but that just made me more tired. Eventually, I resorted to doing jumping jacks outside in the subzero air. My main concern was keeping the fire stoked and the cupboard doors under the kitchen and bathroom sinks open so warm air would keep the pipes from exploding. The pipes froze anyway, but at least they didn't burst. If they had, we would have been out of luck. I wouldn't have had the faintest clue how to fix them, and who was going to come over and do major plumbing work for free?

Diablo's trough was the next thing to freeze. I'd been so busy dealing with the pipes that I let his water level get too low. Instead of just an icy crust that could be easily smashed through with the maul, there was a solid, ten-inch-thick block of ice covering the water in the tank. I spent a few minutes bashing at it anyway and hissing the worst swear words I'd ever heard my father say when he was shoeing horses, but it was hopeless. In the process of nearly dislocating my shoulder, I made little more than an opaque white dent in the ice.

My only remaining option was to go back inside, fill the biggest stew pot I could find with packed snow, heat it to near boiling, and carry it out to the trough. I used pot holders to grip the handles, but the scalding water sloshed all over me anyway as I walked, first burning and then freezing my clothes wherever it soaked in. I hardly noticed. I was too busy thinking of the disaster that would unfold if Diablo didn't have anything to drink. The last thing we needed was a horse with impaction colic due to a dried-out gut. There was no way any vet in town would be willing to brave our snowed-in road, and I shuddered to think what it would mean if I had to put Diablo down myself. If the colic was bad enough, I wouldn't even be able to lead the horse out into the woods for the vultures and coyotes to take care of. I'd have to shoot him right there in the paddock where Mom would be forced to view his carcass from the kitchen window. The sight of her beloved horse with a hole in his head would probably finish her off, too.

Steam burst upward when I poured the hot water into the trough, but the ice didn't budge. It was only after I repeated the process several more times and my clothes were frozen solid that I heard the telltale crack I'd been waiting for. I pounded the ice with the maul, using every ounce of frustration in my body to bring the steel head down as hard as I could, until the block finally gave way in four big chunks. I pulled one of the chunks out and tossed it aside to keep the others from fusing back together, at which point Diablo was able to get a drink. I knew I'd have to keep the water thawed for the rest of the night, or I'd soon be right back where I started. Diablo lowered his head through the steam, and I watched the lump in his throat move back and forth as he sucked in, gulp after gulp. It was like a sped-up video of a hairy python swallowing a mouse over and over, and it was one of the first small victories of that winter.

42

AGNES
DAY 59: APRIL 27

IT WAS THE BEST THING IN THE WORLD, SITTING HIGH UP there on Diablo's back while Boone led him around the paddock. I've been missing out. It's no mystery whatsoever why some girls get obsessed with horses—drawing them, braiding their manes and tails, riding them any chance they get. What was Moira so grumpy about? She looked magnificent in the saddle, like some stout Viking warrior queen.

"I hate that you and Boone are being snippy with each other." We're on our way to school Wednesday morning when I dare to say it.

"It's not like we were great pals to begin with."

"You used to be."

"That was a long time ago, Agnes."

"So?" Sometimes she talks to me like she's my mother.

"So," Moira repeats. "It's . . ." Her voice grows quieter. "Just whatever."

If there's one thing I can't stand, it's when the people I care about aren't getting along. Thinking about whatever rift this is between Moira and Boone brings me right back to the last fight my parents had before Dad finally left for good. I was nine, and their raised voices through the wall separating their bedroom from mine woke me from sleep.

"I can't do this," my father was saying.

"You can't do this? You can't *do* this?" Mom's voice was hoarse, which was a clue the fight had been going on for a while before I woke up.

"I love her so much, but I didn't know it was going to be this hard."

"This is life, Tom. It's just . . . life."

I tried plugging my ears, but their voices got through anyway.

"You're tough, Deb," he answered. "You know how to keep moving forward despite the odds, day in and day out. I don't."

"What are you saying?"

"I'm saying I love her more than I can stand, but I can't do this anymore."

There was a long silence before Mom said the next thing. The final thing. "Well, you can just go ahead and get the hell out, then."

Moira and I ride the rest of the way to school in silence. She parks El-C in the usual spot and opens the door.

"Isn't he supposed to come out to your house again this week?" I ask her.

Moira pauses like she's considering something, but only for a second. "He won't show," she says.

43

BOONE

DAY 58: APRIL 28

I SHOW UP AT MOIRA'S HOUSE ON THURSDAY AFTER SCHOOL
because that's what her dad and I agreed to the last time I was
over there. And I'm not one to go back on my word. Sure,
I could have called and told him I was sick or something. I
could have lied.

I don't know why Moira hates my guts so much, but she
clearly does. I'm not about to let it get to me, though, even if
I have no idea what I did to deserve her wrath. It's the same
old story, really. What have I ever done to deserve anyone's
hatred? Okay, so there was the thing in sixth grade, and that
wasn't cool of me. But, I mean, get *over* it already.

At least I got the truck working again, which means there
will be no question of her offering me a ride. Not that she

wants to drive me anywhere anyway. It was pretty obvious Agnes forced her to pick me up on the side of the road the other day after school. I wish they'd just driven right past.

As soon as I arrive at her house, Moira's parents invite me inside. "We're working from home today," Moira's mom says.

I hesitate for a second, but I don't want to be rude. Moira passes through the living room as I stand there with my hands buried in the pockets of my coat. She takes one look at me and then goes straight to what I assume is her bedroom and slams the door. Her mom looks at me with an unspoken question on her face. I just shrug.

With all the cold, wet weather we had all winter and well into the spring, everyone's behind on tree maintenance. Moira's parents are no exception. Just by glancing at the big elm in their front yard, I can tell it needs about half a dozen branches cut off. A few of them are hanging over the roof, which could cause some expensive damage if those brittle limbs give way. Plus, judging by the amount of wilted, yellowish leaves I can already see this early in the season, I suspect the tree is diseased. I tell them as much.

"Do you think it's serious?" Mrs. Watkins asks when I point the leaves out to her.

"I've seen it quite a bit," I tell her. "My dad knew how to save trees infected with Dutch elm disease. But you might want to talk to an expert. I'm pretty sure the whole tree might have to come down if it's not trimmed back now. Even that might not save it, but we could at least give it a shot."

She looks like she might be about to cry. Moira's dad comes up and puts his arm around her. "I guess there's such a thing as being too much of a tree hugger," he says. "But go ahead, Boone. We trust you. Do what you have to do. This elm's like a part of our family. We want to save it if possible."

I just nod. How did these two have a daughter like Moira? They're so . . . well, gentle and . . . nice. Moira's dad hands me a smallish chainsaw he got from the garage, and I climb up into the highest crook of the elm I can get to. Before long, I'm looking down on the roof, focused on the work, which is a good thing. The last thing I need to do is cut my own arm off because I'm distracted by the bitchy attitude of some girl who clearly has issues that are beyond the scope of my ability to—

The chain hits a knot in the wood and snarls, bounces back toward my face. I manage to push back right before it slices through my nose, but that was close. *Focus, idiot,* I tell myself. I hope Moira didn't see that; not that she cares enough to be watching me or anything.

The rest of the work goes pretty smoothly. I manage to limb the worst of the high branches without dropping them on the roof or on my head. When I'm done, the tree looks a lot better. It might even survive. I don't know why this makes me feel so proud, but it does. I'm pretty sure Moira's parents will think it looks better, too. They went somewhere in the car when I was about halfway done. Before they left, Moira's dad waved up at me. "We put your cash in an envelope on the seat of your truck," he called out.

Now I lower myself carefully out of the elm and half stumble to the back of the house, where I sit on the concrete step with a thud. My saw arm has pretty much gone numb, and I'm about as dog-tired as I've ever been.

"My mom said I had to bring you this." It's Moira's voice, surly as ever, coming from the doorway behind me.

Twisting my body, I look up to see what she's talking about. Then I laugh my not-exactly-friendly laugh. I hope it makes her as uncomfortable as her comment made me. Like she was *forced* to do something nice for the hired help, and it pretty much wrecked her day. "Don't do me any favors," I mutter, reaching up to take the glass of lemonade from her hand. Either she forgot the sugar or she left it out on purpose; when I chug it down, I realize (too late) that it's just really strong lemon water she's given me. I gag a little but keep drinking. For one thing, I'm so parched I almost don't care. For another, I refuse to let her see that she got to me even a little bit.

Her need to always be on the offense drives me crazy. It's like she goes around constantly itching for a fight. I don't understand it. Opposition finds me so easily, and life always gets worse when it does. Why would anyone go looking for it on purpose? Not that I care why Moira does any of the things she does. I'm over it. In fact, I'm done thinking about her at all. This time, I mean it. As usual, though, my mouth is lagging behind my brain. "What the hell happened to you, anyway?" I blurt out.

Moira was already headed back into the house, but she freezes at my words. *Moron,* I scold myself.

She turns around to face me, her eyes blazing with hatred. "Meaning?"

"Meaning . . . I don't know." I'm looking away now, but for some inexplicable reason, I still don't stop talking. I've reached the tipping point where I can no longer keep my rush of thoughts about her from spilling out. "All the . . ." With one grungy hand I motion to my own face, then gesture toward my body with both hands. "All the black . . . everything. Black hair, black makeup, black clothes. You look like walking *death*. I mean, you could mix it up a little, you know?"

A long, bleak moment of silence hangs suspended in the air between us. God, I'm an idiot. Why does this fact always occur to me too late?

"Mix it up," Moira repeats, her voice suddenly too calm, too quiet. "Right, because it's my job to make sure I always look pleasing for a guy. Is that it?"

"Give me a break."

"No," she tells me. "You give *me* a break. Do you even *know* what the statistical probability of a woman overcoming her culturally instilled desire to please men long enough to succeed in the world on her own terms is?"

At which point I just stare at her, dumbfounded. Did she have to practice that line in front of a mirror? Holy hell, I've never been this tired. "No," I say, my own voice calm and quiet now. I feel twenty years older than I am. "I don't know that. How would I know that? How would *anyone* know that? I don't . . . I don't even know what you're talking about right now." I stand up and hand her the glass. "Tell your mom thanks for the lemonade," I say. "Tell your dad the chainsaw is by the back door. Tell both of them good-bye for me. If it's not too much trouble, that is."

44

AGNES

DAY 57: APRIL 29

MOM AND I ARE IN THE POOL AT THE Y FRIDAY AFTER SCHOOL. I tread water in the shallow end and watch as she finishes up her freestyle laps. Her arms sailing through the air and cutting through the water's surface are the picture of strength. Everything about her is long and elegant, from her neck to her arms to her legs.

Just this morning, I logged into the progeria community website for the first time in a while. The memorial page was updated with two new death announcements, one for a thirteen-year-old girl named Marisol in Mexico City and the other for a fourteen-year-old boy in Cleveland. I knew the boy, Daryn. We met on the website's chat forum two years ago. I told him we should try to hang out at a progeria gathering someday, and he said that would be great. When I saw his memorial this morning, I didn't really know what to think. I still don't. I never told Mom about it, either.

I look around at the other swimmers and continue to tread. Mom's almost done with her laps. Thank goodness for the flippers on my feet. Without them, I would have already tired out by now. Some little kids swimming nearby glance in my direction, look at each other with wide eyes, and then paddle away toward the other side of the pool.

45

MOIRA
DAY 56: APRIL 30

WHAT WAS I THINKING, LETTING HIM WALTZ BACK INTO OUR lives like nothing ever happened, like the three of us had no bad history? Agnes and I were perfectly happy (for the most part, anyway), and now she's all caught up in thoughts of Boone hanging out with us again, of Boone being our new best buddy. But what's to stop him from waltzing right back out of our lives, just like he did in sixth grade? I wouldn't care, of course, but it would break Agnes's heart. No. Better to push him away now. In the long run, that's what will be best. For Agnes.

I thought I'd forgiven him for what happened all those years ago. I thought I'd forgotten that feeling of standing there with a knot in my stomach, pressured to do something

I didn't want to do. Something physical, athletic. Dodgeball, horseback riding. Doesn't matter what it is. Those things are all about the body. They're about reflexes and control, fitness and grace. I was always the big, ungainly girl picked last for any kind of sports team. It's such a cliché, and I despise clichés. But this particular one happens to be my life—or at least it was. PE is finally an elective now that I'm a sophomore, but back then, back in grade school, it wasn't an option. Everyone had to participate, even Agnes. And it was like *Lord of the Flies* on that blacktop. The ringleaders and the victims. The killers and the killed.

Take that day when any possibility of friendship with Boone officially imploded. Dodgeball team captains were picked, and the rest of us were sent out to the blacktop to be chosen . . . or, in my case, aggressively *not* chosen, until one team was forced to take me just to keep the numbers even. Even Agnes got picked before me, but at least we were teammates. Boone was on our team, too, but he was acting like we weren't there. Worse, he was laughing about something with Jared Vandercamp, who'd already cornered me in the hallway that year to spit insults in my face. He and Boone were apparently best buddies now that they'd been teammates for all of five minutes.

Jared said something to Boone in a low voice as I headed toward where Agnes was standing, and I caught a glimpse of him sneering. Boone didn't look at me at all, but as I walked past him, he stuck his foot out right in my path and tripped me. I knew it was his foot. Nobody else in the class wore dollar store tennis shoes. This certainty settled into my brain as I spotted the foot (too late) in my peripheral vision and then tried in vain to stop the momentum of my body as it pitched forward toward Agnes. *Out of the way!* I tried to scream at her, but there was barely time to open my mouth before I basically tackled my best friend. I threw my weight hard to the right in an attempt to land on the concrete instead, but it was no use. At least half of her tiny, delicate body was trapped beneath me when I landed. I rolled to the side, and she whimpered a little.

For a long moment, nobody said anything. I expected Agnes to start screaming or at least crying, but she didn't. Instead, in a voice so quiet I almost didn't hear it, she said, "I think something's broken, Em."

I struggled to my feet and told her not to move, that I'd go get Mrs. Johnson, the PE teacher. "Somebody stay with her!" I yelled. I registered the fact that nobody was doing anything of the sort, that our classmates were instead just standing there with their hands over their mouths, staring down at her crumpled form on the blacktop rather than comforting her like any human being with a beating heart would do. And then I heard it: the sound of Jared Vandercamp's laughter followed by the other boys on our team cackling like hyenas, like they'd just witnessed the most hilarious thing ever. A few of the guys on the other team started laughing, too. The only one not laughing was Boone. Not that it mattered. I knew what he'd done to try to show everyone how cool he was, to show how much he belonged. He was no better than the rest of them. It made me sick to think about how Agnes and I let him be our friend. How we'd trusted him enough to let him into our little outcast club.

It turned out something was broken: Agnes's arm. She had to have it reset, which basically meant the ER doctor had to rebreak it, since the first break wasn't clean. "It hurt more than anything," she told me when I saw her at school the next day. She had to wear a cast and a sling for what seemed like an eternity, and her doctor wasn't sure if the bone would ever be quite the same, since it was so delicate to begin with. I could tell how badly it hurt at any given time by looking at her face, even though she tried to hide it.

Boone was suspended from school for only three days. The principal was willing to believe that the whole thing "might have been an accident," which was the most infuriating thing I'd ever heard. I never talked to him again after that, not until our altercation in the cafeteria four years later.

Some people might think it's senseless to hold on to my anger all these years, especially since Agnes's arm eventually ended up healing better than anybody thought it would. And I really did think I was over it. Mostly, anyway. But whether I want it to or not, what Boone did that day on the blacktop still reaches a place buried so far down beneath the layers of who I am that it's almost like I'm not holding on to the memory at all. It's like the memory is holding on to *me*, and I have no idea how to make it let go. Even if he had apologized afterward, which he didn't, I'm still not sure I would have been able to forgive him.

I used to go with my mom to sit *zazen* at a Buddhist retreat on the outskirts of town. We'd meditate with a bunch of other people inside a big white tent and then silently feast on vegan food afterward. It was kind of boring, but kind of neat, too. Maybe we should go do that again. Maybe it would help the stuff from my past loosen its grip. A form of meditation is what I try to do most of the time during school hours, anyway. I sit there, crammed into a too-small desk, trying to convince myself that the suffering is only temporary. That it's a sentence I'm serving, a way of getting through. I do it for Agnes, because Agnes just wants to be a "normal" teen doing normal teen stuff like going to high school. The problem is, normal teens at our school don't want anything to do with Agnes. Sure, they're nice enough to her when they have to be, but it's not because they're genuinely interested in being friends. Who has time for that kind of commitment to a girl they obviously view as a freak? Not that any of them would admit this. We've all had enough training in what you can or can't say out loud to know better.

Sometimes, like now, it occurs to me that maybe my

parents are right. Maybe I *should* get away for a while. Everything's pressing in too much lately, suffocating and confusing me. And it's not like I don't have options. There's always . . .

Berkeley.

But no. I'm not ready for that kind of adventure.

Am I?

A strange noise from the spare room—Grant's old room—interrupts the daydream. I haul myself up from the bed and go in there to investigate.

Bingo is lying on his side in a striped patch of sunlight shining in through the blinds. It's the dog's favorite napping spot in the house, and he gets agitated any time the door to Grant's room is closed. This time, though, his entire body is twitching. No, not twitching. More like convulsing.

"Mom?" I call out. I turn my head toward the doorway so my voice will carry into the kitchen.

"Coming," she calls back.

As I stand there watching, Bingo's legs stick straight out in front of him, and his entire body goes rigid. Sometimes, when he's in a deep sleep, his legs will twitch and he'll make little squeaky barking sounds, like he's chasing rabbits in his sleep, but this isn't a dream. Breathless, I step closer and see that his eyes have rolled back in his head.

"Mom!" I scream this time. "Something's wrong with Bingo!"

46

BOONE

DAY 55: MAY 1

MAY DAY, I THINK AS I BEND DOWN TO PICK A WILD IRIS GROWING by the side of a boulder. *SOS.*

Mom used to love getting flowers. Maybe the bunch I'm picking in the forest now will help her remember that.

It wasn't exactly true, the thing I said about not knowing what Moira was talking about. I actually did understand some of it. At least I think I did. Not the part about the culturally instilled . . . installed? . . . desire women had to please men, maybe, but the part about succeeding on your own terms. Rising above . . . whatever it was she said . . . and fighting for the kind of life you wanted to have. That part I'm pretty sure I got.

Not that I'm anywhere close to fighting for my ideal life.

I'm too busy surviving the tar pit I'm stuck in, the one that keeps trying to pull me down and suffocate me like I'm some sort of prehistoric ground sloth. I'm trying to help Mom survive, too, not that I'm doing a very good job of it. She's as messed up now as she was the day we ran through this forest together, back to where my father lay dying, both of us terrified and desperate. She's just as incapable—or maybe unwilling—to fight.

Moira is screwed up, too, but at least she's willing to confront whatever's wrong in her life. At least she's not some cookie-cutter chick trying to be just like all the other cookie-cutter chicks out there. Maybe that's what she meant about the culture and about women pleasing men. But if she thinks women are the only ones dealing with this crap, she's pretty freaking clueless.

What about the stuff guys are supposed to think and say and do to prove we're manly men, to prove we're in control and strong as iron and fearless? What about the way guys call each other *faggot* in the hallway if one of them accidentally gets too close to another, or the way I have no choice but to fight whenever some punk decides he wants a piece of me. Refusing to fight makes me look like a pantywaist, and then every other guy on the planet wants to hurt me, too. That's just how it is.

Moira acts like she's the only one who has to deal with this kind of bullshit. Okay, so maybe she gets more nasty comments than most people, but isn't she asking for it just a little? Everything about how she looks and acts is so in-your-face. How are people supposed to respond?

Like non-assholes, for starters, I think, answering my own question in my head. *Like human beings who can see when someone has a lot of stuff going on, when someone's in pain.* (Jesus, my old man would punch me right in the face if he was here and knew what I'm thinking.) And what *is* Moira's pain, anyhow? What the hell is she so angry about?

I bend down to pick another iris. I'm not so self-absorbed as to think she went to the Dark Side because of me. Not directly because of me, anyway. But I also know some of this stuff with Moira started years ago. I know this because I was there for it. I was there in sixth grade when she'd come into the Resource room to study with Agnes, and I was there when the three of us started hanging out together at lunchtime and recess. I can't say I felt totally comfortable with that arrangement, but nobody else was offering. A few of the guys in our class were pretty cool to me every now and then, but most weren't. Most wouldn't be caught dead hanging out with the class dunce. Being with the girls was better than being alone all the time.

None of this had ever been a problem until that year. In fifth grade, I'd go to the Resource room at a certain point during the day, and none of the other kids thought a thing about it. But things went south for me in sixth. Maybe it was the specter of junior high on the horizon. Maybe it was testosterone. Who the hell could say? All I know is I basically became an untouchable overnight.

All of that changed one day toward the end of the year. Our class was going to play dodgeball for PE, and I got picked for a team early. I'd never been picked early for anything, unless you counted detention.

"We'll take Boone," Amanda Bevins said. She was one of the captains, and she'd already picked a couple of the most athletic boys in the class, including Jared Vandercamp. He was the one I got suspended for decking after he cornered Moira in the hallway. Stunned by the fact that I'd been picked near the start of the draft, I walked toward the spot where Amanda's guys were standing. To my surprise, Jared raised his hand for a high five. A part of my brain started to work this equation, to weigh the rightness of what was happening, but I shut it down and high-fived Jared back. Who was I to argue if he was calling a truce?

"Shoot, I was going to take Boone." This from Vince Goddard, the captain of the other team.

"Well, too bad, so sad," Amanda shot back.

Were they . . . *arguing* over me? I wasn't sure, but Vince seemed genuinely miffed that I wasn't walking toward his group, and Amanda looked superior, like she'd gotten what she wanted. I could hardly believe it. I looked down at the ground to make sure everyone realized how humbled I felt, that I wasn't encouraging the argument. It's not like I was that great or anything, but could I help it if I was in demand? My head felt light from this new feeling of pride and acceptance. It felt like it might detach from my body and float away.

The remaining player pool dwindled as the captains picked the rest of their teams. Eventually, it was just Moira standing there. She was forced to join our team to keep things even, and you could tell it was killing her. To say she wasn't athletic was an understatement. She scowled as she headed toward us, and I felt embarrassed for her. I felt embarrassed for me, too, for hanging out with her. I knew that was two-faced of me, but it was the truth.

Jared Vandercamp was still standing next to me. "Check out Gigantor," he said under his breath.

I didn't respond.

"I dare you to trip her."

Moira was getting closer. "Shut up. I'm not going to trip her." I made sure to smile when I said it, to show I was keeping his joke between us.

"It's because you love her," Jared taunted in a louder voice now. Moira was about to pass right in front of us. "It's because you *lust* after her. You want to make babies with—"

My foot shot out like it was acting independently of the rest of my body. If I had known Agnes was standing right there off to the side and that she'd be hurt when Moira fell, there's no way I would have let my foot do that. Even now, all these years later, I really like to think I would have stopped it. Instead, it seemed like time froze. I didn't even think Moira would really hit the ground. I figured she'd see my foot and give me the stink eye, maybe tell me I was a jerk as she walked on by. But she did hit the ground. Hard. And Agnes was right there to break her fall. I'd done the unthinkable without even giving it a second thought. I was a monster.

The school called my mom immediately, but because she was down with the flu, my dad had to interrupt his workday to talk to the principal and pick me up early. Once we got home, he told me to go pick my switch from the oak tree outside. I did, and he proceeded to whip my butt with it. He did it behind the horse shelter so Mom wouldn't see and throw a fit. She was always coming to my defense whenever he decided I needed to be punished. I knew I deserved it this time, though. Plus, I was wearing my jeans when he switched me, so it's not like it was that bad.

When my suspension ended and I saw Agnes at school with her twig-like forearm all bandaged, I felt like I was going to throw up. The worst part was that Agnes and Moira wouldn't even look at me. I tried apologizing to Agnes in the Resource room when Ms. Marilyn was helping another student, but Moira appeared behind Agnes's chair and told me where I could stick my apology.

That was the end for the three of us. Maybe it wouldn't have been the end if things had gone differently. Maybe I could have figured out a way to work myself back into their good graces. But the gulf between me and the girls only widened once seventh grade started. They had their lives, and I had mine. Well, at least that second part was true right up until partway through eighth grade, when life as I knew it came to an end as well.

I've picked two big handfuls of irises, and it's time to head back to the house. When I get there, I fill a mason jar with water and try to arrange the flowers as best I can. I clear some bills and dishes and other clutter off the table before setting the jar in the middle, like a centerpiece. Who knows if she'll even notice?

47

AGNES

DAY 54: MAY 2

AT FIRST, I THINK IT'S A WRONG NUMBER.

The voice on the other end of the phone line Monday evening is garbled and hysterical. I check the caller ID. "Who is this?" I demand. "I can't understand what you're saying."

". . . didn't want to call and upset you. I'm calling from the vet's. Bingo had a stroke, and the vet says there's brain damage. We have to put him to sleep, Agnes. He's dying!"

Moira.

"Oh, Em. I'm so sorry. Poor Bingo." An image of the old chocolate Lab appears in my mind: Bingo as a puppy in that picture of sweet, happy toddler Moira. I knew they'd had to take him to the vet the other day, but I had no idea it was this bad.

"I can't handle this," Moira cries. "I love him so much."

"I know," I tell her. "I wish there was something I could do."

We stay on the line for a while without saying anything. After a couple of minutes, Moira's breathing slows down, and her voice gets mostly back to normal. "My parents are talking to the vet now. I should probably get off the line and go back in there."

"Call me later," I tell her. "And, Em?"

Sniff. "Yeah?"

"Bingo is lucky you're his human. I love you."

"I love you, too, Agnes."

BOONE

DAY 53: MAY 3

AGNES IS ALONE IN THE HALLWAY. SHE'S LEANING AGAINST A WALL near the girls' bathroom, looking down at her intertwined fingers.

"Hey," I say. There's something I want to tell her. Moira, too, someday, but I should probably start with Agnes. I'd better do it now before I lose my nerve. "So, remember back in sixth grade when you got hurt . . . when I caused you to get hurt?"

Agnes looks up at me, surprised. If she had eyebrows, they'd be raised. "Of course I do," she says.

"Well, I just . . . I wanted to say I'm sorry. I never did say it back then, so I want to say it now."

"Wow," she says. "Okay."

"I don't even know what I was thinking. I mean, I wasn't thinking. I was just a total assho—a total jerk."

Agnes gives me a little smile. "Boone, it's okay. It was a long time ago." She still doesn't move from where she's standing, though.

"What's going on?"

She glances at the bathroom door. "Moira's in there. She can't stop crying, but she doesn't want anybody with her."

"Crying?" As usual, the moment the word leaves my mouth, I half wish I hadn't asked. She's probably having girl issues.

"They had to put Bingo to sleep yesterday. You know, her old dog?"

"Oh, no." I remember meeting Bingo the first time I went over to Moira's house and helped her dad repair the VW.

"The vet wanted too much money to euthanize him, so they ended up taking him to the Humane Society. It costs a lot less, but they usually just cremate the animals and throw away the ashes. Moira's had that dog forever. She's freaking out."

"Can't they just bury him in their yard?"

"Not according to the city," Moira says from behind me. I jump a little. I didn't see her come out of the bathroom. "They're already on my dad's case about an illegal garden shed he built in our yard."

"Hey, Em," Agnes says.

"I'm sorry about your dog," I tell her.

Moira nods, but she doesn't look at me. Most of her makeup has been rubbed away, and the skin around her eyes is pink and puffy. "At least the Humane Society told my parents we could have Bingo's body, but now there's nowhere to bury him."

"It sucks," Agnes says.

Moira nods again. "So I was in there thinking. And I decided I'm going to put him out in the forest."

Whoa, I think. *Bad idea.* "Were you just going to lay him out there?" I ask her. I remember the two drowned birds I threw over the fence earlier this year. Dead birds are one thing to leave out to become part of the circle of life. A dog's quite another. Especially a big dog like Bingo. I don't want to have to explain why.

"My dad will have to dig a hole," Moira says miserably.

"The ground's still frozen solid a few inches below the surface. You know that, right?"

Moira sniffles, and Agnes puts a hand on her shoulder again. "I guess I didn't. What else am I supposed to do? I can't just have them . . . cremate him and get rid of the ashes so I don't know where he ends up."

Everyone's quiet.

"My place," I tell her.

The girls look at me.

"Bury him at my place. It's outside city limits."

"But the ground—"

"I have a backhoe." It's true. We do have a backhoe. I'm just not sure if it works. It was running rough when I started it up last fall. Now that it's spent the past six months behind the barn gathering hay dust and cobwebs, I have no idea what kind of shape the thing is in. I've been thinking lately that I should try to fire it up again when I get a little spare time, figure out what needs to be fixed. I'll probably have to sell it soon for grocery money if things keep going the way they have been. I don't even want to think about how much it's going to cost to get the engine in good shape, but I'm pretty sure I could get it to run for at least an hour or so. I'm pretty sure I could use it to bury a dog. "I can do it after school, if you want."

"I need to be there," Moira says.

"Me too," Agnes adds.

* * *

That afternoon, I drive the two of them in my truck to go get Bingo's body. Moira wanted to use the El Camino as a hearse, but Agnes worried about her being too upset to drive safely.

"I can bring you back here when we're done," I said as we stood in the school parking lot trying to figure out a plan. I didn't look at Moira when I said it, but not because I was mad. It was because she suddenly seemed delicate in a way

I've never seen her; I didn't want to be the one to push her over the edge with the wrong facial expression or the wrong tone of voice.

We stop at Moira's house first so she can get Bingo's favorite blanket to bury him in. Her parents come out and tell me and Agnes that they already bid Bingo farewell during his final moments at the Humane Society. "You kids take your time saying good-bye to him," her dad tells us.

"Keep an eye on Moira, will you?" her mom asks after glancing back to make sure Moira's still in the house. "This hit her really hard."

Agnes and I both say we will.

When we get to the Humane Society, I park the truck and go inside. The crisp spring air is filled with the sound of barking dogs. I wish I'd left the motor running to help drown out the noise for Moira. A girl in scrubs is sitting behind the receptionist counter, and she looks up at me when I come through the door.

"I'm here for Bingo Watkins," I tell her.

The girl can't be much older than I am. She makes a sad face and tells me to drive around to the back of the building. A few minutes later, I back the truck toward a big metal door that rolls up to reveal a garage-like storage area. I get out of the cab when Moira does. We stand by our respective doors as a couple of techs come out with what I can only assume is Bingo inside one of those extra sturdy garbage bags. Moira gasps at the sight. The techs carry the dog out on a giant platter—a platter!—with a handle on each end. They set the whole thing onto the pickup bed and then slide the platter out from underneath. "There you go," one of the techs says. He looks from Moira to me and back to Moira. "Sorry for your loss."

*　　*　　*

Agnes sits between us on the drive out to my place. She rides backward without a seat belt so she can keep an eye on Bingo and make sure he doesn't bounce around too much. Moira hardly seems to notice, though. She's staring out the passenger side window with her chin in one hand and a blank look on her face. Her other hand is clutching Bingo's blanket.

Thank God the backhoe starts up. I was prepared to get out the pickax and the shovel to dig the hole myself if necessary, but it would have been a tough job. Once I've transferred Bingo from the truck bed to the big steel backhoe bucket, I climb up into the operator's seat and navigate the machine carefully into the big field. There isn't room for all three of us in the cab, so Moira follows on foot with Agnes on her back. The ground is too uneven for Agnes to walk safely out to the grave site on her own. From her piggyback vantage point, she keeps an eye out for prairie dog holes so the two of them don't end up in a heap on the ground.

Once we've gone several hundred yards, I stop and idle the engine. "This is the spot I was thinking about," I call down to them. I've always thought it was peaceful, with a line of trees to the east and a ridge overlooking a small slot canyon to the west.

Moira surveys the area and nods. "It's perfect," she says.

I climb down from the cab and lift Bingo, still covered by the plastic bag, from the bucket. The girls follow me as I carry him to a spot about a dozen yards off, set him down on the ground, and pull the bag away. At first, Moira doesn't want to look. She puts a hand over her eyes but then lowers it. The dog is curled tight and frozen there, like he fell into a peaceful sleep during a snowstorm and never woke up. "Here," she says, handing me the blanket. I drape it over him, tucking it in around the edges.

Moira and Agnes find a tree to sit under while I stab the edge of the backhoe bucket into the earth over and over again, scooping up dirt, rocks, and roots that I set off to one side of the hole. It doesn't take too long, but I want the grave deep enough so there's no chance of coyotes digging it up. Of course, I don't mention this. When I'm done, the girls stand up and come over.

"Agnes needs to use the bathroom," Moira says as I step down from the cab.

Agnes, standing behind her, rolls her eyes. "I can just go behind a tree."

"No, you can't," Moira tells her. She looks at me and says, more softly this time, "She can't." It's a plea.

I squint toward the house. I hadn't taken this possibility

into consideration. It nearly kills me to think of the girls going in there. I tried to clean up as much as possible this morning like I do most mornings, but there's a limit to how clean the house ever seems to get. It's not like desperation can just be swept out the door. Plus, having near strangers in the house would probably give Mom a heart attack.

"Agnes!" Moira calls out.

I whip my head around in time to see Agnes tromping off toward the nearest cluster of pine trees with Moira in hot pursuit. "Talk to the hand," Agnes says, holding a flat palm out like a traffic cop. "I'm peein' in the trees, and don't you *dare* try to follow me!" She says the last part with a southern sort of twang in her voice.

Moira stops in her tracks. She turns and looks at me.

"She'll be okay," I tell her. On a whim, I jerk my head toward where I'm standing, like *Come here.*

Amazingly, she does.

"So, I know this isn't the time or the place," I say when she's right there next to me, both of us contemplating the new hole in the ground. "But I don't think I ever said sorry about what a scumbag I was to you in sixth grade."

"You weren't . . ." she starts to say, but then seems to think better of trying to be too polite just because it's a solemn occasion.

"Yeah. I was."

"Okay, maybe you were a little bit."

"I was a big one," I tell her. "I hurt Agnes. And I hurt you. And I am so sorry. It shouldn't have taken me this long to say it."

Moira doesn't say anything for several seconds, just looks into my eyes like she's trying to remind herself of something. "Apology accepted."

There's movement near the trees—Agnes returning. "It's beautiful here," she calls out. Moira breathes a sigh of relief. As usual, Agnes has the little camera hanging around her neck. She reaches for it and takes a few pictures of me and Moira as she walks toward us. "I wish I could live in the country," she says, sighing. "Hey, seriously? You guys should scatter some of my ashes here when I—"

"Agnes!" Moira's face is whiter than usual all of a sudden, and not just because of her makeup. Even her lips look pale.

Jesus, I think.

"I'm so sorry, Em." Agnes is looking down at the ground. "I don't know what I was thinking."

But Moira's shaken. I can see it. "I just . . . there's only so much I can take," she says. "You know?" Fresh tears well up in her eyes.

Nobody says anything for a few minutes after that. Moira walks off by herself a ways to regain her composure. I stand next to the backhoe, silent. Agnes looks down at the grave.

Finally, Moira returns. Her expression is back to normal, and her voice is steady. "I think it's time."

Nodding, I walk back over to the blanketed dog, pick him up, and carry him to the edge of the hole. Then I lower myself down there so I can arrange Bingo inside his final resting place. After climbing back out and brushing as much dirt as I can from my pants, I look at Moira. "Should we say a few words?"

"Yeah." She takes a deep breath. "Bingo is . . ." She lets the breath out. "Was. He was a good dog." Her voice sounds a little unsteady.

"He knocked stuff over with his tail," Agnes adds quietly, which makes Moira laugh before she starts to cry again. She holds the back of her hand up to her nose as if to stop the tears, but they come anyway. She swipes a finger under her eyes where the mascara and eyeliner are starting to travel, blurring the lines of her face just enough to soften it ever so slightly.

I start to look away out of respect, but then Agnes catches my eye and motions for me to join them. So I do. At first I just stand there on the periphery of the two girls, with Agnes on one side of Moira and me on the other. When a shoulder-heaving sob escapes Moira, though, Agnes hugs her best friend across the backs of her legs. It seems like the least I can do is make contact, too, so I put my arm around Moira's shoulders. For a long while, the three of us just stand there like that on the edge of the freshly dug grave.

AGNES

DAY 52: MAY 4

I KEEP A CLOSE EYE ON MOIRA ALL THE NEXT DAY. THERE'S A feeling in the air like something's about to crack, like ice on a lake when winter finally ends. I can't explain it any better than that.

50

BOONE
DAY 51: MAY 5

TWO WEEKS AFTER MY FIRST RUN-IN WITH OUR NEW NEIGHBOR, the Power Stroke is back. Its diesel engine idles in the driveway like a bad omen.

One glance at Diablo's empty paddock as I'm on my way out the front door to talk to Jackson Tate and I don't even have to ask what the problem is. Tate's timing is unbelievable; not only do I have a test in English first period, but now I'm probably going to be late again, thanks to him.

"Had five hundred yards of gravel all leveled," he yells through the open driver's side window as I approach. "Damn horse cratered the entire driveway."

"Sorry," I tell him. "Old man Wallace used to let him graze there."

"I don't give a rat's ass what he used to do." Tate's face is all tensed up and red, like how I imagine a gigantic hemorrhoid would look sitting on top of his shoulders. "I'll put a bullet in that animal's head if he sets foot on my property again."

Technically, he'd be setting hoof *on your property,* I think, but I know better than to say it out loud. "Don't you think that's—" I start to say instead, but Tate (who I now can't help but think of as Rhoid Face) cuts me off.

"It's my right as the property owner. You understand me, boy?"

As long as I live, I think, *I'll never understand bastards like you.* I take a step forward, and Rhoid Face leans back into the cab of the Power Stroke, away from the open window, his eyes widening ever so slightly.

Before I realize what's going on, an old rage rises up my spine so quickly that it threatens to blot out everything else in my brain. The rage rushes to my fists, too, like hot lava that might incinerate me alive if I don't release it by smashing this son of a bitch's jaw to smithereens. Fighting my instincts, I interlace my fingers to keep my hands under control and to keep myself from doing something I'll later regret. I wouldn't be much use to Mom in jail. "I just need to go grab a halter," I mumble as I turn and walk toward the shed.

Rhoid Face peels out of the driveway, sending dirt flying without so much as offering to let me ride in the bed.

Asshole. Serves him right if Diablo causes more damage in the time it takes for me to walk over there.

The damn horse has always been a Houdini. He used to let himself out in the middle of the night to go visit some other horses a mile down the road. It infuriated my dad, who was always the one to throw the halter into the bed of the truck and spin the tires in rage as he tore out of the driveway. He'd come back slower, with one arm out the window leading Diablo, the lead rope clenched tight in his fist. The whites of the horse's eyes usually indicated he'd gotten more than just a mild talking-to on the way home, and he obviously equated the truck with being punished: it got to the point where he wouldn't let my dad put the halter on him at all unless my dad arrived on foot. Now that Diablo hardly gets any exercise, his behavior's becoming worse. I can't risk the boneheaded animal getting shot, can't even think about what that would do to Mom. Somehow, between school and my job and holding things down at home, I'm going to have to find time to start working him again.

The thought of Rhoid Face having time to change his mind and load his gun in the minutes before I get there clears my head. I grab a halter from its nail on the shed wall and start down the driveway. I cover as much ground as I can while maintaining what I hope looks like a relaxed stride, just in case Mom is watching from her bedroom window. Only when I'm past the house do I break into a run.

51

MOIRA

DAY 50: MAY 6

ON FRIDAY NIGHT, BOONE, AGNES, AND I HAVE PLANS TO HANG
out. Agnes wants to go downtown, which her mom says is okay
as long as I keep an eye out for her and make sure she keeps
her coat on. Deb looks worried, though. She pulls me aside
near the front door while Boone and Agnes go ahead.

"The doctor told her not to get too chilled," Deb whispers.
"So she needs to watch her temperature. Her body fat percent-
age is lower than it's ever been. I hate to have to put restrictions
on the situation, but . . ."

"We'll take care of her," I say.

"Make sure she eats, too."

"I will."

The three of us head downtown, where the monthly Art

Walk is already under way. Agnes seems so happy as we wander through all the different stores and galleries, happier than I've seen her in a long time.

"I wish you guys could hold my hands and swing me back and forth between you," she says.

Boone looks down at her before I can say anything. "It would hurt your wrists, silly. I've already caused a broken arm. I sure don't need any more injuries on my conscience."

I'm a little taken aback by how he just went there and brought up the old injury, but I also feel a flush of tenderness toward Boone at that moment. I know from long experience that it's not easy to set boundaries with Agnes. Once you get to know her, you pretty much want to give her anything her heart desires.

The evening air is warmer than it's been all year. If there's a chill in the breeze, it's easily overlooked. On one edge of the town square, a shirtless contortionist is twisting himself into a pretzel on top of a Navajo blanket. He's not much older than we are, but there are primal symbols tattooed all over his torso. At first, I think the way he's twisting his body must be some kind of optical illusion, but then I realize there's actually something wrong. He's beyond double-jointed. It almost looks like he has no joints in his body at all. A cardboard sign on the ground in front of him says something about needing donations for his upcoming surgery. Agnes steps forward to put a few dollars in a bowl next to the sign, and he nods at her like she's one of his tribe. She nods back.

Nearby, a traveling bluegrass musician couple start a song in the middle of the square. They look like they're in their early twenties. The woman plays a stand-up bass, and she stares at Boone with a dreamy half smile. He smiles back at her, and another kind of flush passes through me at the sight of it. I have a sudden impulse to place myself between the two of them. That would be a ludicrous thing to do, of course. Boone doesn't belong to me. He's allowed to smile at whoever he wants. The bass player's partner is a bearded guy who's playing the banjo and stomping on an antique foot drum. Both of them are dressed in clothes from another time—lace skirt and corset for her, a velvet-collared coat and fedora for him. They look like they raided their great-grandparents' closets before heading out for the night. It's such a cool look that it makes me feel self-conscious about my own getup—an old Bauhaus T-shirt that's so faded and thin it looks like it might disintegrate any second, a long black skirt, and the usual drama makeup.

Next, the three of us head over to a glassblower's studio, where a massive kiln takes up most of one wall. Inside the kiln, a fire blazes so ferociously that I can't look directly at it without my eyes starting to water.

"This is the greatest thing ever," Agnes says. The three of us stand there watching the glassblower turn a transparent, melty glob inside the fire with a pair of long metal tongs. "We should come down here every night during finals break. I've heard there's always stuff going on."

"Oh," I say. "Actually, I won't be here during the break."

Agnes and Boone both frown at me, but it's Boone who speaks up first. "Where are you going?"

I feel caught in the act. I wasn't planning on talking about this tonight. I haven't yet figured out how to explain the thing that occurred to me the day after Bingo died. Basically, I realized life is short, and that this might be my shot. This might be the time in life when I'm supposed to rise above my wussy, uncompromising tendencies and have an adventure. I realized that I should just be brave already and take the opportunity to check out Berkeley.

I started to see how it could work, despite the potential horrors of air travel. I saw myself walking around campus, maybe even passing for a college student. I saw myself laughing with my new college friends, hanging out in coffee shops and bookstores, talking about important stuff, maybe even becoming somebody interesting. Just yesterday morning I asked Mom and Dad to book my plane ticket. Needless to say, they were thrilled.

"My brother has a place in Berkeley," I tell Boone now. "I'm going to stay with them for the week, check out UC Berkeley, that kind of stuff." I'm aware of Agnes's eyes on me, aware that I'm talking too fast all of a sudden. "I didn't want to at first, but my parents sort of convinced me. It should be okay, I guess. It'll go by quick."

"I think it sounds awesome," Agnes says.

Boone just frowns again. Agnes must think he looks cute doing it, because she reaches for the camera hanging around her neck and snaps his picture in the orange glow of the glass-blower's fire.

52

BOONE

DAY 49: MAY 7

SETTING OUT THE HUMMINGBIRD FEEDERS AND THE BIRDSEED IN the impulse-buy zone near the registers, I remind myself to be cool. It's not like Moira and I are dating or anything. Technically, we're not even friends. So I helped bury her dog. So we hung out with Agnes downtown. I know better than to think those things mean more than they do. Besides, Moira is clearly on the kind of upward trajectory I'll probably never be on. She's going to check out a university that she might attend in the not-too-distant future, and what am I going to do while she's gone? I'm going to investigate the new groaning sound that's started up recently whenever I downshift the truck from third to second, that's what. It sounds like somebody's torturing a narwhal under there.

My boss, TJ, walks by on his way to talk to a customer. "How's it going?" he asks as I unbox another bird feeder.

Living the nightmare, I think. "Going great," I answer, giving a thumbs-up for emphasis.

53

AGNES

DAY 48: MAY 8

"YOU DON'T HAVE TO DO THIS, YOU KNOW. I COULD PROBABLY just make something really nice myself."

"Nonsense," my stepmother says. It's Mother's Day, and we're standing outside a store called Chica Bonita where they sell dresses for first communions, confirmations, and quinceañeras. Kid-size mannequins wearing white gowns and veils crowd the display window. Mom said she didn't mind if my dad and Jamey kept me for a little bit on Mother's Day, which was nice of her. This was the only time Dad could watch Isaiah and the twins before Jamey took them to visit her parents in Oklahoma. My stepmother isn't a big believer in nonfamily babysitters. She worries about outside influences. Still, I'm surprised she'd want to go dress shopping on a Sunday, even if she did tell me she was planning to attend the evening service instead of going to church this morning.

"Tuesday night is going to be special for you and your father," she says. She holds the door open for me and smiles cautiously at the middle-aged Latina woman who welcomes us inside the store. "We can go a little fancy. I won't hear of your wearing something homemade or plain."

I'm not sure how to respond. Jamey is pretty much the *queen* of homemade plainness. She wears humility like a badge most days. No makeup, no bra, hair pulled back in the simplest of braids (which is just a complete waste, as far as I'm concerned. If I had long, thick, wavy hair like Jamey's, I'd never tire of finding ways to show it off). Jamey looks just one shade less religious than the Amish people I've seen on TV and occasionally walking around downtown in family groups. But whatever. I can deal with it for an afternoon. I don't want to burst Jamey's bubble or anything, but the truth is I wonder how much of a "special night" this father-daughter chastity ball is really going to be. I've pretty much tried to avoid thinking about it at all.

We spend about an hour in the store. By the time the dress is finally paid for, I'm exhausted and starving, so we hit a drive-thru. Afterward, Jamey pulls into a grocery store parking lot and tells me to sit tight in the booster and enjoy my food while she runs inside. A few minutes later, she comes out with a big bouquet of flowers. "For your mom," she says as she gets back in the car and sets the flowers down on the front passenger seat.

I'm not even sure what to say other than, "Wow, that's really nice of you." Which is true. Suddenly, I feel bad about all the times Moira and I have laughed about how over-the-top my stepmother can be sometimes. When we get to Mom's house, I extricate myself from the booster seat and gather up my stuff. "Thank you so much for the dress," I tell Jamey before opening the door of the minivan. "Have a good trip to Oklahoma. Happy Mother's Day."

"I thought I might say hi to your mom," she says. "If you think it would be all right."

"Oh. Okay." Actually, I'm not at all sure it's going to be all right, but what am I supposed to say?

Jamey carries the dress and some other stuff so I can carry the flowers. Once we're inside the house, I call out to let Mom know I'm home.

"Be right there, sweetie," she calls back from her room.

"Um . . . Jamey's with me."

Silence. I glance at Jamey and try to smile.

She's cringing a little. "It's okay," she whispers as she heads for the door. "Maybe another time." She's just about to step outside when Mom appears in her old sweats and weekend hair. She's not wearing any makeup, and it's clear she's been having one of those hedonistic days we both love so much—days when you never change out of your pajamas and you eat whatever you want while simultaneously watching a movie, reading a trashy novel, and painting your toenails. When I hand her the flowers, she gasps and tells me it's the prettiest bouquet she's ever seen. "Thank you so much for bringing Agnes home," she says to Jamey.

"Oh, it's no problem."

"And please excuse the way the house looks," Mom adds with a laugh.

Jamey smiles at her. "Your house looks like you have a live-in maid compared to mine." This isn't true, but it's kind of Jamey to say it anyway.

"So, did you get a dress?" Mom asks me.

I nod.

"It's really pretty on her," Jamey says. "We brought it back here so you could see it if you wanted to. And happy Mother's Day, by the way."

"Happy Mother's Day to you, too," Mom says.

It's good to see the two of them talking and smiling like they actually don't mind hanging out, but it's also awkward. When Jamey says she'd better be getting home, I thank her for everything and give her a hug.

"Huh," Mom says when she's gone. There's an absent sort of look on her face.

"You okay?" I ask her.

She snaps to attention and runs her hand across my wigless scalp. Other than my dad, she's the only person who ever touches my head, weird looking as it is. "Yeah, honey," she says. "Yeah, I am. I just hate having the wrong idea about a person for so long, that's all."

54

MOIRA

DAY 47: MAY 9

"OH MY GOD. YOU'RE GOING TO LOOK LIKE A CHILD BRIDE."

I don't even try to hide my despair as Agnes pulls the dress from its zippered garment bag Monday afternoon. The thing could not possibly be any whiter or frillier or poufier. Only someone like Jamey would force her stepdaughter to wear such a monstrosity. And, of course, Agnes's dad won't do anything to stop it, because he's totally Jamey's bitch. Ugh, *Jamey*.

I will never forget the first time I met the stepmonster. We were in eighth grade, and I had purposely applied my eyeliner that day to look like it had been drawn on by a toddler with a Sharpie. Also, I was wearing a T-shirt with the words MODERATION IS OVERRATED stretched in big block letters across my already-colossal boobs. Jamey tried to impress Agnes by acting all accepting and Christian lovey-dovey with me, but she still managed to come off as self-righteous and condescending. "The Lord loves all of us," she told me in a sad whisper, shaking my hand and then holding on to it for too long afterward. She looked like she might be about to cry.

"Yeah," I answered, removing my hand from hers. "Uh . . . thanks."

"Jamey wanted to have it dyed lavender," Agnes says now as she stares down at the dress. "But there's not enough time."

I drop my head into my hands and moan. I'd rather see Agnes dressed in the gingham prairie-girl getup Jamey made for her when she first got together with Agnes's dad. And that's saying something, because the prairie-girl outfit? It was an abomination, pure and simple.

Agnes holds the thing up to herself. The fabric actually makes a *sound*, like itty-bitty claws scratching against a cellar door. "It was the smallest one they had in this style," she says. "It's made for an eight-year-old, but it's too big on me. I swear, I tried on, like, twenty of these. I'm positive whoever makes them gets paid extra for using the itchiest taffeta they can find." She looks less than thrilled with the dress, which surprises me a little. Agnes usually adores over-the-top girly stuff like this. "But wait," Agnes says with a flat voice. "There's more." She reaches toward the bottom of the garment bag, unwraps the item she finds there, and holds it out.

"A flipping *tiara*?"

Agnes nods. "I liked the veils they had there. They covered up my head and my face, which is never a bad thing, but Jamey wouldn't go for it. She was nice about it and everything, but she said I looked too Catholic. She said it would offend people at a Protestant function."

All I can do at this point is just sit there and rub my temples. "You're hurting me now, Agnes," I tell her.

55

AGNES

DAY 46: MAY 10

DAD PICKS ME UP AFTER SCHOOL ON TUESDAY AND DRIVES ME TO Mom's house so I can pick up the dress. As soon as we get to his and Jamey's house, I head upstairs to change. With Jamey and the kids in Oklahoma, the place is eerily quiet. I can't remember the last time Dad and I spent time alone. Seventh grade, I think? Or maybe it was even earlier than that, around the time Dad and Jamey started dating ("courting," Jamey preferred to call it). I remember sitting across from him at a fifties-themed diner downtown. I was sipping a strawberry milkshake, and he seemed nervous.

"This may come as a bit of a shock," he said, "but I've met someone special. She's a good Christian woman."

I sat back against the soft booth cushion. A good Christian

woman? What did that even mean? What did such a person look like, and when had my dad become interested in finding one? He and Mom had only been separated for a few months at that point. The divorce wasn't even final yet. "Are you going to get married?" I asked him.

Dad chuckled. "Let's not go putting the cart before the horse."

But I wasn't putting the cart before the horse. Not too long after that conversation, I met Jamey for the first time and found out they were engaged. "You are a unique child of God" was the first thing my future stepmother said to me. Honestly, the look in her eyes creeped me out a little, but I tried not to let it show. Before the ink from the judge's signature dried on the divorce papers, Jamey and my dad were married.

When I get upstairs, I find a note taped to my bedroom mirror: *I know you and your father will have a blessed time at the ball. -J.* Jamey has also set out the wig I'm supposed to wear, which is golden blond with long curls that fall halfway down my back. It's not the kind I'd normally choose, but it does somehow go with the rest of the outfit. I wrangle the dress over my head and zip it up before securing the wig into place. Then I attach the tiara.

Dad is sitting downstairs at the kitchen table in his rented tux. He looks up when I enter the kitchen, and his mouth falls open a little.

"Pretty fancy, huh?" I say, feeling suddenly shy and a little depressed. I do my best to keep my voice peppy.

"I . . . uh . . . Honey, you look so pretty."

"Thanks. Jamey worked really hard on this."

There's a long silence, and then my dad says something I'm not prepared for. "You don't really want to go to the ball, do you?"

I bite my bottom lip. The last thing I want to do is hurt his or Jamey's feelings. "I mean, you guys seem to really want me to go, so . . ."

"But it's not about me and Jamey," he says. "It's about you."

I walk over to his chair and place one of my hands on top of his. "Dad," I tell him, "I want to go. Really."

"Well then," he says, smiling at me. "In that case, let's go party."

*   *   *

A man's deep voice booms out a welcome the second we set foot inside the conference room the churches have rented for the evening. It's the new preacher, the one I offended by laughing during his sermon. He and my dad shake hands, and then he turns his attention to me. "Well," he says. "Now, that's a dress, young lady. Why don't you give me a twirl?"

At first, I don't understand what he means. Then the preacher makes a little twirling motion with his index finger.

"Um," I say. "Okay." Dad frowns a little as I do the best twirl I can. My hips and knees have been aching all day, so it's more of a slow circle.

"I have some rings for the two of you," the preacher says, bending down toward me. There's a big smile on his face, but he looks a little uncertain about this part. "They're promise rings. They represent a promise you're making to, uh, stay faithful to your father here as well as to your Father in Heaven." He opens a little box. "With this ring you promise to, uh . . . remain abstinent until you are, you know . . ."

"Married?" I ask him, trying to hide my own smile.

The preacher clears his throat. "Well, yes," he says. "That's the idea."

I look past him and into the conference room. Teen and preteen girls are milling about with their fathers near a bunch of tables set up for the fancy dinner. A banner hanging above a podium at the front of the room reads CHASTITY. PURITY. GODLINESS. Without warning, I've had enough. I can't do this anymore. Dad was right. I really, *really* don't want to be here. "So, basically," I say, meeting the preacher's eyes, "you guys are really freaked out by the idea of females having sex before a certain time that you consider appropriate."

He stands up, wide-eyed. "What did you . . . ?"

"Is there a chastity ball for males?"

"Of course not. That would be—"

"Then this is just totally hypocritical and ridiculous," I say, interrupting him. "Even if there *was* one for guys, the whole thing is pretty creepy in my—"

Dad takes my hand. "Agnes," he says. I feel a lecture coming on, and the thought makes me sigh. I'm not trying to be mean. I'm not even trying to be disrespectful. I'm just so tired. Just so, so tired.

"What, Dad?" I say, my voice a little hostile now. The preacher straightens up and snaps the ring box shut, clearly getting ready to set me straight, to instruct me in all of my moral failings.

"Let's get the hell out of here," Dad answers, cutting the preacher off before he can say another word.

*   *   *

An hour later, we're driving home from the burger joint where we stopped for dinner and where other customers openly stared at the two of us as we walked through the door. I had taken off the itchy wig and left it in the car, which meant I entered the restaurant looking like Cinderella's bald, shrunken doppelgänger. I momentarily wondered if I should have left it on.

"I guess we're quite a sight," Dad said, grinning.

Dad caved in to my begging and let me sit up front for this part of the drive. Now I'm messing with the radio, trying to find a decent station. I land on one that's playing old-timey music, and he says, "Oo, wait! Leave it here!" He pulls the car into the parking lot of a strip mall we were just about to pass. "I love this song. Do you know it?"

I shake my head. It sounds familiar, but I couldn't name it. It's catchy, though. I move a little in my seat to the rhythm.

"The Temptations," Dad says. " 'Ain't Too Proud to Beg.' One of the all-time greats." Then he holds out a hand. "Care to dance, my lady?"

I look at him like he's crazy. "Here?"

"Why not?" He has parked in the big, empty lot, and he cranks the radio up so loud that I have to plug my ears. It's like being in Moira's car. Leaving the engine running and the headlights on, he opens his door, gets out, and comes around to my side. I'm starting to get the picture. Smiling, I take his hand and jump down onto the concrete in all my finery. "Why, thank you, kind sir. I believe the dance floor is this way." I lead him toward the front of the car, and the two of us start dancing right there in the glare of the headlights.

"Here's how we used to do it," Dad says, breaking out some of his best moves from the Stone Age.

"Oh my God! Dad, no!" I can't stop my mortified laughter from bubbling up. "It looks like you're being attacked by killer bees!"

"Okay then, whippersnapper. You show *me* how it's done."

I respond by showing him some of the moves I've seen in videos recently, moves I sometimes practice in my room when

I'm bored. The chastity ball dress throws sparkles everywhere, all over Dad's tux, out across the parking lot, and onto the windows of the closed stores. I'm like my own disco ball, my own laser light show.

Dad watches me, openmouthed. "You never could have gotten away with that at the chastity ball," he says.

Ten minutes later, we're breathless and boogied out. I can't remember the last time I felt so physically exhausted and so happy at the same time. Who cares if dancing in the glow of headlights is the stuff of cheesy inspirational movies? This time, it's *my* movie, and I can't imagine anything better at this moment than dancing with a guy I love.

56

MOIRA

DAY 45: MAY 11

IT'S ONE OF THOSE BALMY SPRING DAYS THAT MAKE A PERSON
want to *do* something. I'm as amped up as a Chihuahua on
crack after school on Wednesday, and I need to get out of the
house.

Unfortunately, Agnes has a cold again. She's already told
me she's not up to going anywhere.

"Let me come over and bake for you, then," I said when
we talked earlier. "You could just sit there and watch."

"I feel too crappy, Em. I just want to stay home, eat some
chicken noodle soup, and nurse my stuffy head."

"You're no fun."

"I know," Agnes said. "I'm sorry."

And then there's this: ever since I decided to take my
brother up on his offer, I welcome any distraction that will

help put the Berkeley trip out of my mind. It's just four days away now. My stomach gets queasy and my hands get shaky anytime I think about it. Driving always helps. Baking, too. Not to mention eating the things I bake. God, I've probably gained ten pounds in as many days. My dad's been pretty good about helping me power through trays of brownies and batches of cookies, but I can tell even he's getting sick of the stuff at this point. And my mom won't touch all the processed sugar and bleached flour. Now it looks like Agnes and Deb are out, too.

Which is probably why I find myself navigating El-C around turns in the endless dirt road leading to Boone's place. *And why not?* I reason to myself. *My homework's done, and I've been ready for finals since winter break. Maybe I can help Boone study.* I stay under the speed limit to avoid toppling the stack of baking supplies I piled into a cardboard box and set on the passenger seat before leaving the house. I'd run out of most of my ingredients, but miraculously, my mom had a bag of real chocolate chips in the pantry, buried under all the carob. There was a bottle of her good homemade vanilla extract in there, too, the kind she makes by slicing a bunch of rubbery vanilla beans and stuffing them into brown glass bottles filled with cheap vodka. I also grabbed a few sticks of unsalted butter from the freezer and eggs from the fridge before leaving, but sugar was a problem. All Mom had was raw turbinado or agave nectar. I'll have to count on Boone being one of those teen guys who oversweetens his breakfast cereal and his coffee with nutrition-free white sugar.

The dirt road keeps me focused by shifting beneath El-C's tires like it did the first time I came out here. It's like driving across marbles. The washboard ruts don't help, either. Boone is out chopping wood in front of the dilapidated little house when I drive up. He straightens when he spots El-C, rests the ax blade on a stump, and squints at me. I give a little wave, but doubt descends quickly. It was probably stupid to show up uninvited like this. What was I thinking? Then again, I did try calling him before I left, just to make sure he was home. His cell phone was maybe out of minutes, because all I got was a generic recording.

What the hell. I'm here. May as well see it through. "I keep feeling like I need to thank you for . . . stuff," I proclaim as I open my door and extricate myself from El-C. "You know, all the . . . stuff you do for Agnes . . . and me." What a doltish thing to say. Haven't I already thanked him enough? Isn't all that "stuff" already behind us? Plus, I need to stop talking so fast.

"You don't have to thank me," Boone says, coming closer. He looks a little wary, confused. It's not what I was expecting. Well, what *was* I expecting, exactly? A parade and confetti?

On top of the doubt, I'm flustered. I hate being flustered. To cover it up, I dive toward the box sitting on the passenger seat. "Look," I say, holding up the chocolate chips and the vanilla. "Stuff for cookies!" As soon as the words leave my mouth I think, *Enough with the "stuff" already. Kill me now.* Jesus, why am I so awkward around him all of a sudden? Movement in a window of the house behind him catches my eye and provides a welcome distraction. "Is that your mom?"

Boone turns to look at the window and nods. He holds up a hand and waves, but she's already disappeared behind one of the curtains. His face is grim.

"It's her horse I rode, isn't it? If you can call what I did *riding*, I mean." I'm still babbling, but I'm grateful for the change of topic at least.

"Yeah," he says. "Used to be hers, anyway. She's not too interested in him now."

"Well, I'd like to thank her, but if I'm not welcome . . ."

"It's not that," Boone says. "It's . . ." His voice drops off.

"You know what? Never mind. This was a bad idea. I'm sorry." It *was* a bad idea coming out here, but at least I know what to do now that it's clear neither of us is going to get over the awkwardness. To hide my disappointment, I turn my face away from him. I'm reaching toward the cardboard box to put the chocolate chips and vanilla back when a soft yet firm voice says, "I taught you better manners than that, Boone."

I startle a little at the unexpected sound. Straightening up, I turn to see Mrs. Craddock standing in the open doorway of the house.

BOONE

DAY 44: MAY 12

IT'S NOT POSSIBLE TO OVERSTATE MY HUMILIATION AT THAT moment, when my mother decided to make an appearance out of nowhere. All a person had to do was behold the state of her, the state of the house, and the state of my entire life to know that this was not going to end well. Mom just stood there in the doorway, like she's safer in doorways or something, like an earthquake's going to level the place at any moment. She said what she said about manners, and then she motioned for me and Moira to follow her inside. It was surreal.

As we entered the house, I felt dizzy, like all the blood was leaving my head and draining toward my feet. I tried to see the place as Moira must have seen it: the worn carpet and old television circa 1988; the cobwebs and soot graying the walls; the living room coffee table covered with a partially completed jigsaw puzzle of dogs playing poker. There were loose pieces everywhere. *The shrapnel of my mother's life,* I almost said out loud, but didn't, thank God. Looking at my house through Moira's eyes was like being disemboweled without anesthesia. If Moira felt uncomfortable or disgusted, though, she hid it really well.

Strangely, the day ended up sort of okay after that. It was only a little weird having Mom wandering around the house as if being around other humans was a foreign experience for her. Which it kind of is.

For the rest of the afternoon the two of us hung out, just making cookies and goofing off. At one point, when Mom was in her room, I threatened to lick the wooden spoon before we'd finished using it to drop dough onto the baking sheet. Moira tried to take the spoon away from me, and I resisted. In response, she wrapped an arm around my waist to brace herself as she wrestled it from my grip and then pointed it at me like she'd had quite enough of my shenanigans. She couldn't hide her smile, though, and I didn't allow my brain to linger for too long on the warm softness of her body when she'd pressed it against me. She was even stronger than I'd suspected. Both of us were out of breath afterward.

Later, while the cookies cooled on sheets of newspaper, Moira and I sat facing each other at the old wooden table. A thick slice of sunlight slanted down through the air between us, and all I could think looking at her through that light was, *This will do. This will do just fine.*

AGNES

DAY 43: MAY 13

I MUST HAVE BOOGIED A LITTLE TOO HARD THE NIGHT OF THE chastity ball, because now, three days later, I still don't feel good. More specifically, I feel like I was "drug through a knothole backward," which is something I once heard Boone say. Mom would kill Dad if she knew about our late-night dance party in that parking lot Tuesday night. It was worth it, though, even if my head does feel like it's stuffed with cotton and sand.

59

BOONE

DAY 42: MAY 14

AGNES IS STAYING AT HER DAD'S HOUSE FOR THE WEEKEND, SO Moira and I decide to hang out at my favorite downtown dive, a little hole-in-the-wall diner where they serve fifty-cent coffee with free refills. "I've heard that new movie about undead circus clowns is supposed to be pretty cool," I say once we've settled into our booth. The seats are covered with cracked vinyl, and the Formica tabletop is etched with decades' worth of graffiti. We're the only customers at the moment. As usual, I'm struggling to find a topic of conversation that won't make me sound like a complete tool. I've always sucked at small talk, but I remind myself that it's okay. We're just hanging out. It's not like I'm trying to impress her or anything.

Moira perks right up when I mention the movie. "Oh my God, I want to see it *so* bad."

"Let's go, then."

"When?"

"Tonight."

Moira hesitates for just a second. Then she says, "Okay." Gives me a little smile, even.

I can't believe I'm being so bold. For one thing, it's not like I have wads of spare cash lying around. TJ has shown no sign of increasing my hours beyond the every-other-weekend crap I'm doing now. Antler sales have been slow, and wood sales won't pick up for another six months, at least. And what if Moira thinks I'm asking her out on a date? What if I *am* asking her out on a date? *What the hell,* I think. *She's going to be gone soon anyway. For an entire week. Maybe even longer, if she decides she loves California, and why wouldn't she? What the hell is there to keep her here?*

Well, okay, there's Agnes.

We hang out at the diner for a while, getting overly caffeinated, and then I drive home to finish some horse chores and get dinner ready for Mom: reheated food bank lasagna. I shave and then take a quick, mostly cold shower, since I don't want to waste water by waiting for it to warm up. Then I stand in the middle of my room in my boxers and socks trying to fend off a panic attack about what I'm going to wear. *Get a freaking grip,* I tell myself. *You're going to a movie, not getting married.* I finally choose a casual button-down shirt and the cleanest jeans I have. They're not pristine or anything, but at least they don't reek of horse manure or transmission fluid. I knock on Mom's door and tell her I'll be home later. There's no response. I tell her to call me if there's an emergency. Saying it makes me feel a little better about leaving her alone after dark.

I pick Moira up at her house. I sit in the truck for a minute, trying to decide if I should go to the door or just wait outside. There's a new hole in the Chevy's exhaust pipe, so I'm sure she heard me pull up. Going to the door would be more respectful, obviously, but it also seems more date-like somehow. If Moira was one of my guy friends (not that I have any), I'd just tap the horn and wait behind the wheel. That's what guys do, right? Then I think about her parents and how cool they were about paying me to do stuff around their property. I could use going to the door as an excuse to say hi to them. I'm halfway up the walk when Moira comes out of the house. She's dressed fancier than usual, and she's gone a little lighter on the war paint. Her hair is pulled back from her face with shiny clips. "Let's go," she says.

"I was going to say hi to your parents."

"They're busy." She walks past me and toward the truck quickly, with her head down. Reluctantly, I follow.

*　　*　　*

Once we get to the movie theater, I still have all these unanswered questions in my head. Moira insists we go Dutch, so is it a date, or isn't it? Am I dressed okay, or do I look like a total hick? God, I wish I could just pull it together and relax already, just live in the now. But being out at night with Moira like this, just the two of us, it's like my brain stem activity has been compromised. As if to prove it, I'm distracted by something sparkly in the lobby. My eyes simply latch on and follow the shimmer of their own accord. I'm not even aware of what it is or even that I'm staring, but it turns out the sparkly thing is a girl. She's about our age, and she's wearing a sequin top that looks like it's a few sizes too small.

"Um, hello?" Moira is glaring at me.

I snap to consciousness. "Hi. Uh, what?"

"I mean, I know this isn't, like, a date or anything, but still. It's so disrespectful." She crosses her arms in front of her chest.

"What?"

Moira looks in the direction of Sparkle Girl, who has joined a group of her friends, also sparkly. They're wearing short shorts, low-cut tops, makeup, and shiny jewelry.

"I mean, I'm right here," Moira says. She looks away when I turn to her.

Was she . . . is she . . . *jealous*? Heat surges through my chest. I want to tell her that I've never been good at multi-tasking, at doing things like thinking and keeping a reasonably intelligent expression on my face at the same time. But I also don't want to make the situation worse. Did she say this isn't a date? "I wasn't—" I start to say.

"Yes, you were. Just admit it already. God."

I don't know what else to do, so I just stand there looking ashamed. I make a show of ignoring Sparkle Girl, which isn't at all difficult. I may have been looking at her, but it's not like I was *seeing* her. I glance back over to where she's standing with her too-skinny, wannabe-fashion-model friends. Now I do see her. She's pretty, sure, but she's not amazing or anything.

She's not Moira.

*   *   *

The movie is stupid as hell, but it's also terrifying. I mean, clowns start off creepy anyway. Once they get killed by zombies and then turn into zombies themselves, the situation becomes truly horrific. During a few of the more graphic scenes, Moira practically jumps out of her seat and clutches my arm. Every time she does it, I have to close my eyes and focus on my breathing.

Later, the two of us sit in the truck as it idles in front of her house. I know she has to pack, but I'm also not ready to part ways yet.

"So," I say.

"So." She looks at me sideways with one eyebrow raised.

"You're leaving for California tomorrow."

"Yup."

"Are you excited?"

"Kind of."

"Are you nervous?"

Moira looks down. "Yeah. Yeah, I am." She doesn't say anything more after that, but she does turn her face toward me and smile again.

I wonder, briefly, if I should kiss her. Just lean forward and do it. Moira's looking at me strangely now. I wonder if she wonders if I'm going to kiss her. Within seconds, the moment passes. Moira opens the door and gets out.

"See you when I get back," she says.

And then, just like that, she's gone.

MOIRA

DAY 41: MAY 15

MIRACULOUSLY, I MANAGE TO FIT INTO MY ASSIGNED SEAT, BUT it's not exactly roomy. I'm wedged in next to the tiny lozenge of a window, and a woman with a baby is in the center seat next to me. The baby is fussing, whining, pulling at the woman's hair. I don't blame the kid. We've been sitting on the runway for almost an hour. According to the captain's overly soothing voice coming through the speakers, this sort of thing happens. None of the other passengers seem too worried about it, but I have to actively remind myself to breathe so I don't pass out.

The plane lurches into motion, a slow turn into position. "Ladies and gentlemen," the captain says, "we've been cleared for takeoff." A few people clap. Moments later, the roar of jet engines fills my ears. I'm pressed back into my seat like I'm on the Gravitron ride at the county fair. It's so loud that even the baby next to me is spooked into silence. I dare to peek out the window, where clumps of grass and weeds next to the runway are blurring past. The plane is tilting back now, making me feel like I'm on a lounge chair at the beach. My stomach feels like it might float right out of my body.

And then, just like that, I'm flying.

AGNES

DAY 40: MAY 16

I EXPECTED TO MISS MOIRA SO BADLY OVER FINALS BREAK THAT I wouldn't be able to eat or sleep or do anything else. And I do miss her.

Just not so much that I can't function or anything.

When Moira first announced that she'd be gone for the entire week, I felt my heart sink. It literally felt like my heart was hanging lower in my chest. Which was silly, since she's only going to be gone for a week. Then I got a cold and we didn't get to see each other before she left, either. We did talk briefly on the phone the day before, but that was it.

"I want to see you before you go, Em, but I still feel like death on a cracker."

"It's okay," Moira said, her voice softer than it was the last time I spoke to her. I thought she'd be more upset, considering the fact that we hadn't seen each other in several days.

"When's your flight?"

"I need to double-check. All I know is I have to get up at the crack of butt."

This made me giggle. "I'm jealous, you know."

"I know," Moira told me. "I wish you could come, too."

I wondered if this was really true. I've heard the excitement in her voice lately any time the trip has come up in conversation. It makes sense, that excitement. Moira's going to be traveling and exploring and hanging out in a new city, like an actual adult. I'm proud of her.

Still, it's only Monday, and I'm already starting to get a little restless and bored. Mom is subbing today at a nearby school that doesn't have finals break. I've done some studying, but it's a relief when Boone shows up. A few minutes after hearing the rumble of his truck outside my bedroom window, I open the front door to find him standing there with his hands in his pockets.

"Wanna chill?" he asks, looking down at me.

"Definitely," I tell him. "I'm over my cold and bored out of my mind. Come on in."

Mom would have no problem with us hanging out in my room together with the door closed, since it's totally obvious nothing would ever happen. Even if something ever *did* happen with a boy (which it wouldn't, of course—a person has to take just one look at me to know this), it's not like

I'd get pregnant or anything. Not with my octogenarian ovaries.

Boone stands with his back to me, looking at the picture wall where I've tacked up hundreds of photos over the years. There I am with the mayor of the town. There I am as the grand marshal of the Fourth of July parade. There I am with the governor of the state and a team of doctors from Massachusetts. The doctors were working on an experimental cure and convinced my parents to sign me up for the clinical trial. "You know, Agnes," Boone says, "someone should write a book about you."

"They tried. It didn't work."

He turns around to face me. "Why not?"

"I don't know. They weren't telling the story right, and I guess I didn't want to be one of those kids where it's like, 'Oh, she has such a hard life, but she's so inspiring.' You know? So, I told the writers I didn't want to do it. I didn't want people to see me as the innocent victim of some dreadful, rare disease, which was basically the whole idea behind the book. But it's like people can't help it. They can't stop seeing me that way. The latest thing is a bunch of businesses in town got together to sponsor a trip to Disneyland for me and my mom."

"That's pretty cool," Boone says.

"It's good PR, is what it is. At first, I wasn't even sure I wanted to go."

"Wow. Seriously?"

"Yeah, but I said yes anyway. Look, I don't mean to sound

ungrateful. I *am* grateful. It'll be good for me and Mom to get away for a little while. I just . . . I don't want people feeling sorry for me. But I can't stop them from feeling sorry for me. It sucks." I can't remember the last time I've talked so much about myself and my condition. Usually, talking about it is the last thing I want to do. Right now, though, I feel . . . *fierce* about it for some reason.

Boone's smiling at me. "I don't feel sorry for you," he says.

"Thanks." I start to smile, too, but then immediately close my mouth over my ugly teeth.

62

BOONE

DAY 39: MAY 17

I WAKE UP AT THREE A.M. AND IMMEDIATELY START THINKING about the meal I ate last night at Agnes's house. It was quite possibly the best thing I've ever eaten in my life.

"You're staying for dinner, aren't you, Boone?" This was what Deb asked as I headed toward the front door. My stomach rumbled at the mention of food. I tried not to look too eager as I nodded.

Honestly, I hadn't planned on hanging out for dinner. I half figured I'd already overstayed my welcome. Plus, there were evening chores still waiting for me at home. The longer I stayed in Agnes and Deb's clean, comfortable house ignoring that fact, the more unpleasant the chores were likely to be when I finally got to them. So far that day, I'd eaten only a couple of Slim Jims, which were on sale at the gas station, two for one. "Uh, I guess I could stay," I told Agnes's mom. "If it's not too much trouble." I called Mom to let her know I'd be home a little later than expected, but there was no answer. She was probably asleep already.

The scent of dinner went to my head the second I walked into the kitchen. Deb said something about the recipe being from Morocco. All I knew was that it smelled like cloves of garlic and chunks of juicy meat being juggled by baby angel unicorns. And the taste of the chicken when the three of us finally sat down to eat—oh God, the taste. I tried to pace myself. Reminded myself to chew each bite thoroughly before swallowing and to come up for air occasionally. I also tried to remember to sit up straight and keep my elbows off the table—those manners Mom reminded me about when Moira came over to bake cookies.

All told, I had four helpings of the Moroccan chicken and the couscous side dish. I was ashamed to eat so much, but not ashamed enough to stop shoveling forkfuls of heaven into my mouth. Deb seemed happy to see me enjoying the food. It was probably a rare sight for her, since Agnes seems to survive on portions that would leave a pygmy mouse begging for more.

After dinner, Agnes asked her mom if we could watch TV in the living room. She pulled me out of the kitchen by my sleeve and pointed to the big couch. "You can put your feet up," she said. "We don't care."

I knew better than to put my feet up on someone else's couch, but I did recline the upper half of my body against a bunch of pillows piled at one end. It was insanely comfortable. About five seconds before falling into a hard sleep, it occurred to me that I was like Goldilocks or something. Entering a strange house, eating the porridge, trying out the furniture . . .

I woke more than an hour later with Agnes standing over me grinning and holding a box of tissues. "It's for the drool," she said.

Deb came into the living room from the kitchen. "Your mom's probably wondering where you are," she added as I stood up fast and tried to clear my head.

"Whoa," I mumbled. "Sorry. I must have fallen asleep."

"Ya *think*?" Agnes giggled.

Deb just smiled. "Nothing to be sorry about. Here." She handed me a brown paper shopping bag with the top rolled down to seal it closed. "I packed a container of the chicken for you to take home. Maybe your mom will like it, too."

I took the bag from her. It was warm. "Thank you," I said, but I couldn't look at her for too long. I was afraid I'd do something psycho, like start crying out of gratitude.

Throwing off the blankets and getting up from bed, I head to the kitchen in the dark, open the fridge as quietly as I can, and pull out the container of leftover Moroccan chicken.

Mom woke up after I got back from Agnes's house last night, and she had some of it, too.

"This is delicious," she said.

"It is," I agreed. "It's almost as good as that one chicken recipe you used to make. What was it again?" I knew the answer, but for some reason I wanted her to say it. I wanted us to have an actual conversation.

"Chicken cacciatore," Mom said, studying her plate.

"That's right. It was really good."

"Not as good as this." She smiled at me for about half a second. I'd take it, though. I'd almost forgotten what her smile looked like.

"Yours was definitely as good as this," I told her, bending the truth just a little, since nothing was as good as this. "It was just different."

Not much was said after that. Still, a part of me hoped that maybe this could become a new thing. Maybe we could sit down to a meal together once in a while and chat like a normal family.

Now I close the door of the fridge and grab a fork. I don't even bother to heat up the food first. I just sit at the table and eat it cold, right out of the container. A lump starts to form in my throat again.

It's been so long since anybody has taken care of me.

63

MOIRA

GRANT LIVES IN THE WORLD'S TINIEST APARTMENT ABOVE A Greek delicatessen on Telegraph Avenue. I sleep on the twin futon that takes up his entire living room. When I wake up in the morning, it's to the sound of traffic on the street below and the smell of meat and exotic spices ribboning in through the heater vent. My first morning here, the first thing I thought about was how I survived the flight despite the lightning bolts of adrenaline that shot down my spine every time we hit turbulence and also when the landing gear clunked into place. Three days later, I'm still proud of myself for not coming unglued.

Fern comes by while I'm folding up the futon. She doesn't have to work her library shift until this afternoon, so the two of us head downstairs for an early lunch. I have no clue where to even begin with the menu.

"Everything's good," Fern advises as we walk through the door of the delicatessen. "Believe me." A man behind the counter smiles at her. "Hi, Gregor," she says.

As I'm trying to interpret the menu, clearly lost, he points to me and says in a thick accent, "You: gyros and souvlaki."

I hesitate. "Both of them?"

Gregor smiles and nods.

I look around to see who might be listening, to see which of the college students packing the place is going to make a crack—*Hey, fatty. Why stop at two? Why not order three or four entrees?*—but nobody gives me a second glance. Except for one guy sitting behind an open biology textbook near the back wall. He's wearing retro-frame glasses, and he is not unhandsome. He brings a gyro to his mouth, takes a big bite, and gazes around the room. Our eyes meet briefly.

I pay for my two items (because, okay, why not?). As I'm waiting for Fern to pay for her stuff, I scan the deli again, looking for a place where we can sit down. Bespectacled biology guy is still looking at me, smiling this time. It's not a creepy smile, and it's not a mean one. It seems . . . Could it be a genuine signal of goodwill from an attractive stranger of the opposite sex?

This does not compute. I just stand there and stare blankly back, unsure of what to do next. Should I return the smile?

Flip him off? What's the protocol here? Clearly, I think about it too long, because a blush rises to the guy's face and he looks down at his food.

Fern's eyebrows are raised when I turn back to her. "Looks like somebody has a fan," she says.

"What? Oh, please."

"I'm just saying."

I feel color rising into my own cheeks. I hope the extra pale foundation I'm wearing today (China Doll #728) is enough to cover it. When I get up the nerve to look back at the guy one more time, he won't look at me. *Smooth move,* I tell myself. *Way to terrify the locals.*

*   *   *

Later, when we're back out on the street, wandering into and out of the various shops, a woman in a wraparound sari-type dress and big hoop earrings walks in front of us. She's about the same size as me, but unlike me she holds her head high and sways her ample backside proudly from side to side as she strolls. I watch the eyes of people walking toward us to see if they're going to laugh or say something insulting, but nobody does. If anything, I catch a few oncoming females looking at the swaying woman with admiration. Several of the men look at her with something different, something more like adoration. From the back, I can't tell if she returns their stares with smiles or dirty looks or what. I'm guessing smiles, probably secret ones. Not that it matters. Clearly, this woman is moving through the world for herself and herself alone, with little concern about what other people might think.

More than anything else, at this moment I want to reach forward and tap her on the shoulder. I want to offer to buy her a cup of coffee so I can pick her brain and ask her how she got this way. Maybe I could be her apprentice. For the first time in my life, I'm looking at a big, mighty, curvaceous gal like myself and thinking, *This. This is who I want to be.*

64

AGNES

DAY 37: MAY 19

IN THE MIDDLE OF FINALS BREAK, BOONE TAKES ME WITH HIM TO
haul water.

I'm waiting on the front step when he pulls up. A jumbo
fiberglass tank is strapped into the bed of his truck. "Our cistern's almost dry," he calls out to me from behind the wheel.
"Not that water hauling is much of an adventure, but you said
you wanted to get out of the house."

I check with Mom, who says it's fine. She says she knows
I'll be careful.

"That thing looks like a big white space pod," I tell Boone
as I walk toward the truck and climb in.

"I've always thought it looked like an alien egg," he replies.
"Like it's going to hatch and a thousand alien babies are going
to come out and take over the world."

"Ew." There's no booster seat, and I have to hold the seat belt strap to keep it from covering my face.

As we approach downtown, we see a truck parked in a dirt lot with a For Sale sign in the window. The truck is beat-up and yellow with a thick brown center stripe. Boone stares at it as we drive past.

"Looks like an old banana," I say.

"Yeah, but it's not as old as this one." As if in response, his Chevy lurches and sputters. I'm thrown forward a little, and Boone sticks an arm out to brace me, just like Moira would.

"Sorry about that," he says, cranking the stick shift into a lower gear and stomping on the gas to keep the engine from dying.

Next, we pass a billboard advertising a local mattress outlet. The model is wearing a silky negligee. She's sleeping on a bare mattress with a big sexy smile on her face and long brown hair fanned out all around her shoulders.

"Who sleeps like that?" Boone says. "I mean, at least put a *sheet* on the bed, for crying out loud."

"She has the prettiest hair, though," I tell him, sighing. "It's like . . . religious hair."

He's laughing now. "What does that even mean?"

"You know . . ."

"Um . . ."

"Oh come on," I say, swatting at him. "Hair! Hair that's,

like . . . blessed or something. It's like . . . childbirthing hair."
I play with a few strands of the curlicue wig I put on this
morning.

"Okay, now you're just scaring me." Boone turns onto a
narrow side road and navigates the truck under a long hose
hanging from a standpipe that's connected to the city water
tower. He turns off the engine and looks at me.

My arms are crossed over my chest now. "You're never
going to understand this," I tell him. "Try to imagine what
it would be like if you had no hair."

"I'd be cool with that." Boone opens the door and gets out
of the truck.

"Shut up!" I open the door on my side and jump down
to the ground. With help from Boone, I climb up onto the
open tailgate and watch as he unscrews a cap from the fiberglass tank so he can place the standpipe hose inside. He fishes
a bunch of quarters from his jeans pocket and feeds them into
a coin-op machine. Seconds later, water roars down through
the hose and whooshes into the tank, making the entire truck
rumble beneath me.

Boone finishes feeding quarters into the slot and leans
against the tailgate. "Seriously, I'd totally rock as a bald guy.
I'd be like Yul Brynner or something."

"I don't know what that is."

"Yul Brynner? *The King and I*?"

My face is blank.

"Seriously?" Boone takes a step toward me and holds out one flat palm.

"What are you doing?"

"Shall we dance?"

Silence.

"And you accuse me of being out of the loop with your whole 'religious hair' thing," he says. "Please tell me you've heard of *The King and I*."

When I shake my head, he does something I wouldn't have expected in a million years. He takes a deep breath, holds both arms out, and begins to sing. *"Shaaaaaaaaall weeeeeeee DANCE! Bom bom bom!"* He launches to the left in a spin, one arm held low in front of him now, as if on a lady's waist. He holds the other hand higher, at about ten o'clock, like he's holding his partner's hand aloft.

I sit there, stunned, on the bed of the truck as it lowers under the weight of roaring water.

Boone keeps singing about flying on a cloud of music, his voice deep and strong. It only falters a little bit on the higher notes.

The sound of the water in the tank is suddenly muted. There's a gurgling, and then the water is overflowing. It runs down the side of the space pod and sloshes into the truck bed before I can get out of the way. In an instant, my pants are soaked and I'm shrieking. I'm only a little surprised when Boone whirls back, punches the emergency stop button on the coin-op, picks me up from the tailgate, and twirls me along with him all in one fluid motion.

I watch the horizon to keep from getting too dizzy as Boone spins me around, still singing. Then he stops and our dance ends. He sets me down and looks at my clothes. "Oh, boy," he says. "I'm so sorry, Agnes. I don't know what got into me. My mom loved that movie. Man, you're soaked. I must have put too many coins in by mistake." The look of concern in his eyes is one I've rarely seen from anyone other than immediate family members. It's the look of someone who's seeing past—seeing through—my veiny scalp, my crooked teeth, my beak of a nose.

Above all else, this is the thing about Boone that I'd put inside a sealed jar on my bedside table if I could. This is the thing that makes me . . . what?

Like him as more than a friend?

Maybe even . . . love him a little?

Well, yes. There's that.

MOIRA

DAY 36: MAY 20

GRANT DRIVES US ACROSS THE BAY BRIDGE AND INTO SAN Francisco so I can see the Haight-Ashbury district.

"It was the heart of the flower child movement," Fern says from the backseat of the Subaru. We're driving high above the choppy, slate-blue water of the bay. Sunlight glints off the tips of waves like a million stars, as if the inverted night sky is below us.

San Francisco—with its wisps of fog swirling just out of reach, the Muni buses and trundling trolleys, the people in all shapes, sizes, and colors wearing the kind of perfectly cobbled together, edgy outfits I'd pretty much kill for—is a wonder. When we get to the Haight, Victorian houses line the streets. They're not so different from my own house, really, but these are all painted different colors, like they're Easter eggs and Haight-Ashbury is the basket.

We go into an enormous music store, and when we come out half an hour later, a man in a full formal suit and fedora is standing outside the store playing an upright bass. There's a carnation in his pocket, and he reminds me of Boone somehow, with that stature. I feel a pang of homesickness. Not that I don't love it with all my heart here, and not that I don't appreciate everything Grant and Fern are doing for me. I just wish Boone was here to experience this place with me. Agnes, too, of course. Grant puts a few bucks in the bass player's tip jar.

We check out a store filled with wigs in all different cuts and colors, everything from conservative and gray to wild and neon. Agnes would flip. Feather boas and irresistible tights, in patterns I've never before considered, hang from dozens of racks shoved close together in the small space. It's obviously a store for drag queens, but I couldn't care less. I buy a pair of tights with a swirling, psychedelic pattern in reds and blues and oranges. It's way more color than I ever wear, but I can't help myself. Maybe I'll wear them under the full-length black skirt I made last month in the home ec room, just to know they're there. On second thought, maybe I'll whip up a black miniskirt when I get home so the tights are fully visible. It would be almost refreshing to give the simpletons at school something new to torment me about: *Hey, Rotunda,* I imagine them saying as they gawk at my ginormous rainbow legs. *Nice . . . colors.*

273

BOONE

DAY 35: MAY 21

I WONDER IF SHE'S THINKING ABOUT ME AT ALL, MAYBE EVEN just a little, like I'm thinking about her.

Which is totally brain-dead of me. Moira has probably been out on the town this entire past week, meeting college guys who have their shit together and are almost as smart as she is, things I could never in a million years claim to have and be. At night, she's probably sitting in cafés with those same guys, drinking fancy coffee and discussing art and politics and philosophy while they lie drooling at her feet.

I force myself to think of something else. Like sitting down and studying for finals, which I haven't done nearly enough of. The thing is, I feel more prepared than I probably should, considering the fact that I don't get as much extra help in school as I used to. I don't want to be full of myself or anything, but it's nice to feel confident about even one small part of my life for a change.

MOIRA

DAY 34: MAY 22

THE THREE OF US ARE HANGING OUT AT GRANT'S APARTMENT on my last morning in Berkeley. "So what do you think?" Fern asks. "Is Cal at least going on your college maybe list?"

I've finished packing my carry-on for this afternoon's flight, and Grant's in the kitchenette getting some cheese and crackers for us to munch on.

I just smile and nod. The Bay Area is obscenely expensive, and I don't know how I'd ever manage to afford it. My parents would no doubt figure out a way to help me like they've helped Grant, but I wouldn't want to bleed their bank account dry. Still, I almost feel like I have no choice but to do whatever it takes to move here someday. There's so much to see and do. From the food and the architecture to the people and the fashion, this entire place is amazing. It's like nothing I've ever seen or dared to imagine for myself. *I am Paradise,* it seems to say. *And I will be here when you're ready for me.*

Fern lowers her voice and glances toward the kitchenette. "So, I know Grant asked you this when we were at your house, but it was probably hard to answer with everyone there. What's the boy situation like back home? Any special guys in your life?"

Blushing, I look down. "Not really. I mean, there's this one. Kind of."

"Aw," Fern says. "What's his name?"

"Boone Craddock." My voice is so small that I half wonder if I said his name at all. Maybe I just thought it, like I'm always doing lately.

It's no surprise when perfect Grant, with his gift of perfect hearing, chooses that moment to return with the cheese and crackers. "Boone Craddock? I remember that kid. What about him? He was kind of messed up, wasn't he?"

I stare at him. "What? No. Nothing about him. Fern was just asking if—"

"I was asking if she knew any guys with kind of . . . unusual names. You know, like we have?"

Grant frowns. "My name's not unusual. It was a president's name."

"Yeah, yeah." Fern smiles and rolls her eyes. " 'Who was

buried in Grant's tomb' and all that. But you have to admit, it's not a *common* name. Just like Moira and Fern aren't common."

And with that, the brilliant woman who I dearly hope will be my sister-in-law someday effortlessly changes the subject.

68

AGNES

DAY 33: MAY 23

"DO YOU MIND IF WE WAIT IN THE COMMONS?"

"Go right ahead," the front desk receptionist tells me.

Mom and I head toward the main area of the senior center with its floor-to-ceiling picture windows looking out over the town. Today was the first day back to school after finals break, I think I might be in love, and I have another appointment with Dr. Caslow. I guess when it rains, it pours.

Kitty is there, as always. She looks up from her mah-jongg game and waves us over to the big circular table where she's sitting with five other elderly female residents.

"My girlfriends and I all had debutante balls," one of them is saying.

"Oh, we used to get sozzled at those," another chimes in. "Afterward, we'd go out to the lake. I'm not saying there was skinny-dipping involved, but I'm not saying there wasn't, either."

The others throw back their heads and cackle.

"Young women think the saddest thing about old ladies is that we just haven't experienced Johnny or Jimmy or whoever the magic man du jour is," the old woman continues. "But they're wrong. We have experienced them."

"Mine was Walter Anderson," Kitty pipes up. "Oh, but he knew how to woo a girl."

"We thought the same thing about the old women of our day," the one who brought up the debutante balls says, looking at me now. "How sad it was that they'd missed out. Let me tell you something, honey. Just in case you're wondering, old people haven't missed out on anything. In fact, they've likely experienced more than most young people ever will, the way the world's going. Everyone hiding behind their electronic screens."

Her friends murmur their agreement and get back to the game.

"So, who's yours?" Kitty asks me.

"My what?"

"Your Johnny or your Jimmy, or whoever."

I look away, my face hot. "I don't have one."

"Pah!" Kitty waves her hand in the air. "Sure you do."

A few minutes later, when Mom's in the bathroom, I whisper, "Well . . . maybe there's one."

"Out with it."

"His name's Boone. And he's . . . he's just so . . . He's perfect. But you can't tell anyone, Kitty. Promise?"

The old woman pinches her thumb and forefinger together and zips them across her lips. "I know a thing or two about keeping secrets from parents," she whispers. "Is he kind to you?"

I'm unable to stop the corners of my mouth from curling upward in a goofy grin. "Oh man, Kitty. You have no idea."

"No idea about what?" Mom asks, coming back to the table.

Thankfully, a nurse comes over right then to tell us the exam room is ready.

* * *

"Feeling good?" Dr. Caslow asks me when he comes in. He and Mom shake hands.

I nod. "We're going to Disneyland."

The doctor raises his eyebrows at Mom, who says, "It was a gift from some local businesses."

"I wasn't that into it at first, but I finally decided to go," I add. "I can go on the rides, right?"

"Not the awful ones," he tells me. "Like the roller coasters and such. The milder ones should be fine."

This makes me happy. Once I decided to accept the trip to Disneyland, I actually started to get excited about it. Knowing now that I'll be able to go on at least some of the rides makes it even better.

69

MOIRA

DAY 32: MAY 24

I'VE BEEN BACK AT SCHOOL FOR TWO DAYS, BUT I STILL DON'T feel like I've come back down to earth.

On Saturday, the day before I came home, Fern took me to get my hair hennaed. Afterward, we took a yoga class where we pressed our palms together at our foreheads and then brought them down to our hearts. We did poses like Downward-Facing Dog and Happy Baby. Five minutes in and I was exhausted. I didn't care, though. Strangely, my body seemed to crave that kind of silent, flowing movement.

It was during Warrior Two that something inside me shifted. I can't say what it was exactly. But standing there in front of the mirrored wall of the yoga studio, with sweat running down my face and my entire body centered and poised as if ready for battle, I understood for the first time how much better it feels to appreciate my body for what it can do rather than constantly despising it for how it looks.

At the end of class we all lay there in the dark. Final relaxation, the instructor called it. "Take a deep breath," he told us in his soft, reassuring voice. "Now let . . . go."

And so I did. For the first time in maybe forever, I let go.

BOONE

DAY 31: MAY 25

I NOTICED THE CHANGE IN MOIRA RIGHT AWAY WHEN I FIRST saw her Monday morning. Of course I noticed it. I'd have to be blind not to. But it's taken me a couple days to get up the nerve to say anything. I'm not even sure I *should* say anything. Or, if I do, how I should say it. I should probably just keep my mouth shut. But, "You look . . . different," I tell her on Wednesday during lunch, my mouth racing ahead of my brain. As usual.

Moira smiles down at the ground when I say it, but then she lifts her eyes to mine.

Different's not quite it, though. What she looks is transformed. Morphed. There's hardly any makeup on her face, for starters. No more black lips, no black eyeliner. She looks more vulnerable, like she's starting from scratch. Her hair is different, too. It's still black, but there are some reddish-brown strands mixed in now.

Since the weather's been so nice and the girls are done with their home ec dresses, the three of us have been hanging out on the grass in front of the library most days to eat.

"What I mean is," I say, trying not to stumble too much over my own tongue, "you look . . . really pretty." Agnes is looking down at her lunch and not saying anything. She's probably embarrassed for me.

There's a long pause before Moira takes a deep breath. "Thanks," she says.

71

MOIRA
DAY 30: MAY 26

AGNES WANTS BOTH OF US TO COME OVER BEFORE SHE LEAVES for Disneyland tomorrow.

Boone and I pull up in front of her house at the same time, and we go in together. Deb is busy with last-minute packing, so the three of us hang out in the kitchen.

"I'm going to miss you guys," Agnes says.

"You're going to have an incredible time," I tell her. I hope it's true. Even though I know Deb had to work, part of me wishes they could have made this trip during finals break; Agnes's coloring looks a little . . . off somehow this week. Lately, she's had more colds and other annoying stuff going on with her health than I can count. I hope the two of them don't overdo it in Anaheim. But what am I thinking? Deb's even more protective of her daughter than I am. Plus, they'll have tomorrow and then the long Memorial Day weekend to take their time in the park and not feel like they need to rush.

"Please tell Ariel the mermaid that I'm her biggest fan," Boone says, distracting me, as usual, from worry. I elbow him in the ribs, but lightly, as Agnes beams up at him.

She and Deb have an early-morning flight, so we don't hang out for too long. When it's time to go, Boone gathers his coat and gets ready to head out the door behind me.

"See you when you get back from the House of Mouse," I say, bending down to give my best friend a hug.

Outside, Boone and I say good-bye, get into our vehicles, and pull away from Agnes's house at the same time, just like we arrived.

It's when we're both waiting at the stoplight near the first major intersection that Boone taps his horn. When I look over, he's gesturing for me to roll down my window, so I do.

"Hey," he calls out over the rumble of the truck's engine.

"We have to stop meeting like this," I call back. Not my most original line, but Boone laughs anyway.

"Do you want to maybe, I don't know, go get something to eat?"

I force myself to act like I'm thinking about it for a second, but I can feel the corners of my lips tugging themselves upward. Finally, I nod and just let my smile do its thing. "I'll follow you to the diner," I tell him.

72

AGNES

DAY 29: MAY 27

OUR HOTEL HAS A CANDY THEME. FAUX CANDY CANES THAT ARE taller than I am frame the entrance doors, fabric lollipops serve as couch cushions, and there are dishes full of real candy everywhere. Other guests in the lobby rubberneck in my direction like I'm a Disney cast member—one of the Seven Dwarfs, maybe—who wandered away from Fantasyland.

That first afternoon, Mom and I ride the air-conditioned hotel shuttle to the park and meet our VIP escort. His name is Carl, and he's a sociology major at a nearby university. I didn't think an escort was necessary, but it was part of the package the businesses in our town paid for when they set up this trip. Carl gives us a tour of Main Street, which smells like flowers and waffle cones. Afterward, we ride in a horse-drawn carriage and take the train all the way around the park.

The only real ride we have time to go on that evening lifts us up and makes it seem like we're flying above orange groves, snowy mountains, and the ocean, like angel-bird hybrids. When it's over and our feet have touched back down on the concrete floor, I look over and see tears in the corners of Mom's eyes. "That was . . ." she starts to say. "Well, it was just amazing, wasn't it?"

BOONE

DAY 28: MAY 28

I'M LEANING AGAINST THE MUCKING FORK ON SATURDAY, HARDLY noticing as Diablo grips the wheelbarrow handle with his teeth. It's part of his oral fixation. Only if he starts chewing on the wood will I shoo him away. We can't afford a new wheelbarrow.

Looking at Moira across the table of the diner after leaving Agnes's house, I'd barely been able to eat. It was ridiculous.

"You're looking at me the way Agnes looks at you," she said.

"What does that mean?"

"Just . . . you know."

I didn't know, but it didn't matter. Other than that, neither of us said much.

When we did speak, it was always at the exact same time.

"I think Agnes is going to love . . ."

"I'm so jealous of Agnes getting to go to . . ."

"You go first."

"No, you go first."

It was an awkward sort of torture, but I didn't care. I could stare at Moira all night.

In one quick motion, Diablo bites down on the wheelbarrow handle and raises his head, flinging the load of manure everywhere. I just sigh. *That'll teach you to think about some girl rather than paying attention to me,* I'm pretty sure the gelding's saying.

74

AGNES

DAY 27: MAY 29

ON OUR THIRD DAY IN ANAHEIM, WE DECIDE TO WALK TO THE park. Yesterday, we stayed at the hotel all day, and we both feel ready to stretch our legs again.

The only problem is, riding the shuttle on day one masked the distance. Neither of us realized how long it would take on foot. It's not the nicest walk, either. It's over a mile of concrete, and you see things walking that you don't notice as much from inside a vehicle. Things like vandalism and sad-looking people at bus stops and trash all over the place.

"I'm going to hail us a cab," Mom says.

"Don't," I tell her. "It's fine. We're almost there." We're standing under a storefront awning, taking a break in the shade. And that's when I see him.

He's in a wheelchair holding a cardboard sign with the words DISABLED VETERAN—ANYTHING HELPS scrawled across it in fat marker strokes.

Try as I might, I can't stop staring.

"Everything okay?" Mom asks.

"No," I tell her. "Look at him."

"Agnes, I don't think—" she starts to say, but I leave her side before she can reach out to stop me.

The guy stares at me as I approach him. One of his eyes is scrunched shut, like Popeye's in those old cartoons. I can't tell much about him other than that. Every inch of his skin is covered with either whiskers or grime. "Is you old?" he asks in a raspy whisper when I'm close enough to hear.

"Sort of," I answer. "What about you?"

"As the hills," he says. A sound comes out of him that I assume is a laugh, but it's more like a couple of rusty cans being rubbed together. Most of his teeth are missing.

"I'm Agnes."

He looks at me for a minute longer and then finally holds out what I realize is his only hand. His other arm ends in a stump just a few inches below the shoulder. "Sarge," he says.

"Honey." It's Mom's voice behind me. Worried but firm.

I ignore her and shake Sarge's hand. "Is there anyone who can help you?" I ask him. "Family or friends?"

"Afraid I burned those bridges a while back, little mama."

"Where do you sleep?"

"You ask a lot of questions, you know that?"

I look down at my hands, at my knobby fingers entwined and fidgeting with one another now. "Sorry."

"Bet you get a lot of questions, too."

"Not really," I say. "People stare at first, but then they pretty much just pretend not to see."

"Yeah," Sarge says, nodding. "Yeah, I hear ya."

*　*　*

He stays on my mind for the rest of the day. An hour after meeting him, Mom and I stand posed in front of the It's a Small World castle so Carl can take our picture. He gives us free mouse ears and a bunch of coupons for food, too. I get some curious looks, as usual, but most people are too busy fanning themselves in the heat and navigating the crowds to pay me much attention.

It's only once we're on It's a Small World and floating in our boat through the darkened indoor waterway surrounded by singing dolls that I finally understand what's been gnawing at me lately. It's that I'm tired of being treated like a child, like everyone's extraspecial princess. I don't want to be the town mascot anymore. I don't want to be the charity case for local businesses to use in their advertising. We float into the last major part of the ride, where the dolls are illuminated in all different colors and waving at us now. The song that won't leave our heads for days reaches a seemingly endless crescendo, and all the signs say GOOD-BYE in dozens of different languages. Mom is sitting perfectly still, looking off to the side of the boat. Out of the corner of my vision, I see her reach up and swipe a tear from under her eye. I'm guessing it's because our trip is almost over, and who knows when, if ever, we'll be able to do something like this again. Swallowing hard, I lean toward my mother and rest my head on her shoulder as the boat gently rocks us back into daylight.

MOIRA

DAY 26: MAY 30

IT SCARES ME HOW MUCH I'VE BEEN THINKING ABOUT HIM lately. It also scares me how happy thinking about him makes me. I do my best to play it cool when we're together, though. And with Agnes gone, we're together a lot.

Alone in my room, I take off all my clothes except for my bra and underwear and stand in front of the mirror. I try hard to see myself, to really *see* myself. It's excruciating. It's almost impossible to avoid my years-long habit of only glancing, of just allowing a quick glimpse of this body part or that. I've been dissecting myself with my eyes that way for most of my life. After all, why would I want to look at my entire body all at once? The few times I've accidentally seen myself naked, the litany of names I've been called since grade school plays in an endless loop inside my brain. The only time mirrors have been tolerable is when I've practiced my death scowl. But I won't let myself do that now. I force my expression to stay neutral.

I want to see who I really am, not what other people tell me I am.

Turns out I am . . . well, I'm big, for starters.

I'm also mighty.

I am Rubenesque.

And I am capable of moving through this world for myself and myself alone, with little concern about what other people might think.

76

AGNES
DAY 25: MAY 31

ON TUESDAY MORNING, AS WE'RE HEADING TOWARD OUR LOCKERS and groaning about the long weekend being over, I ask Moira if she wants to study for finals after school tomorrow.

"I might be busy," she says after a pause. "But definitely Thursday, okay?" She doesn't look at me when she says it, which is kind of weird. I don't think too much about it, though. She's been acting different—kind of distracted or something—ever since she got back from Berkeley. She hardly asked me anything about my trip.

"Okay," I tell her. "Thursday it is. How about after dinner, at six o'clock?"

"Perfect."

That night, Dad calls and asks if I want to go out for ice

cream with the kids. I tell him sure. When they come to pick me up, I climb into the back of the minivan with Nevaeh and Obi. Isaiah offered to put my booster in the front seat, but I told him it was okay. The booster can't go up there because of the airbags, and the seatbelt restrains me in all the wrong places when I try to ride like a normal passenger. Plus, I know it makes him feel grown up to sit next to Dad.

Nevvie gives me a big hug as soon as I shut the door. It's a little *too* big of a hug, actually; I feel a slight pop in one of my ribs when she does it. "Ouch!" I cry before I can stop myself. Dad's worried eyes fill the rearview mirror, and Isaiah turns to shout at his sister. "Careful! Agnes is *delicate*!"

Nevvie looks like she might cry. "I'm sorry, Agnes," she says, her lower lip trembling.

"Oh, sweetie, it wasn't you," I lie. "I just kicked the seat and hurt my toe."

"Oh, phew." She grins, and I notice that she's lost another baby tooth. At the sight of the empty space, I feel a pang in my heart to go with the one in my rib cage.

We go to the same ice cream place where Dad used to take me when I was the twins' age. At first, a small, jealous part of me feels resentful that we're all there together. I've always sort of thought of it as a special place for just the two of us. But as I watch my brothers and sister eating their cones and describing the insects they're learning about in homeschool, I end up wishing we'd all come here together sooner. "We should have made this a regular thing these past five years," I say out loud.

Dad looks at me. "We still can," he says, but his eyes look sad.

I feel an arm wrapping around mine. It's Obi's. He gives my arm a gentle squeeze and rests his head on my shoulder. "Nobody can replace Agnes," he says. The words momentarily stop my breath. Dad and I exchange a look.

"That's the truth," he says. He clears his throat and tousles Obi's hair. "Nobody can replace Agnes."

77

BOONE
DAY 24: JUNE 1

IT'S WEDNESDAY AFTER SCHOOL, AND THERE'S NO PLAN. AGNES is being picked up by her mom, and all Moira and I know is that we want to hang out together today, just the two of us. We're not headed any place in particular. We're just driving.

"I want to play BioHaze for you," Moira says.

"Is it any good?"

"I don't know. Is the *Mona Lisa* any good? Is Beethoven's Fifth any good?"

"I guess," I say, laughing.

"You guess." Flabbergasted, Moira looks up at the roof of the car. "He guesses," she tells God.

The song begins, and it's not a song at all. It's an aggressive wall of noise. I can't make out any specific instruments, but I'm pretty sure there are a few screaming guitars in there. There are also electronic drums and what sounds like a ukulele being played by a honey badger on methamphetamine. Someone might be singing, too. That, or it's a recording of a guy choking on his own tongue. So much for Berkeley mellowing this girl out. "You're going to ruin your hearing," I holler at the top of my lungs.

Moira just reaches for the volume knob and turns it up. "It's worth it," she yells back.

"You're going to ruin *my* hearing!"

The "song" finally plays out, and we ride in silence. After a while, I pull something from my jacket pocket. It's an old cassette tape I found in my dad's collection. I eject Moira's tape from the player and replace it with mine.

"What the hell is this?" Moira's face twists in confusion as the opening slide guitar strains of "Whiskey Bent and Hell Bound" snake out through the speakers. "*Country* music?"

"Don't you remember me telling you about Bocephus?"

"Who the hell?"

"Hank Williams, Jr. My dad had the same name."

"Your dad's name was Hank Williams, Jr.?"

"Close enough. His name was Henry." I reach for the volume knob and turn it up as Moira rolls her eyes. There are so many other songs I could introduce her to. "Sweet Dreams" by Patsy Cline, Willie Nelson's "Till I Gain Control Again." Nanci Griffith and Lucinda Williams sing a version of "On the Wings of a Dove" that will make you want to cry, but am I going to tell Moira this? No. She'll just have to miss out on her own. I cross my arms over my chest at the thought, but then Moira reaches for the eject button. I reach my hand out to stop her. "Just give it a chance," I plead as Hank wails about hearing a sad song and getting his emotions all balled up.

Moira's hand stays there, hovering near the eject button, and my hand stays there, too, covering hers. I don't want to distract her from the road, but I also don't want to so much as breathe in case it makes her pull her hand away.

*   *   *

Later, when we're hanging out on a picnic table at the park, she says, "What are you thinking?"

"I'm thinking the same thing I thought in sixth grade before everything went wrong," I tell her. Maybe I'm emboldened by our music war, maybe by the sun warming the skin of my back through my T-shirt, I don't know. Moira tenses at the mention of the Year That Shall Not Be Named, but I put my hand on hers again, like I've been doing it forever. "I'm thinking you're the most beautiful girl I've ever seen." I don't know how she's going to take it, and I don't really care. It's the truth. I'm sick and tired of hiding it.

There is a long (eternal, even) silence before Moira leans in toward me. Her eyes are almost closed as she presses her lips to mine. I've never felt anything like it. I'm pretty sure kissing Moira could fix just about anything that's ever been wrong in my life. No, strike that. I'm certain, beyond the shadow of a doubt, that kissing Moira *has* fixed anything that's ever been wrong in my life.

She pulls away a few millimeters, and we stay like that for a while, our faces almost touching but not quite, until I vaguely register the sound of her voice. It forces me out of paradise and back to consciousness.

"How are we going to tell Agnes?" she's asking me.

"I don't know," I whisper against her lips. "I think she'll be happy for us."

Moira pulls back. "That, right there, just proves how clueless guys are when it comes to love," she says.

"Mmm-hmm," I murmur. All I want to do is pull her back to me, pull her back under the surface of life to where I am now, to where bliss resides. "Are you saying you love me?"

"No," Moira says. "That's not what I'm saying at all." There's a slyness in her eyes, though, and she gives me a playful little shove. "Shut up."

78

AGNES

DAY 23: JUNE 2

I EAT DINNER EARLY ON THURSDAY, AND THEN MOM DROPS ME at Moira's house just before six, like we agreed. Finals start on Monday. That's just a few days away now, so we'd better get cracking if we want to be prepared. I haven't seen much of my best friend this week, other than at school. I'm looking forward to studying with her and catching up.

"I'll wait here until you get inside," Mom says as I unbuckle myself from the booster seat and get out of the car. I nod and sling my backpack carefully over my shoulder.

I'm about halfway to the Watkinses' front door when a sound coming from behind the old elm tree in their front yard catches my attention. It's probably Moira's mom out garden-ing. I step closer, preparing to say hi, but then I realize it's not Moira's mom at all. It's Moira. She's leaning against the tree with her eyes closed and her arms raised. They're draped across Boone's shoulders, those arms, the wrists crossed behind his neck as the two of them stand there pressed against each other, kissing and kissing and kissing. It's the longest kiss I've ever seen. It makes the earth start spinning at roughly ten times its normal rate. I try not to make a sound, but I fail. My horrified gasp gives me away before I can stop it. As I turn to run back the way I came, back toward Mom's waiting car, Boone and Moira pull apart.

"Oh my God," Moira says behind me, her voice blurry. "Agnes, what are you doing here?"

"We're supposed to study, remember?" I've stopped on the flagstone walkway, but my back is still turned toward them. It's all too much.

"Oh my God," Moira sputters again. "I totally forgot."

"Why didn't you tell me about this, about you and Boone?" My eyes are filling with tears. And because my funky, lashless eyelids are too thin and stretched out to hold them back for more than a second, the tears start streaming down my face almost immediately. I turn around to face the two of them anyway.

"I didn't think—"

"You didn't think what?" I challenge her. "You didn't think it mattered if you got together with Boone behind my back? Because it's not like I'm really even in the running or anything, of course. I mean, *look* at me. Right? Am I right?" My voice has reached such a high pitch that I wonder if they can hear me at all. Maybe I sound as invisible as I feel. Maybe only dogs and dolphins can hear me now.

"Agnes—"

"*Stop saying my name.* You go away to get your head screwed on straight, and while you're gone, I . . . Boone and I . . ." He's standing right there, so I don't say what I was going to say, which was . . . what? That Boone and I were somehow romantically involved? I'm not going to let the question get me off track. The point is, Moira deserves to hear what I'm saying right now. She needs to hear this. "And then you come strolling back in here, la-di-da—"

"Strolling?" Moira is looking at me with her head tilted, trying to comprehend.

"Just never mind. Forget it." I feel suddenly dizzy.

"No. Agnes, I want to know."

The girl who used to be my best friend is too pretty in this moment, her voice and hands too soft and feminine. Between the time when she got back from Berkeley and I left for Disneyland, I didn't have a chance to get used to how much she had changed. This new, lovely girl is not the Moira I know. This is not a Moira tough enough to protect me.

"Agnes, wait." It's Boone's voice this time.

"And you!" I say, pointing at him. He flinches like he's just been zapped by a cattle prod. "You made me . . . You made me think . . ." I'm struggling for breath a little now, panting. I have no idea where this anger inside me came from or where it's been hiding. I feel righteous, all-powerful, and more than a little sick all at the same time.

Boone's looking at me almost like he's scared. "Agnes, I'm so sorry."

"*You* don't say my name, either! Moira and I were fine before you barged into our lives again. We never should have let you back in."

At that Moira takes a step toward me, but I hold up a hand to stop her. "Mom!" I cry, running back toward her car that's just now starting to pull slowly away from the curb. "Mom, wait!"

MOIRA

DAY 22: JUNE 3

WHEN BOONE CALLS ME THE NEXT MORNING, I TELL HIM IT WAS all a mistake. That we should have just left the past in the past. I force myself to be strong, to not back down. It's the only way.

He doesn't want to hear it.

I tell him I should have known better, that I shouldn't have led him on.

He says I didn't.

I tell him not to call me.

He says he wishes I'd rethink that.

I tell him not to call Agnes.

He says he won't call her if not calling her will help.

I tell him Agnes and I are going to make up, that I'm sure of it.

He says he's sure of it, too. That it's all going to work out. That he'll be there to help. Whatever we need.

I tell him to just leave us alone.

He doesn't say anything more.

AGNES

DAY 21: JUNE 4

MOM TRIES TO TALK TO ME. SHE INVITES ME TO CURL UP IN HER big king bed on Saturday night like I did when I was younger. "Having a boy in the picture complicates things, doesn't it?" she whispers.

I don't answer right away. I'm glad it's dark. I don't want to have to monitor the look on my face in case it gives something away that I'd rather keep private. "Sometimes I just think it would be better for everyone if I wasn't here at all," I say after a while. "If I was just . . . out of the picture."

Mom sits there in silence for a minute, breathing slowly in and out. "It won't help for you to not be here," she finally says. "You do realize that, right?"

"But you're so tired all the time. And sometimes you seem so sad."

"I am sad sometimes," she tells me. "Tired, too. But all mothers are tired. Every one of us is tired, Agnes. Do you understand me? So don't think for one second that your not being here will help me. Okay?"

"Okay," I whisper. After that, sleep comes easily.

81

BOONE

"I CAN'T DO THIS TO HER" WAS ALL MOIRA SAID AS WE STOOD IN the middle of the street watching Deb's car drive away. We were both out of breath, having realized the futility of trying to chase down the car after Agnes got back into it. I'd like to think Deb would have stopped if she'd looked in her rearview mirror and seen me and Moira running after them, hollering for them to please wait. Probably, she'd been too worried about Agnes to even check her mirrors.

More than anything, I wish I'd noticed Agnes sooner. That's my biggest current regret. When I came up for air from Moira's luscious lips and opened my eyes, Agnes's face was the first thing I saw. Her eyes and mouth were frozen into three little round Os.

Before leaving Moira that night, I took her hand and held it between my own hands. "It's all going to work out," I told her. I hoped I sounded convincing since I wasn't at all sure that what I was saying was true. Then I leaned in for a hug, but she leaned away.

"It's not . . ." she said. "I can't." She hadn't been able to reach Agnes on the phone in the half hour since they'd driven away, and she seemed to know better than to go over there. She didn't want Agnes to get so upset that she made herself sick.

82

AGNES
DAY 19: JUNE 6

FINALS START TODAY, AND I DON'T EVEN CARE. I'VE BEEN GIVEN an extension due to the fact that I've been "going through a rough time lately—on multiple levels," as Mom wrote in her note to the school staff. I can even use the first week of summer vacation to finish everything if I want to. I'm also allowed to take my exams open-book, but I've decided to take them closed-book and in one sitting like everybody else. What's it really going to matter, anyway?

For this last week of school, I've been assigned a new chaperone to walk with me between classes. Moira tried to accompany me to first period this morning as usual, but I told her to go away. She tried ignoring what I said, so I planted my feet near my locker and refused to move. The two of us stood there in the hallway for about five minutes after the last bell rang. We were both late enough to our classes that the secretary from the office was sent to find us.

"What's going on, girls?" she asked, sighing.

I was the first to answer. "I don't want Moira walking me to class."

"She needs someone to protect her," Moira protested.

The secretary nodded at Moira and tilted her head at me. "Everything okay, Agnes?"

I didn't answer.

"I think Moira's right," she told me. "It's important for you to have someone to keep you safe in the hallways, don't you think?"

"As long as it's not her." I stared down at the hallway floor when I said it so I wouldn't see the look on Moira's face.

Moira's replacement is a sophomore named Brittany who needs some quick extra credit to avoid summer school.

"Mrs. Deene is applying this to my home ec grade," Brittany tells me when we meet in the main office. "She says it's a form of community service. Otherwise, I'd totally fail."

"How does someone fail home ec?" I ask, slightly incredulous. I can tell by the look in her eyes that the question doesn't win me any points with my new handler.

Still, while we're waiting in the cafeteria lunch line, I laugh when Brittany says, "Ew, potatoes au gratin. More like au *grossen*," even though it isn't remotely funny. I laugh so Moira will see me laughing. Boone, too. I notice that the two of them aren't standing in line together. In fact, there are about twenty people separating them, but that doesn't make me feel better. It doesn't make me feel anything.

As we're looking for a place to sit, Brittany's friends try to wave her over to their table. Brittany makes a sad face at them. She points to me and shakes her head, doesn't even try to hide it. A minute later, she starts to sit at the corner table Moira and I used on the rare occasions when we'd eat in the cafeteria instead of the home ec room, but I tell her I don't want to sit there. Not that it ends up mattering; I see Moira walking quickly toward the exit with her tray of food.

"God, you're lucky you're so skinny," Brittany says when we finally find a decent spot. "You can probably eat anything you want."

Sometimes there are no words. This is one of those times. If Moira was here, there would most definitely be words. I don't allow myself to wonder what they'd be, though.

After lunch, instead of chaperoning me through the busy hallway and back to my locker like she's supposed to, Brittany stands outside the cafeteria and checks her phone. She also makes blinky eyes at every handsome upperclassman that walks past as I sit on a nearby bench twiddling my thumbs.

Moira appears from around a corner of the building. She comes over to the two of us, sizes Brittany up, then makes a disdainful sound with her nose.

Brittany tears her attention away from her phone long enough to glance at me and then at Moira. "Um?" she asks.

Moira ignores her. "So this is it, then," she says to me.

"I guess." I don't look her in the eye. "It's not like we have to make a big drama out of it or anything." I'm aware of how soon we could start sounding like we're reciting lines from some after-school special if we're not careful. I'm aware that doing so might make one of us laugh, and I'm not at all ready for that. I'm still mad. I'm still *betrayed*.

"If this is your decision . . ." Moira starts to say.

"This is my decision," I tell her.

I don't expect those words to have an actual taste leaving my mouth, but they do. They taste the way I imagine old, tarnished coins taste—bitter and metallic.

They taste final.

BOONE

DAY 18: JUNE 7

I'VE PICKED UP MORE TIME AT THE FEED STORE. IT'S JUST A couple of hours after school, but I'm not going to complain. For one thing, it's a good distraction. For another, I'm going to show TJ that I'm a team player if it kills me. Maybe that way he'll be willing to bump up my hours permanently when summer vacation starts in a few days.

Just before closing, I see my neighbor's truck pull into the parking lot, and then Jackson Tate himself gets out. Heading toward the front entrance, he tips his hat and smiles at one of the register girls who's loading a case of canned dog food into the trunk of a customer's car. I'm stacking bags of alfalfa cubes at the end of an aisle near the doors, which means Tate can't avoid seeing me when he comes in.

"Help you?" I ask him as I lift one of the fifty-pound bags onto the stack and then reach for another. I try to use the same tone I use for every other customer. There hasn't been any drama between us for over a month, and I'd like to keep it that way. That last time Diablo escaped, the hoofprints he left in Tate's driveway gravel were so laughably faint that I could barely even see them. And Tate hasn't brought up the fence line in over a month, no doubt because he realized how off his measurements were. *That's probably not the only thing he's mismeasured*, I think to myself, smiling. Tate must see something he doesn't like in my smile. He must see all the stuff that's been simmering inside me since the first time we met, because he shifts his gaze away from mine and says, "No, thanks. I'm good."

After work, I head home and grab my favorite pistol, the one called the Judge. Somehow, the weight of the blued steel always feels comfortable in my hand. I also grab the box of ammunition I've set aside for emergencies. Mom's in her bedroom. I can hear her walking around in there, so I know she's okay.

Dead pine needles crunch beneath my work boots as I head out into the woods behind the pasture. The air feels like it did the last time my father took me woodcutting with him, the last day I saw him alive.

Nobody else is at the gravel pit, which means I get to be alone as I shoot at the junk others have left behind for target practice. I start with an old stove, then move on to plinking beer cans. Finally, I decide to shoot the shit out of an old refrigerator somebody dragged out here years ago. There's still enough of the old, rusted steel left to make a satisfying sound when it's punctured. For a long while I stand there bracing my wrist against the kickback as I unload round after round before reloading and doing it all over again. I refuse to think about the money I'm blowing on ammo. For once, I couldn't care less about the waste. In fact, maybe I just need to let myself not care about anything for a while. My old man would kill me if he was here, but he's not here. Henry Everett Craddock will never be here, or anywhere, ever again.

"You're not here, are you?" I shout at the refrigerator, startling myself a little, as I fire off another several rounds. "Answer me, you sonofabitch! You're not here! You're not anywhere! You couldn't help me then, and you can't help me now. *You're* the useless one, not me!" My voice cracks a little on the last part.

And just like that, in my mind, I'm an eighth grader again. It's right before the holidays, and I'm back at the wood-gathering spot that's not too far from where I'm standing now.

My father was done cutting big rounds from the felled tree trunks with his chainsaw. As we each carried a last armful of wood up the steep, forested hill toward where the truck was parked, he noticed the rear tire on the driver's side. It was flat as a pancake. "Shit," he said.

"Should we change it?" I asked him.

"What do *you* think? No, let's just drive home and ruin the rim, shall we? It's just money, right? Numskull."

By then, I was pretty much used to the hair-trigger temper he'd had since falling off that roof and losing his job more than a year before. Plus, I knew he was tired from the day, tired from the responsibilities and the money worries that constantly seemed to be crushing both my parents back then, but my father's tone still struck me as unnecessarily sarcastic. Why did he have to be like that? I'd only asked an honest question. I'd only thought that maybe the forest floor was soft enough to allow us to get home, where Mom would say "Here are my men" when we walked through the door. For that's what I was now, wasn't I? A man? Maybe she'd even make cups of hot apple cider or her special hot chocolate with vanilla and cinnamon and heaps of those miniature marshmallows stirred in. Maybe there was still hope for things to go back to the way they'd been once upon a time.

The only jack we could afford was meant for a regular car, not a pickup. It was too light-duty for such a heavy work truck, especially a truck loaded down with more than a half cord of wood. I started to remind my father of this, but he grabbed the jack from behind the seat anyway, ignoring me.

"Truck's on a hill," I said. I knew I was really pushing it now, but it seemed like he was being too reckless, even for my dad. "Want me to at least find a big rock to put under the good front tire so she won't roll?" I thought using the word *she* was a nice touch, like we were two sailors at sea and the Chevy was our battered but trusty ship. I thought it might calm him down. I was wrong.

"So," he said, his voice almost friendly for about half a second, "are you going to shut the hell up and stay out of my way, or are you going to keep yammering like a useless girl?"

"I just thought chocking the tire—"

"Just shut the hell up, Boone!"

With that, my father confirmed what I'd been thinking for a while: I *was* useless. I was always in the way, nothing but a nuisance. Obviously the ground wasn't soft enough to drive on without wrecking the wheel rim. Duh. And of course he knew what he was doing, brain injury or no. My father was right: I was a yammering idiot. Maybe not a total girl, but no better than a dimwitted little boy. It didn't matter that I'd start high school next year; I was still nothing like a man, not even close. Even when I was an actual, physical grown-up, I probably wouldn't be anything like a man.

84

AGNES
DAY 17: JUNE 8

THE MEMORY OF BEING LIFTED OFF THAT TAILGATE AND SWUNG around by Boone as he sang still comes to my mind at the oddest times.

Apparently, my wonky senior-citizen heart is broken, and it sucks. Heartache isn't like it seems in romantic movies. There's no swelling violin music following me wherever I go. All I want to do is hang out alone in my room listening to Mazzy Star and watching old black-and-white movies.

"Agnes?" I listen to Mom's soft knock on the door. It's a regular thing lately, this knock. "Are you okay?"

I know she's been worried about me lately. I can tell by her fingernails chewed down to the quicks and the bags under her eyes. This is the kind of thing Mom always assumed

I was immune to, after all, this kind of teen heartache and angst.

"Yeah," I call back, forcing my voice into the most convincing, cheerful lie I can muster. "I'm fine. Just resting a little."

*   *   *

On Wednesday afternoon, with my last final on the horizon and only two more days to go until summer vacation, there's a lockdown at school. It turns out to be nothing, just some idiots setting off firecrackers behind the gym, but nobody knows that at the time. It happens during biology. As soon as we all hear the popping noise that sounds like gunfire, Mr. Gund locks the door and closes the blinds. He orders everyone to take cover and stay quiet, but I refuse to hide under the lab table like I'm supposed to. My classmates are down there on the floor, some of them staring up at me in the half dark, all of us listening for screams outside, for the gunshot sounds to get closer. "Get down here, Agnes," a few of them hiss, but I won't listen. I remain at my desk like a statue, a wee figurine. *Que sera, sera,* I think. *Whatever will be, will be.* Finally, Mr. Gund crawls over to me on all fours like an army guy, his forehead covered in sweat. "Agnes," he whispers. "You need to come down here with the rest of us."

In response, I continue to do what nobody expects; I disobey authority by shaking my head and looking away. It's not that I want to get shot. It's that I need to start practicing things like defiance and toughness, the kind of things Moira has always been so good at. Everybody always thinks of me as this delicate thing. Well, I'll show them.

Still. That night before falling asleep, images of Moira and Boone keep coming to me. I can't help it. I miss them both. I'd be lying to myself if I said I didn't. But I'm still so angry I could cry. The only thing bigger than that anger now is the fear that I may have pushed them too far when I pushed them both away, that I might have said things I can't ever unsay.

BOONE

DAY 16: JUNE 9

"MR. CRADDOCK, WOULD YOU CARE TO JOIN OUR LAST MATHE-matical conversation of the year, or would you rather we not interrupt your nap time? Mr. Craddock?"

My own name invades the dream I'm having, a dream of somebody screaming, some faceless person needing my help, but I'm paralyzed and unable to reach them. I sit up flustered, not knowing where I am.

Geometry. I must have fallen asleep at my desk.

MOIRA

DAY 15: JUNE 10

FINALLY, IT'S THE LAST DAY OF SCHOOL. I SHOULD BE HAPPIER about that than I am, especially since it's only a half day and I aced most of my finals. After the last bell rings, I clean out my locker and then instinctively look around the hallway for Agnes. She's nowhere to be found.

It's only when I'm pulling out of the parking lot, listening carefully to what I think might be one of El-C's pistons mis-firing, that I spot her. She's sitting alone on the curb where the buses usually park, but the buses have already left. She's not wearing a wig. Instead, the blue-gray scarf from home ec is tied around her head.

"Hey," I say, rolling down the driver's side window.

There's no response.

"What's going on?" I press.

Agnes looks away from me, squints toward the bright horizon. "Nothing," she says, finally.

"Where's Brittany?"

She shrugs.

"Wasn't she supposed to stay with you until your ride came?"

Another shrug. "She had . . . stuff to do."

"That bitch."

"It's no big deal." Agnes shifts her eyes ever so briefly in my direction. "My mom's coming to get me."

"Can we talk?"

Silence.

"Agnes, please get in. Just hang out with me and El-C until Deb gets here. We miss you. Look." I swat the driver's side door to get her attention. It works. Agnes glances up, and I point to the side-view mirror. "Even El-C's mirror is drooping."

"What happened?"

Sighing, I explain. *"Allegedly,* I *might* have sideswiped the mailbox while I was backing out of the driveway the other day." (Agnes can't hide her smile.) "But that's according to my dad, who happened to be present at the time. Personally, I admit to nothing."

As I'm talking, Deb pulls up and gets out of her car.

"Moira and I are going to hang out for a while," Agnes tells her. My heart leaps in my chest. "Is that okay?"

"You bet it's okay." Deb walks over to El-C, leans in through the window, and gives me a hug. "I've missed you," she says.

"I've missed you, too."

*   *   *

I drive us toward the west-side park where we sometimes used to sit on the swings and talk. We're about halfway there when Agnes murmurs something.

"What was that?"

"I said *slug bug*." She points at an oncoming Volkswagen and then punches me in the arm. Hard.

Five minutes later, we're at the park, sailing back and forth through the air. The swings sound like elephant calls, like whale song.

"I should have told you what was going on," I say.

"Yes, you should have."

"I'm really sorry, Agnes. I mean, I'm *really* sorry. You don't even know."

"It's okay."

"No, it's not. Because the way you found out was just shi— It was crappy. And not fair."

We've stopped pumping our legs and are letting the swings come back to earth. "Em," she says, "it's okay."

I have a hard time believing she really means it. I saw the

look in her eyes when she caught me and Boone kissing. The image makes me cringe all over again. "The thing is, all this stuff came out of the blue. I didn't even know I felt that way about him until—"

"Moira," Agnes says.

"What?"

"I love you, okay?"

"Yeah," I say. "I know."

"I've been thinking about all of this. A lot. You're my best friend. And Boone's a close second. I just . . . got my feelings all mixed up for a minute. It felt like I was trapped in a flipping . . . damn . . . love triangle. And I hate love triangles."

I raise my eyebrows at the language. Swearing definitely doesn't come naturally for Agnes.

"Anyway," she continues, "you two belong together."

This takes me by surprise. "You think?"

The swings have come to a complete stop. Agnes rolls her eyes at me. "I've thought so since sixth grade."

For a minute, neither of us says anything more. "I don't know who I'd be without you, Agnes Delaney," I tell her finally.

"We should talk to Boone," she answers.

"Yeah. I guess so."

When she stands up from the swing, the chiffon scarf slips from her head and falls to the ground.

"Ha!" I cry, grabbing the scarf and holding it tight in my fist. "Mine again. I *win!*"

"You're a dastardly villain, Moira Watkins."

"Don't I know this." To prove it, I put on my toughest gangster face, but a smile breaks through despite my efforts.

Agnes and I, we are *so* back.

AGNES

DAY 14: JUNE 11

WE GO TO THE Y AS SOON AS IT OPENS ON SATURDAY.

The first thing I notice is that Moira seems more confident in her swimsuit than she used to. It's a black one-piece, and she stands there at the edge of the pool, not bothering to tug the hip panels down like she normally would. Maybe my best friend is finally figuring out how fabulous she really is.

In contrast, I feel like an extraterrestrial. As always, I'm wearing flippers and water wings to help with propulsion and buoyancy, even though wearing them hurts my shoulder and toe joints more than I let on. The trade-off is worth it, though; with hardly any fat to speak of, my body's natural tendency is to sink like a stone.

The pool's not crowded yet, which is nice. I affix my nose

clamp and dog-paddle away until Moira is at the other end of the lane, but I feel her keeping an eye on me anyway. I wonder for the millionth time what it would be like to swim unattended and unadorned, like a normal person, without the stupid clamp and flippers. Without someone always having to watch over me.

BOONE

DAY 13: JUNE 12

THEY'RE AT MY DOOR. I DON'T THINK TWICE ABOUT INVITING them in.

Mom stands half inside her room and half outside it, sheltered in the doorway, weird and twitchy as ever. I expect her to back up and lock herself in, but she doesn't.

It's awkward. Nobody seems to know what to say.

"You go first," Agnes tells me. She looks rough: there are dark circles under her eyes, and she's paler than usual.

I bend down so I'm looking right at her. "Agnes, I'm an idiot."

"I know," she says, nodding. I assume that's the end of it. That's what they came to hear, and now they're going to turn around and leave. It would serve me right.

But they don't go anywhere. Instead, Agnes opens her tiny arms wide and motions at me and Moira. "Come here, you two."

Moira and I haven't even said anything to each other yet. We exchange a glance, and then we step toward Agnes, both of us careful, crouching so she can reach us. Unfortunately, I'm not a very good croucher, so I lower myself to my knees instead. The three of us stay like that for a long time, our arms wrapped carefully around one another.

"Group hug," Agnes sings in her high-pitched voice.

Honestly, it's the most bizarre thing I've ever done, especially with my mother standing nearby, hugging herself and practically vibrating out of her pilly cardigan from social unease. But at this point I don't even care. The cardigan is a step up from the bathrobe as far as I'm concerned.

"We are *such* dorks," Moira says into my shoulder. God, the feel of her breath.

Once again, all is right with the world.

AGNES

DAY 12: JUNE 13

DR. CASLOW COMES INTO THE ROOM AFTER I'VE CHANGED INTO a gown and climbed up onto the paper-covered exam table. Right off the bat, I don't like how he's smiling at me. It looks like he had to arrange his face before coming in here. I know my doctor's real smile, and this one isn't it.

Sitting in the magazine chair, Mom notices, too. "What's wrong?" she demands before he can even get a word out.

The smile falters. "I don't like the look of the latest round of scans and blood work," he tells us. Exhaling, he looks at me. "I was reviewing some of your tests from a couple of years ago, some of the baseline stuff we did."

"And?" Mom looks worried.

"And the news is not necessarily good," he tells her. "This

latest round of results indicates that we could be getting into some issues with the heart. Specifically, I'm concerned about the condition of Agnes's arteries. The statins don't seem to be doing as much as we'd hoped."

I swallow involuntarily. *So here it is,* I think. *The bogeyman that's been hiding under my bed for the past fourteen years, ever since I was first diagnosed.* I recall the tightness in my chest recently, the episodes of breathlessness I haven't wanted to tell anyone about. Now it's all coming down to this: *issues with the heart.* It's what almost always gets progeria kids. Cardiovascular disease. Heart attacks, stroke. I shouldn't be as shocked as I am. I had the blood vessels of a seventy-year-old by the time I was in fourth grade.

"Are there other options?" Mom asks him.

The doctor looks doubtful. "There are experimental drugs being tested, as you know. But there's no magic fix for this artery issue. How I wish there was."

Mom pulls a tissue from a box on the counter next to her. She holds it to her nose and stands up abruptly. "Excuse me," she says, her voice breaking. "I have to leave for a moment."

As soon as the door closes behind her, I look at Dr. Caslow. "It's all downhill from here," I say, "isn't it?"

The fact that he doesn't answer right away is answer enough. "Well, we're going to try not to think that way, Agnes."

"But it's the truth, right? What's the point of trying not to think about the truth?"

He puts one of his hands on top of mine. "We're going to try to keep a positive outlook." A vein on the side of his head has started to throb.

"I'm sorry," I tell him. I grab a tissue from the box and wipe at my eyes. I want these tears gone by the time Mom returns. "I'm really not trying to be a pain. It's just that my parents are going to have a really hard time with this, and . . . it's a lot of pressure, you know?"

"It's more pressure than I can imagine. But your parents are strong, Agnes. You need to let them be there for you."

When Mom comes back into the room, Dr. Caslow says, "Agnes and I were just talking about how important it is to stay positive, even though this is a scary time. So, I want to have some more blood drawn today, just to verify what I'm seeing. I've also scheduled a conference call for tomorrow afternoon with some specialist friends of mine back East. I'm putting a rush on the blood work, so I should have the newest results back when I talk to them. I will call you as soon as I have more information, okay?"

Mom nods.

"Until then, chin up," he tells her, forcing another smile. "Still okay to leave a message on your machine?"

"Yes," she says, looking at me. "It's fine."

The phlebotomist has a heck of a time finding a vein, which means I'll have to wear a long-sleeved shirt tomorrow to cover the bruising from the needle. Once I'm all bandaged up and we're back in the car (which is warm from being parked in the sun), Mom immediately goes into disaster-management mode. "I need to call your father, tell him what's going on. That things are . . . not going in the direction we'd hoped with that medication."

"Mom," I tell her, "it's okay. I feel fine." Of course, that's not true. I don't feel *fine* at all. I haven't felt fine for a while now, and Dr. Caslow's news doesn't exactly help. But we knew this day was coming. It's not like anything he told us is a surprise, not really.

So why is it still such a hard pill to swallow? So to speak.

"Dr. Caslow was right," Mom's saying, changing tactics. "We need to stay positive. Just tell me what I can do to—"

"You don't have to do anything," I snap. "It is what it is." Not only am I sick of the word *fine*, I'm sick of the word *positive* all of a sudden, too. I'm also irritated by how hard she's trying to make the situation seem less awful than it is, even though I know it's not fair of me to feel this way. She's scared. I need to be strong for her. I take a breath and soften my voice. "Do what you need to do," I say. "Just let me be the one to tell Moira, okay?"

Mom just nods. She looks like she might burst into tears again at any second.

I let out a long sigh. Then, so she doesn't think I'm sighing in annoyance, I reach over and put my hand on her shoulder. I pat her gently, the way one pats a frightened child.

Sometimes, the effort of keeping up appearances exhausts me. But this is new territory we're in. I have to be careful to not upset her more than necessary. If she starts panicking now, she's going to burn out by the time I really go into decline. And she'd never forgive herself for that. More than anything, I wish she didn't have to travel the road ahead. It's not going to be pretty.

90

MOIRA

DAY 11: JUNE 14

"HOW WAS THE APPOINTMENT?" I ASK.

"Same old," Agnes says, but there's an instantly recognizable note of false cheer in her voice. Plus, she won't look me in the eye when she says it. I wonder if part of her is still mad about the thing with me and Boone. Whatever it is, I'm going to tread carefully.

I don't want to lose her again.

91

AGNES

DAY 10: JUNE 15

IF MOM COULD HEAR THE MESSAGE DR. CASLOW LEFT ON THE answering machine, she'd freak. Fortunately, she's in the shower, getting ready for tonight.

". . . sitting here looking over the latest blood work again," he's saying. "I still don't love what I see. But you already know that. I'd like for you all to come in, if possible, so we can discuss . . . options."

I'm not stupid. I know what those options are. Surgery on my arteries at the very least, on my heart at most. Extended hospital stays. Side effects from the loads of antibiotics and other medications. Recovery time that might not end in recovery at all. More wishing, more hoping, diminishing odds. Tons of money spent on all the things insurance probably won't cover. And for what? So I can live a long, healthy life? No. That ship has sailed. The possibility of my living a long life died the day I was diagnosed as a toddler. Actually, it died even before that, probably when I was still just a microscopic blob of unstable cells dividing in my mother's womb. As of today, my sixteenth birthday, I've already lived longer than most progeria kids. I'm one of the lucky ones.

Dr. Caslow doesn't even try to hide the emotion in his voice that comes through the tiny speaker next. "I'm just . . . I'm really very sorry."

A rush of heat flows to my face, and I feel my eyes tearing up. It's not so much the news that makes this happen. It's the fact that Dr. Caslow is such a good guy. It's the fact that this "news" is going to hurt everyone I care about. I hear the sound of the shower shutting off, hear Mom moving around in the bathroom. Unsuccessfully blinking back tears, I reach my hand out toward the phone. I need some time to think about all this. I need some time to decide what I want to do before I'm checked into the hospital and stuck full of needles and tubes for good. I just need some time.

Mom agreed to let me spend the night at Moira's house tomorrow night, which is no small miracle. If she knew about Dr. Caslow's message, there's no way she'd let me go over there. He'll eventually call and leave another one, of course, but I'm hoping that will take a few days. I don't want the start of my sixteenth year being defined by this news. My finger hesitates over the answering machine only briefly before pressing the delete button.

*   *   *

At my birthday party that evening—dinner and *tres leches* cake at my favorite Mexican restaurant, Piñata Loca—our group looks like any other happy family out celebrating. Dad is there, as are Jamey and the kids. Isaiah sits next to me and acts all grown up while Obi and Nevaeh take turns wearing my birthday hat and asking Mom all sorts of random, whispered questions. Nevvie: *Did you used to be married to our dad?* Obi: *Do you know who Wolverine is?* Nevvie: *Are you married to anybody now?* Obi: *Do you think I look like Wolverine?* The interrogation goes on like this for a while, cracking me and Mom up, until Jamey gets wind of it and shuts the twins down with a Look of Doom. "I am so sorry," she tells Mom, blushing.

"What did they do?" Dad asks her. When Jamey tells him, he groans and puts his face in his hands. Then he looks up at Mom, grins, shrugs, and rolls his eyes.

For some reason, it's not even weird to have the three adults together in one place like this. It's just . . . good. It fills me with gratitude.

When it's time to say good-bye for the evening and everyone's giving me hugs, I look each one of them in the eye and whisper, "I love you." Dad and Jamey look a little shocked, but they whisper it back to me, as does Isaiah. Obi and Nevvie giggle and squirm at first when I whisper it to them. Each of them hugs me a second time afterward, though, and it almost seems like they don't want to let go.

*　*　*

"That was the best birthday ever," I tell Mom later, when I'm in bed and we're saying good night.

"It was pretty great," she agrees. She bends down to give me a kiss on the forehead. "Happy sweet sixteen, my extraordinary daughter." She looks radiant. She looks happy. What I know everybody was thinking tonight but nobody said out loud is that we're lucky; I wasn't ever expected to make it this far. Thank God I erased Dr. Caslow's message, or this night never would have happened the way it did.

She's heading toward the door when I respond. "Hey, Mom?"

"Hmm?" She stops and turns around.

"Thank you for everything," I tell her.

"You've already thanked me, silly girl."

"No," I say. "I mean for *everything*. Everything you've ever done for me for all these years, ever since you first found out you were going to have me. You're the extraordinary one."

"Oh, honey," she says, coming back to wrap me in a hug. "You don't have to thank me for those things. I'd do it all again in a heartbeat. I'd do it a hundred times over."

BOONE

DAY 9: JUNE 16

"YOU'RE NOT GOING TO PLAY 'UNHAPPY BIRTHDAY' FOR ME?"
Agnes asks her.

"No," Moira says, staring straight ahead through the passenger side windshield of the Chevy. "I don't have the Smiths tape with me. Besides, it's too late. Your birthday was yesterday."

El-C is out of commission again. Something to do with the starter, I assume, based on the symptoms Moira described to me over the phone earlier. She also said Agnes was begging to have another night out with the two of us as a sort of post-birthday celebration, since she spent her real birthday with her family.

"Is Deb okay with it?" I asked her.

"Agnes told me she was."

I picked the girls up from Moira's house, and now here we are, the three of us cruising along in my truck listening to Waylon Jennings and Tammy Wynette instead of The Cramps or Violent Femmes.

"Yeehaw," Agnes says.

I figure even Moira won't be able to resist "Stand By Your Man," especially the part where Tammy basically disses the entire male species. But she's too distracted to notice.

Agnes chose the destination. To get there, we have to drive way out into the country and over a steep, curvy hill. More than a few local teenagers have gotten themselves killed on this road over the years while driving home drunk from the reservoir. It's been the biggest party spot in the county since it was first constructed in the sixties, and it's where Agnes insisted she wanted to be tonight.

She also demanded that she ride on the seat between me and Moira, unbuckled the whole way due to the fact that there are only two seat belts. Nothing we could say about safety or the law would change her mind. For a second, idling there in front of the Watkinses' house, I thought we might not go anywhere at all. But Moira finally relented after Agnes stared at her for a full, silent minute.

There aren't any other cars in the reservoir parking lot tonight. I park near the start of the trail that leads up to the water, and the three of us step out among the beer bottle caps and cigarette butts strewn all over the ground. A nearby sign says NO SWIMMING, NO CAMPING, NO FISHING.

It's not an easy hike to the water. About halfway up the trail, Agnes's breathing becomes labored. "I don't think I can go any farther," she says. "Can we rest a little?"

"Let's just go home," Moira answers. I know she doesn't like having Agnes out here one bit.

"No," Agnes says. "I just need to catch my breath."

I turn around and back up to her. "Well, hop on up, little lady," I say, crouching as low as I can.

Agnes hesitates, but then, with Moira's reluctant help, she climbs onto my back and wraps her delicate arms around my neck. She weighs next to nothing. She definitely weighs less than she did the day I danced her around near the city water standpipe.

We keep climbing, slowly, up the trail until finally we're standing on the bank of the reservoir.

"It's so beautiful," Agnes says, lowering herself down from my back. "I wonder if there's a place we can sit."

"Looks like some old fire pits and stuff over there." I point about a hundred yards west.

"I'll go check it out," Moira says. "You stay with Agnes."

When she's gone, Agnes tugs on my sleeve. "Boone, you should go with her. I'll be fine."

"I think I should stay with you."

"Why? Because I might be eaten by a bear? I'm right here."

Sometimes, it feels like no matter what I do, it's the wrong choice. This is one of those times. I decide to walk away. Maybe both the girls need some space. Maybe I can just distance myself a bit while still keeping an eye on them. You never know when some Freddy Krueger type might make an appearance in a place like this. The three of us have already created the perfect setup for a teen slasher flick by not bringing flashlights to a spot in the middle of nowhere where there's no cell service.

I've gone about twenty-five paces when I hear a scream. It's accompanied by a splash.

"Agnes, no!" Moira's running toward the spot where Agnes and I stood just a minute ago.

I whip around and scan the bank. She isn't where I left her. I break into a run, and I'm almost back to the spot when a moving glint in the dark water catches my eye. Agnes. Her head is just above the surface, and she's doing this gasping cough thing that makes it impossible to tell if she's drowning or just clearing reservoir water from her pipes. I'm running toward her, ready to dive in fully clothed, when the coughing subsides.

"I'm okay," Agnes croaks. After she clears her throat, her voice sounds heartier than I've ever heard it, no doubt from cold shock. "Take off your clothes and jump in!" she calls to us.

"What are you *doing*?" Moira screams at her. "Get *out* of there!"

"You of all people should know how well I swim," Agnes responds.

"Swimming isn't allowed here, and you're going to get a chill!"

"Maybe *you* should chill."

Moira looks like she's been slapped. "Agnes!"

"I think she's okay, actually," I say in what I hope is a calming voice.

"You don't know shit."

Agnes is clearly working hard to keep herself afloat. "Come in, Boone," she hollers at me. "You too, Em."

"Like hell," Moira says. "We have to get her out of there. She doesn't have her flippers or her wings."

"She actually looks like she's doing fine out there."

"Are you kidding me?"

I hate to ignore the girl I love, but I do it anyway. This time, it's Agnes who has the right idea. I start with the top button on my flannel shirt. Then I keep going until I get to the end of the button fly of my jeans. I pull my T-shirt over my head, kick off my shoes, and shimmy the jeans carefully down to the earth so that I'm standing there in nothing but my boxers. "I can't believe I'm doing this."

"What the hell *are* you doing?" Maybe it's wishful thinking, but I'm pretty sure Moira's eyes linger on me for just a few seconds longer than they need to after the question leaves her mouth.

I shrug in response. "Going in, I suppose." With that, I walk to the edge of the reservoir, hold my arms over my head, and dive.

"Woo, Boone!" Agnes hollers when I'm in midair.

A few seconds later, I emerge beside her. "Holy cheese, it's cold!"

"I know," Agnes says. From this close, I can see her teeth chattering, but she looks like she's having the time of her life.

"Dude," I tell her. "You know Moira's going to kill me if I don't convince you to get out, right?"

We both glance toward the bank, where Moira's standing. She's holding herself tight, arms crossed over her belly.

"No, she won't," Agnes whispers. "Watch." She takes a deep breath and calls out, "I know you're many things, Moira Watkins, but I never figured you for a chicken. Looks like that's exactly what you are, though."

Moira's mouth falls open, and her arms drop to her sides. "Give me a break, Agnes."

"Bok."

Moira doesn't try to defend herself. Instead, she starts lowering herself into the water with her clothes on.

"Nuh-uh," Agnes calls to her. "If I can do it, so can you."

Moira looks at me, but I just hold my hands above the water, palms up, like I have no power here. I try, unsuccessfully, to hide my smile. "What can I say? She's right."

Moira starts unbuttoning her shirt. "I'm keeping my bra

on," she informs us. "Also my slip. These items are nonnegotiable." She commands me to turn around, so I do. *"Don't look,"* she says.

I don't, but only because of something like divine intervention that keeps my back to her and my eyes focused on the reservoir stretching out in front of me.

There's a series of splashes followed by the sound of Moira shrieking. Next to me, Agnes's breathing is starting to get a bit more labored, but she still manages to giggle.

"Can I look now?" I ask her.

"I think so," Agnes says.

Moira is already in the water when I turn back around, and she's grimacing from the cold. Only her shoulders and head are visible above the dark surface, which means I have to imagine the rest of her, all those endless curves. The skin that I can see is luminous in the moonlight. It appears to be lit from within.

"It's not that bad," she says, dog-paddling toward us. When she gets close enough, she motions for Agnes to climb on her back, like a baby seahorse, so Agnes can catch her breath. After that, just Moira and I are left treading. Occasionally, our fingers and toes brush against each other as they move slowly through the water. For several minutes that pass more like seconds, the three of us stay like that in the almost silence, none of us making a sound.

*　　*　　*

"I have a horse blanket in the truck," I offer uncertainly when we're standing on the bank again.

"Get it," Moira says. The girls are clutching their clothes to themselves. They don't want to put them on until their skin dries off some. Thank God it's a warmish night. The breeze, when it kicks up, is still chilly, though.

"Please hurry," Agnes adds, her teeth chattering harder now. As if I would do anything else.

"Use my clothes as towels," I tell them, handing over my T-shirt and jeans. Then I stuff my feet into my tennis shoes and jog back to the truck in my soaking boxers, wondering what else I might have that they can dry themselves off with.

By the time I reach the still-empty parking lot, I'm all but dried out from the sprint. I pull the blanket from the back of the truck and give it a good shake. It's hairy and probably smells like Diablo, but at least it'll be warm.

Before heading back up the trail, I start the engine and crank the heater up as hot as it will go. Fortunately, the cab always warms up fast.

Back on the bank of the reservoir, Moira doesn't look like she's dried off much. Agnes has, though. It's clear that, after I left, Moira used her own clothes instead of mine to blot as much water as she could from Agnes's skin. She's standing there shivering, wearing little more than she entered the water with. I force myself not to look below her eyes, which are locked on to mine.

In the truck on the way back to Moira's house, there is no scolding, no "I can't believe you did that, Agnes." There's nothing of the sort. It's like Moira and I have an unspoken agreement to act like everything's normal, even though nothing could be further from the truth. With hot air from the heater vents blasting on us full strength and the rocking of the truck as it lurches back toward the paved road, Agnes falls asleep almost immediately.

It's a couple minutes before midnight when we get back to Moira's house. Agnes wakes up and allows me to carry her from the truck to the doorstep. "Should I bring her in?" I whisper.

"I think it's best if you don't," Moira tells me, but it doesn't seem right not to. It seems unchivalrous to leave two freezing girls on a doorstep late at night. Still, I know better than to argue. Moira knows what's best for Agnes and herself. She always has.

93

AGNES

DAY 8: JUNE 17

MOIRA'S PARENTS ARE UP LATE WATCHING AN OLD MOVIE WHEN we get inside the house. A rental DVD case sitting on the entry hall table has the word *Koyaanisqatsi* typed across the front. Whatever that means. From the brief glimpse I get of it on the TV screen in the other room, the movie looks indie and artsy and deep.

"We've been waiting up for . . ." Moira's mom starts to say. Then she notices Moira's still-damp hair and rumpled clothes. I must not look too put-together, either, because she gasps when she looks at me. "Oh my God. What did you girls do?"

"Mom, it's no big deal," Moira tells her. "Agnes is fine. We just went swimming."

"Swimming?" Her mom looks astonished, and not in a good way. "I need to call Deb."

I beg her not to. "It will just ruin her night," I insist. "I'm fine—look!" I do a slow twirl. "See?"

She still doesn't look convinced. "Mom," Moira says. "She's okay. We just got a little goofy."

"Well, you were obviously soaking wet at some point. Really, Moira, I thought you'd use better judgment than this!"

I watch Moira shrink in the face of her mother's disappointment. I've never seen Mrs. Watkins this way. "You guys," I say, trying to get their attention. "I think I'd know if I wasn't fine. Jeez. Helicopter much? Maybe I'll have to run around the block in my jammies just to prove—"

"No!" they both cry out.

Moira's mom draws a hot bath for me. As I soak, I think about our night. How Boone's big body shattered the moon's reflection on the water when he dove in, and how the pieces of light started squiggling back together almost instantly when he was under the surface. It almost made the water seem alive.

The truth is, I might not be quite as fine as I was trying to make them believe. Well, duh. Dr. Caslow's message on the answering machine Wednesday was proof enough of that. But there's a certain new quavery shortness of breath that has started up only in the past couple of days, like my lungs need a good long nap. As we hiked up the trail to the reservoir, I felt bad for saying I couldn't go any farther, but it was true. When Boone backed up and told me to climb onto his back, part of me—a big part—wanted to say, "Boone, don't." Because I knew where it would go for me, I knew how it would end up making me feel. It was okay, though. I still maybe love him a little, but it's nothing I can't handle. Plus, the simple fact of the matter is that he has to be with Moira. I need for them to have each other. To be strong for each other. Stuff is coming soon that neither of them should have to handle on their own. I've never been able to piece that thought together until right this second, but there it is: the inescapable truth.

After Boone carried me all the way up the trail and I stood looking at the water of the reservoir, I remembered a documentary I once saw about people in Finland, how these old men came running out of sauna huts built next to a frigid lake. All of them ran down the pier naked and jumped into the near-freezing water. It was supposed to be good for their circulation or something. After Moira and Boone had both walked away, I tried not to giggle at the thought of what I should do next.

It took me less than a minute to shed my clothes. Like those Finnish men, I decided to make a splash.

The water was so cold, it stopped my breath. In the black silence beneath the surface, I thought, *Now you've done it, Agnes.* I imagined my body pulled from the water, my blue face frozen into a permanent mask of regret. The image made me kick my legs faster, but it was hard to propel my fat-free body very far without the help of flippers. Trying not to panic, I looked up toward the underbelly of the water's surface and found the moon shining through like a sign that I shouldn't give up. I kicked some more until I didn't think I could kick any harder. I wasn't wearing my nose clamp, and some water got into my nose.

Moira's scream was the first sound I heard when my head finally broke through. *Calm down,* I wanted to call out to her. *Just calm down, will you?* But I was too busy gasping for air. My too-large underwear ballooned around me in the frigid water. At least it had stayed on.

When I watched Boone strip down to his boxers on the bank and saw him for the first time without his clothes, I gasped again, and not just from the cold. I felt a sharp twinge in my chest. I couldn't help it. It was a twinge of longing with just a dash of white-hot jealousy, and then it was gone.

When Moira got in, too, I could hardly believe it. She looked like some earth-destroying goddess returning to the sea. She looked like she was made of light and the absence of light, with a little bit of rage and grace mixed in. I wanted to hold on to that thought of her so I could write it down later, but I knew I'd probably forget it. My friends were so stunning that it almost made me weep. I thought of the stars above, a billion tiny peepholes for angels to look through. I hoped angels were watching the three of us in the water and laughing at what they saw. I bet they were. God knows, we were a sight to behold.

Now, from downstairs, I hear Mrs. Watkins demanding an explanation and Moira, near tears, saying, "I didn't *know*, Mom. I didn't know she was going to jump in."

Half an hour later, in the spare trundle bed, warm, safe, a little dizzy maybe, a little overtired, I register Mrs. Watkins coming into the bedroom. She sits on the edge of Moira's bed and says, "I sure love you girls. That's the truth."

"Love you too, Mom." We say it in unison, just like we've done since my first sleepover here in fifth grade. Back then, this room was decked out in tie-dye.

Mrs. Watkins peers at me in the dark and puts the back of her hand to my forehead. "Do you feel okay, honey?"

I nod. True, I have a little bit of a scratchy throat, probably from inhaling that reservoir water. I'm definitely not going to mention it now that everyone has finally calmed down.

"Well, don't be alarmed if I come check on you in the middle of the night, okay?"

I nod again, or try to, at least. The truth of the matter is, my head is so heavy and I'm so tired that I can't . . . even . . .

*   *   *

I wake from the strangest dream, but then realize I'm still having it, that the dream's tentacles are still wrapped around me even though I'm no longer asleep. In the dream, a large, long-haired white cat is sitting on my chest, heavy and warm, watching me with half-closed eyes. The cat is purring an uneven *thumpity-thump* type of purr. I know it's a dream from this fact alone, because Moira has never owned a cat—her mom and dad are both allergic. I want to say something, but lying in the dark of Moira's room I find myself without the ability to speak. My voice is simply gone. I try to lift my hand, but it's as if my limbs turned to lead while I slept. I'm like somebody trapped in a spell, a zoned-out princess in a high tower.

*   *   *

I don't know how long it is before I hear the next voice. It's gentle, but with a note of panic woven through. "You're going to be okay," Moira's mom says from above me. Somehow, I am in motion. I am being carried. I open my eyes and look up as her voice starts to fade away. She glances worriedly down at me, her hair like a curtain framing her face. "Your mom's going to meet us at the hospital."

94

MOIRA
DAY 7: JUNE 18

"I'M SO SORRY, I'M SO SORRY!" THOSE WERE THE ONLY WORDS I could say when I saw Deb running down the hospital corridor toward me, toward the temporary room they'd wheeled Agnes into. "It's all my fault. I'm so sorry."

There's no way Deb could have been prepared for what she saw, for how small and pale—almost translucent—her daughter looked lying there in the hospital bed. It was like Agnes was hardly there at all, but where had she gone? How could she have started to disappear so quickly? It was only hours ago that we'd . . .

"It's not your fault," Deb told me without taking her eyes off Agnes. "It's nobody's fault."

Now, only twenty-four hours later, Agnes is firmly encased

in the coma-like state that she kept slipping into and out of yesterday. She's hooked up to more tubes and machines than I can keep track of, and her doctor told us it doesn't look good at all. Out in the waiting area, Boone and Agnes's dad are pacing around, drinking too much coffee. A few hours ago, Mr. Delaney came in, and Deb and I left so he could be alone with Agnes. Now we're back, sitting in a huddle next to the bed, propping each other up with our eyes closed.

BOONE

DAY 6: JUNE 19

Mom is in her room when I'm about to leave for the hospital. I knock softly on her door. Yesterday I hung around the Intensive Care waiting area in case Deb or Moira needed anything, and I've called in sick to the Feed & Seed so I can go back there today. First, though, I just need to talk to somebody. I need to get my head screwed on straighter if I'm going to be of use to anyone else. It was too much of a shift, from utter bliss at the reservoir Thursday night to the way my gut felt like it dropped through the earth when I found out Agnes was admitted to the ICU on Friday. Life doesn't seem quite real. I knock again.

"There's a piece missing," my mother finally responds. Her voice is distant and timid on the other side of the door.

"What? Mom, are you okay?"

"From that puzzle you brought me last week. The optical illusions one." She sounds bereft.

"I'm sorry," I tell her, trying to keep my voice as steady and encouraging as possible. "I'll get you another puzzle."

"I want to finish that one."

Now I can feel the mercury rising. It's clear my mother can't handle any more stress today. She's already dealing with the life-altering trauma of a misplaced piece of cardboard, for God's sake. *Why are you acting like such a child?* I suddenly want to yell at her. *Why the hell are you so weak?* Of course, I don't say either of those things.

I'm full to bursting with exhaustion and helplessness. I can feel it starting to leak out through my pores, like I might start weeping at the smallest thing, howling for somebody to wrap me in a warm blanket and tell me everything's going to be okay. To top it all off, my father's disapproval scrolls across the backs of my eyelids, which are clenched shut. *Damnit*, why can't I stop thinking about that bastard, especially now? I'm needed at the hospital, and I'm going to be wrecked enough without fighting off the memory of that last day, when he barked at me as he changed the tire.

"Mother of Christ," my father hissed after pulling the tire off the hub. I stood a few paces behind him on a mound of dead pine needles and sticks, chewing at a hangnail and trying to just shut up and stay out of the way. Something under the chassis had caught his attention. I never found out what it was. When our neighbor, old man Wallace, came out to the spot a few days later to help us get the truck home, he said there was nothing amiss with the axles or the transmission or anything. Still, my father wiggled his body under there so that only his belly and legs were sticking out from underneath the running board. I wondered what he'd found, but there was no way I was going to ask. Hopefully, it wasn't something that would keep us out in the woods all night. Mom would worry.

The creaking groan that came just before the truck rolled off the jack sounded like an old dungeon door closing. It's the same sound I hear in my nightmares to this day. Without warning, our trusty ship filled with wood was starting to roll down the hill as I stood there, helpless. Useless. I opened my mouth to scream, but no sound came out. I reached my arms out as if to stop the truck or to yank my father out from under it, but my feet were attached to the forest floor as if they'd sprouted deep, sudden roots. The Chevy lurched upward as the wheel hub plowed across my father's chest, instantly crushing his rib cage. Then it rolled another twenty yards or so before colliding with an enormous pine, the hood folding like a fortune cookie around the tree's trunk.

MOIRA

DAY 5: JUNE 20

PLEASE LET HER LIVE.

I'll do it all over again if I have to. I'll protect her better this time.

People can call me the worst names they can think of. They can throw food at me. Forks and knives, even. I don't care. I won't resist.

I'll even smile when they do it.

97

BOONE

DAY 4: JUNE 21

IT'S BEEN FOUR DAYS SINCE AGNES WAS ADMITTED TO THE ICU, and everything is madness. If I started giggling right now, I'm pretty sure I wouldn't be able to stop. At the hospital, where I spend every waking moment that I'm not here at home, there's talk of minimal brain activity, of the machines that are breathing for her, of arrangements that must be made.

Agnes's dad paces in the hall while Moira and her mom and Deb cocoon together in the waiting room and sometimes in the chapel. People go home separately to sleep in shifts. I stay with them as much as I can, but I have to drive back home at least twice a day to take care of things here.

Now Diablo's been fed, the house has been cleaned, and Mom is as nonresponsive as ever. She's damn near as nonresponsive as Agnes. I find myself in the pasture, walking in no particular direction. As the moon's pale light washes over me, another tsunami of dark memories swells and crests overhead. I've held it at bay this long, but there's not enough left of me now to keep it from crashing down.

There was never any hope for my father. The simple, obvious truth was that he never should have jacked up the truck on a hill using subpar equipment, and he should have let me put a rock in front of the tire to keep the truck from rolling. These things were just common sense. I should have taken his damaged brain more seriously. I should have forced him to listen to me somehow. But all those *should*s couldn't do squat to change the situation after the fact.

I recall my father's mouth trying to form words after I uprooted my feet from the earth and scrambled to where he lay in a bed of pine needles. To this day, I wonder what he was trying to say as I stood there, mute, looking down at his ruined body. "I'll go get help," I finally said, my voice nothing more than a hoarse, cracked whisper. And I ran back through the woods, my stomach roiling, tripping over dead tree limbs, running headfirst through whiplike branches that slashed at my face. More than anything I wished I'd ridden Diablo out to meet my father at the wood-cutting site so I'd be able to kick the horse into a flat-out run now. My father was dying—no, my brain wouldn't allow that thought—but it was maybe true anyway, and here I had to rely on my own inadequate legs, legs that had just come through yet another growth spurt and were, at the time, abnormally long and didn't quite fit with the rest of my body. I kept running, stumbling, and tripping until I reached the back door of our kitchen.

My mother turned from the counter where she'd been spinning salad. "Back already?" she asked. She smiled, but just for a moment, just until she saw the blood from all the cuts on my face running down my neck and drenching the front of my T-shirt.

My mouth was moving like my dad's; no words came out. My whole body shook, and my breath heaved until there was something other than breath there. It was the roiling in my stomach again, rising up and up, uncontrollably up. I tried to move toward the trash can in order to vomit there, but I didn't make it and got sick all over the linoleum floor instead.

Before we left the house Mom screamed into the phone, tried to describe to the paramedics where we were going, how we could be found. Then she was running back through the forest with me. My brain registered the smell of wood smoke in the air as our feet snapped twigs and crunched dead pine needles. Her apron kept getting snagged on branches, but there was no time to stop and take it off. Also, she wasn't wearing proper shoes for the forest. They were little more than thin slippers, really, the flats she was wearing. She cried out at one point but kept going, even though the pinecone she'd landed on had embedded itself in the arch of her foot, and she'd later—in the oily blur of the days ahead—have to get stitches.

Meanwhile, with one clear sliver of my brain, I berated myself. If only I'd tried CPR, tried something other than panicking and running home when I saw my father's mouth opening and closing like the mouth of a hooked fish thrown onto dry land.

But it's pointless to let myself drown in those memories. I need to get cleaned up and head back to the hospital. I'm aware that my face is wet with tears and snot. My throat is dry from sobbing. I've cried so hard and for so long in a sort of wandering daze that my face hurts. I shake the fog from my head and start walking back toward the house.

It's when I'm inside the paddock, latching the gate, that Diablo intercepts me. The gelding's breath forms barely visible plumes of steam in the cool night air as he ambles up to me and exhales gently onto my face.

I step even closer, so that I'm standing right next to his shoulder. Then I wrap my arms around the thickest part of the horse's neck and bury my face in his mane, breathing in the salty-sweet scent. He lets me stand there like that for a long minute before he gets impatient and starts nibbling on my clothes, looking for a treat. I let go of him and walk back to the house, surprising Mom a little when I walk through the door. I no doubt look like hell.

"Boone . . ." she starts to say. She looks lost.

"It's not okay," I tell her. "I'm not okay."

In response, she gives me her classic zombie eyes, her usual Danny's-not-here-Mrs.-Torrance stare, but I'm not having it this time. I don't care if we've both finally gone off the deep end. I won't put up with her refusal to speak or her refusal to be a real live human mother. Especially now when I need her to help keep me sane so I can be a real live human friend to the other people who need me—Agnes and Moira and their mothers.

"Mom. I mean it. I need to talk to someone. If not you, then a shrink, somebody who can help me. And you need it, too." For the tiniest fraction of a second, my words seem to snap her out of her haze. For the first time in I don't even know how long, it actually feels like she's present, like she's there in the room with me instead of loitering miserably in the atmosphere, just out of reach.

The moment doesn't last long. Drawing back once more into whatever dark, miserable corner of her mind she's been going to ever since my dad died, she stares down at the ground. "I wouldn't even know where to start," she says in a voice so quiet and broken that I have to strain to hear it.

"Then we'll have to find the starting point together," I tell her, refusing to let the conversation end there. "We can just think of it like a puzzle. And this piece right here is as good a piece to start with as any. Right? Right, Mom?"

She still won't look at me, and that's when I figure I've lost her. A dull throb starts up at the base of my skull and works its way slowly up the back of my head, settling in my temples. But then my mother does something truly surprising. She steps toward me and puts a hand on my shoulder. How long has it been since she last did something maternal? I don't even dare to let myself think that this might be what hope looks like. Even so, at the touch of her hand, the thing that's been trapped inside of me for way too long breaks free, like a massive boulder from the side of a hill. It doesn't go crashing down, though. It doesn't smash any cars or kill any innocent bystanders when it goes. Instead, it flies up, up, and away, as if it wasn't made of stone at all, but of something even lighter than air.

MOIRA

DAY 3: JUNE 22

AGNES HAS BEEN IN THE HOSPITAL FOR FIVE DAYS, BUT IT MAY as well be five decades. People going out, people coming in. *Ball of confusion.* That old song my parents blast on the stereo sometimes about running and running and running, but not being able to hide.

I'm dizzy with all the new bits of information darting in and out of my head like minnows. "It's not looking good." That's all the doctors have said for the past twenty-four hours (it's the only thing that sticks in my mind, anyway). And all I know is this: without Agnes there will be nothing. Just nothing at all worth having or seeing or doing.

I leave the hospital and drive the curvy road out to the reservoir without really knowing where I'm going. By the time

I park near the trailhead, my face is wet with tears. I grab a handful of spare napkins from the glove box to mop up. Then I'm climbing the trail and standing breathless on the bank where the three of us stripped down to almost nothing less than a week ago. I stare at the spot where Boone stood in only his boxers. The sight of him was at least as responsible as the cold water was later for taking my breath away. It momentarily made me forget to worry about Agnes bobbing in the water nearby, bluish, but happier than I've maybe ever seen her.

What if we had done something differently, Boone and I? What if we'd been stern with her for once? What if we had simply said, *No, Agnes. We're not going out to the reservoir, and that's final?*

But we didn't do those things. We didn't act like parents. We acted like teenagers, and Agnes acted like a teenager, too. In that water, the three of us had the kind of communion people flock to church on Sundays to find. And whether I like it or not, whether I agree with it or not, I know that's all Agnes ever wanted.

BOONE

DAY 2: JUNE 23

I'M HOME AGAIN, BUT I CAN'T STAY TOO LONG. I'M GOING TO feed Diablo, check on Mom, and then get back to the ICU. Things could be over any minute now. That's what the doctors and nurses keep saying. Not in so many words, maybe, but they're constantly saying it with their eyes, with their concerned checking of the clipboards and monitors and printouts that seem to spit more worthless data into the air every time I turn around in that sterile nightmare of a room.

The gate to the paddock is open, and Diablo is gone. An image of our neighbor, Jackson Tate, appears in my mind. *Here we go again,* I think. I'm about 99 percent sure Rhoid Face will shoot the horse, if only to keep his word. If that's the case, I'll soon have two burials to attend.

But Diablo hasn't escaped at all. When I scan the pasture for one last look, shielding my eyes against the bright sunlight, I spot the horse out in the arena. Guiding him in slow figure eights from the saddle is my mother.

100

AGNES
DAY 1: JUNE 24

I OPEN MY EYES.

It's just for a millisecond, but it's long enough for Moira to whisper, "Agnes," and reach for the button next to my bed that signals the nurses' station.

Moments later, I'm watching a nurse rush out to the waiting area, and then everyone follows her into my hospital room. They're all running—Mom, Dad, and Boone. Everyone's shouting, and that's me in the bed below, colorless as ash. My mother's hands are covering her mouth as if to trap the words and breath that might escape. My father is reaching toward me as if I might save him. And Boone. Boone just stands there behind everyone else, shaking his head in disbelief, smaller than I've ever seen him.

"She was here just a minute ago!" Moira cries to nobody in

particular. "She opened her eyes and looked at me. Make her open her eyes!"

Their voices rise up toward me, intermingled like multicolored streams of smoke tangling together. They are wailing my name. My body's name.

The real me is drawn out into the hallway of the ICU, where a light flashes above the door of my room. Code blue. Over at the beverage dispenser, a guy in a hospital gown fills a cup with apple juice and wonders about the alarms going off. There's at least a six-inch gap all the way down the back of his gown. My little brother Obi was right. Human butts are hilarious. How did I never fully understand this until now?

The moment I think of my brother, a window at the end of the hall beckons me toward it. It's open just a crack, but as soon as I wonder if I could fit through the opening, I'm already outside, high above the hospital roof. I'm part of the night air. I look down and see the west-side park where Moira and I sat on the swings not too long ago. To the left of it, I recognize our high school and, farther on, the tree-lined street where Dad and Jamey live. I pause to focus on their house, and then I'm in their room, watching Jamey sleep from above. It wasn't really fair, the way I always judged her. I get that now. I did it because I thought she was judging me, but the truth about Jamey is that she's doing the best she can, just like most other people. My stepmother stirs a little and turns over.

Obi and Nevaeh come briefly to mind, and then I'm in their

room, too, *floating near their lime-green bookcase. I don't want to wake them, so I don't stay too long.* I love you guys, *I think in their direction.* Be good.

Isaiah's next. I hover above where he's sleeping, not wanting to wake him, either. But he wakes up anyway, says, "Hey, Agnes." *I'm so shocked by the sound of his voice and the fact that he's looking right at me that I almost don't say anything at first. There's no time like the present, though, so I finally say,* Hey, Isaiah. *I don't say it with my mouth, since I no longer seem to be in possession of that or any other body part. Instead, I think the words at him, the same way I thought my love at Obi and Nevvie.* See you around, okay?

Isaiah smiles up at me. He's been sleeping with the covers pulled up to his chin and his fingers wrapped around the edge of his Star Wars comforter. He lifts those fingers now and gives me a sleepy little wave before closing his eyes again. An ache passes through me like a shadow passing over the sun. It's the ache of wanting to stay but needing to go. At the same time I register the sensation, I feel myself pulled away, almost like I'm being sucked into a giant vacuum. It draws me backward and away from everything—away from Isaiah, and the house, and the neighborhood, and the city, and the country, and the planet—away from the only life I have ever known.

EPILOGUE:

MOIRA

NOT TOO LONG AGO, IT WOULD HAVE DONE MY HEART GOOD TO see a room full of people dressed in black from head to toe. Now it's just one more random detail to add to all the other details of the past week since Agnes died.

"It's wrong to have it here," I whisper to Boone when he comes up the mortuary steps to shake my dad's hand and hug my mom. "Agnes would have preferred a park or the field where we buried Bingo." I'm wearing the gray silk dress I made in home ec in honor of Agnes never getting to wear hers.

Boone's mom came with him to the memorial service. She's waiting for us at the top of the steps and looking a little pale and unsure about being surrounded by so many strangers.

"She started back on meds," Boone whispers to me as we head up to meet her.

"Is that a good thing?" I whisper back.

"Does a one-legged duck swim in circles?"

There's an easel set up outside the big room where the service will be held. Inside the room, the Priscilla Ahn song Agnes loved most is playing, the one about a little girl who grows old and gray and dreams of flying away through the trees. Somebody found a new recording of it to play today, one that isn't all warbly like the one on her old mix tape. I can't really listen to the song now. I register the fact that it's playing, but that's all. If I let myself think about all the times Agnes made me listen to it while we were driving around in El-C, I won't be able to put one foot in front of the other and get through this. I'd collapse in a blubbering heap on the maroon carpet of the funeral home instead, and that would be that.

Agnes's dad, Jamey, and their kids are already seated in one of the front rows of seats. Our group sits in the front row opposite with Deb in the middle of us. Once we're all settled, I turn to survey the crowd. A bunch of teachers from school are here, and some students, too. I don't remember any of those kids paying much attention to Agnes when she was alive, but it hardly seems to matter now. Agnes's doctor is here with his wife and children. Also, Kitty from the senior center. She flashes a beaming smile at me and gives a little wave.

Then she points up toward the ceiling and makes an A-okay sign with her fingers. She's wearing a floral silk pantsuit in a riot of colors.

Agnes, I think at my best friend, wherever she is, *you are the most loved person I've ever known.*

The music fades out, and Mr. Delaney goes up to the front of the room. He thanks everyone for being here and says that if anyone wants to say a few words, they are welcome to do so. Sitting next to me, Deb grabs my hand and grips it hard, like a lifeline.

After a while, people start going up one by one to tell their Agnes stories. Most of them talk about how sweet and inspiring she was, even though they barely knew my best friend. The more I listen, the more restless I become. My hair is tied back with the bluish gray chiffon scarf that Agnes and I used for our running game of keep-away. Rather than being a comfort, the scarf pulls at the sensitive baby hairs at the back of my neck. "I need to get out of here," I whisper to Boone.

"It'll be over soon," he whispers back.

After the last person has finished speaking, a slide show plays on a big TV screen at the front of the room. It's a collection of all the pictures Agnes took over the years. When her dad was looking for images to use for today, he found them all in a folder on her laptop, edited and everything. I don't want to look, but I can't stop myself.

Mostly, the slideshow is filled with pictures of her mom

and her dad, Jamey and the siblings. The picture of me and Boone in grade school is there, as is the picture she snapped of Boone that day in the cafeteria when he and I almost got into a fistfight. There's one of Boone in sunglasses leaning against a locker, followed by a picture of me and Kitty at the senior center. There are some shots of us the day we buried Bingo, along with a bunch of self-portraits that I never knew she took. I look annoyed in most of the pictures I'm in. Seeing larger-than-life images of myself flashing across a screen for all to see would normally make me want to stick a fork through my eyeball. Now the experience hardly registers. I just feel numb.

*   *   *

When the service is over, I say good-bye to my parents. Boone drives his mom to the afternoon shift of her new job at the food bank before going home, and I drive Deb back to her house. I stay with her for a few hours, until she says she's ready to take a nap and that she'll be okay in the house by herself. That's when I head out to Boone's place.

There's something different about the inside of his house when I get there. Something's missing, but it takes me a minute to realize what it is: there are no jigsaw puzzles anywhere, not a single puzzle piece or box to be seen.

Just before sunset, Boone and I drive out into the back

pasture. I sit close to him in the truck cab, in the middle of the long seat. Diablo, who has been out grazing, follows the truck, holding his head low and swinging it slowly from side to side as he walks. Boone parks near the tree line, and we get out. The air is heavy with the scent of vanilla from all the pine trees.

The spot we pick isn't far from where Bingo is buried. I visit my dog's grave for a few minutes, kneel down and talk to the mound of dirt in a voice that's too quiet for Boone to hear. He knows I'm ready when I stand up, look at him, and nod. My mom gave me a little earthenware jar for the portion of ashes Deb held back for us. I retrieve the jar from the truck now and walk back toward him. "We should say something," I whisper.

Boone nods and looks down at the ground. "Agnes Delaney was an amazing person," he begins.

"She was my best friend," I add before falling silent. I don't know what else to say. It was careless of me to not have something more formal prepared. A lump starts to form in my throat, but it doesn't turn into anything worse, probably because I'm all cried out from the past week. Still, I can almost sense her there, above us maybe, somewhere up by the tops of the trees, urging me on.

I open the earthenware jar, cup Boone's hand in mine, and pour some of the gritty ashes into his palm. It's the smallest of handfuls; as tiny as she was, Agnes didn't leave too many ashes behind, especially once all the parts of her that could be donated to progeria research were taken away like she wanted. Boone and I each fling the ashes toward the trees. I take a breath and let it out.

As the dust that remains of my best friend swirls away from us on a warm breeze that seems to come from nowhere, I feel my lips forming into a smile. Boone looks perplexed until I say the words that have finally come, at just the right moment. "She knocked stuff over with her tail."

ACKNOWLEDGMENTS

TO MY PARENTS, NANCY AND DON, AND THE ENTIRE MCINNES FAMILY: There's so much in this life that I couldn't have done and/or learned without you guys and gals. I love you all to the stars and back.

To Corwin Leonard for your unwavering support during the writing of this book and your excellent feedback on the manuscript at all stages.

To Allenna Leonard for your keen insights as a beta reader.

To Stacey Glick: agent, friend, and all-around brilliant book advocate.

To editor extraordinaire Joy Peskin and the entire team at FSG/Macmillan for providing the perfect home for Agnes, Boone, and Moira's story.

To librarians and independent booksellers, the frontline champions of books that might not otherwise find an audience.

Finally, my deepest gratitude to kids everywhere who show courage by facing fear in all its many forms every day. You are my heroes and my inspiration.

AUTHOR'S NOTE

If you'd like to learn more about Hutchinson-Gilford
Progeria Syndrome and the efforts to find a cure,
visit the Progeria Research Foundation at
progeriaresearch.org.